Prelude. Chapters 1-14

If you're wondering why the chapters in this book start at 15, you obviously haven't read the first book, 'Dire Straits - The Choke Point'.

Shame on you.

If that is the unfortunate case, then let me help you catch up with the story so far...

Peter and Ray, two washed out ex RAF pilots were unceremoniously 'volunteered' by Le Boustarde and a couple of henchmen to take part in a top secret operation to clear the Strait of Hormuz of mines.

This would involve a souped up ex RAF display Vulcan bomber, five thermo nuclear warheads, a host of technical wizardry and a lot of good luck to pull it off.

... And of course the destruction Fulbeck and Bandar Abbas.

Chapter 15. Shockwave

After we released the final bomb, I pulled the aircraft around to the right and did one of our shuttle climbs, to get the hell out of it as fast as I could. I had no intention of getting caught up in the shock waves from that lot; especially the last 'big one'.

It was a case of brute force and ignorance at this stage. This was the only bit in the whole operation where 'they' couldn't help us.

Not because they weren't there, but because they didn't know how to.

Nobody had ever done what we had done, so there was no precedent or scientific knowledge to fall back on.

Only guess work.

If it was any other aircraft that Ray and I were flying that night, I can assure you that you would not be reading this now. When those combined compression waves hit us we were vibrated like pneumatic drillers in hell...

It wasn't possible at that moment, but after ten minutes in the galley, and hot coffee laced with French cognac from our secret store that even Le Boustarde hadn't found, I managed to do it.

We could see the southern Pakistani coastline as far as Karachi.

We didn't bother interfacing the TV camera, we weren't going that way. The job was only half done, and we had the rendezvous to consider, at least Ray did.

I was a passenger for the rest of the trip.

'They' who must be obeyed at all times, back in the tanker, had made all the arrangements, from the Gan take off to our eventual return.

Unless we saw any message on page two of the communications VDU, we were just to get on with it. This was set on the port screen in front of Ray, giving them instant control.

It was still green at the moment. Then it flashed to a blue background, with the following message,

: Stage One complete. Clearance to continue with Stage Two:

They were obviously in contact with the United Nations building in New York, or we would be on our way back to Gan after the rendezvous. I was glad I was out of it, because there was going to be some heavy diplomatic flak flying around somewhere after those first five weapons detonated...

I'd hate to think what was going to happen later on!

"I've got contact, Peter; they are flying the pattern as planned.

I'll send the signal, and let them come to us."

We carried out the same plan as we did with the two Tornadoes, to allow the tanker to find the Vulcan, and when we saw it turn in towards us, we left it to do its job.

The tanker crew had been given their instructions:

Fly on a southerly heading as far as the southern Pakistani coastline, no further; then north again until contact was made.

It was their job to link up with the Vulcan, in case the latter was incapable for any reason. An inspection of the airframe was essential, then if all was satisfactory, Stage Two would continue.

The heavy aircraft had taken off from its base, and had been flying on its tracks for about half an hour. They had seen the night turn into day, and therefore knew that the first part of the operation had been successful, but they didn't have much hope of finding us...

It was therefore a mixture of surprise and relief when they picked up our homing signal. It took fifteen minutes to get to the same area as the Vulcan, and another ten before the Captain had manoeuvred his aircraft into a position where Ray could get close in behind it for the inspection.

They used white flood lights, and took photographs with both infra red and high definition TV cameras.

It was then that they found out about the paint being stripped off, and the fusing of the panels. The x-ray cameras showed flawless welds, and we were declared safe for Stage Two on the communication screen.

Not a word had been spoken between the two aircraft; it had all been done on the computer via Skynet. There was a final message on the screen.

: Close up on the rear turret:

We got ourselves prepared, then Ray moved the Vulcan up one hundred feet, and forward two hundred, until it was right behind them.

We saw the flash of the hand held camera, then pulled back again as we had done with the Concorde; only this time instead of going upwards, Ray took it downwards.

The TV camera was operating, giving him a full view of the ground below. I would control the navigation from the rear, whilst he controlled the aircraft.

* * *

The tanker captain was Michel Novotny.

Like us, he had been 'recruited' by Le Boustarde, along with the other four members of his crew.

He had picked them up at the Borogontsy logging camp in Siberia, where they were carrying out 'light work', for some minor misdemeanour against the state.

It comes to something, when they were more afraid of what Le Boustarde could do to them, than what 'the state' had already done.

That guy certainly added an international flavour to the scene.

Michel's crew mate, Piotr, had done most of the inspection, and he fed all the signals back to Gan for the final analysis and decisions. It was his suggestion about the photograph which Gan approved.

The aircraft vibrated as the four contra rotating propellers reduced revolutions, as Michel pulled back the throttles of the four Kuznetsov NK-24 turboprops for his descent.

This stage of the flight had all been arranged by Gan during the inspection, and his instructions were in front of him already, on page two of his communication VDU,

: Land at Kandahar. Refuel. Return to Gan as soon as possible:

The big converted Tupolev TU-20 Bear bomber, obtained from the Soviet Air Force four years ago, growled its way through the air towards the new

Russian base at Kandahar in south Afghanistan, adjacent to the ancient pilgrimage route between Istanbul and Kathmandu.

* * *

Before the Russian armies moved into Afghanistan during Christmas 1979, the pilgrims used to travel by buses from Western Europe, many of them forging lasting relationships.

It was a wonder that some of those vehicles managed to travel along the Afghan roads. The pot holes used to be big enough to swallow whole trucks, but not now.

The Russian troops needed rapid communications, so they had bulldozed the old broken down buses and trucks off the sides of the road; and constructed a modern motorway and dual carriageway from the Kushka railway terminal in southern Russia to Herat, Kandahar, Kabul, and back to Russia through the Hindu Kush mountain range, to the rail terminal at Termez on the north Afghanistan border.

Rapid communications were what they needed, and this road network gave it to them. There was no danger now of their buses breaking down... It could be fatal!

* * *

Michel saw the motorway bypassing the Russian base, as he approached for his landing. He heard Piotr remark on the intercom system.

"I'll be glad when we're down and out of here. It's too close to home for my liking..."

It only took them two hours.

They were each given a crate of the best Cossack vodka and a box of caviar, then poured back into their aircraft and sent on their way.

It was obvious that the old camaraderie exists in the Russian forces as well, at least between the United Nations forces, official or unofficial!

* * *

Ray had picked out the same motorway and was using it as his main navigation aid. It was just like driving down the M1 to London, only much higher, and a darn sight further away.

"On course Peter, send out the VDU message now please."

I punched the keys to let 'them' know where we were, and awaited their reply.

"Time for a coffee," I said.

Neither of us had mentioned the last explosion.

We had decided not to.

And we had the same agreement for Stage Two.

We both sat silently, drinking our black sweet drinks, with our private thoughts.

The brain is similar to the computers that we were operating.

Put too much in and it crashes out.

We didn't want ours to crash, so we didn't think about it...

For the moment...

Chapter 16. Dambusting

Abdul Rahid Muhammad had lived in Afghanistan all the thirty five years of his life.

He had been nineteen years of age when the Russians moved into his country and, as with most of his countrymen, he resented their intrusion completely. He had lived with his parents in Girishk, which is about one and a half hour's drive, due west of Kandahar by fast car on the new motorway system.

The town is on the river Helmand, which has its source in the Koh-I-Baba mountain range to the west of Kabul.

His father and uncle had helped to build the Helmand river dam for the Americans, who needed electrical power for their various services.

The Americans had moved out of the area years before the Russians invaded, and had removed much of the electricity generating equipment.

The proposed major base at Kandahar needed the power requirements of a small township, therefore the Kremlin had decided to utilise the river for its hydro electric capabilities; but after all the necessary calculations were made, it was found that the old American dam was not large enough...

So they built another one...

With Afghan help of course!

It was to be about three hundred feet downstream from the old dam, and thirty feet higher. This would give the required head of water to supply the turbine alternators fitted into the new dam.

The power output would be fed into a new aluminium wire high intensity grid system, which would follow the proposed motorway around the country to Kabul and Herat.

Abdul was one of the many young men drafted into the new Soviet system, and had been placed in one of the construction teams for the dam.

That was many years ago.

Under the new system, young men had to do the equivalent of two years work of hard labour, during one year of their natural lives, and many did not survive.

But Abdul was tough.

He was also a natural leader, and a good worker. Both the Afghans and the Russians came to respect him over the years, because he was intelligent as well.

He spent two years at Moscow University, learning electrical engineering, after which he returned to the Girishk Hydro-Electrical Power Station... as it had now become.

* * *

The new dam was four hundred feet in width, and eighty five feet high; with the outputs for the turbines along the base, leading out to a wide expanse of concrete where the water sluice gates were built.

There were twelve tunnels, one for each turbine. Each was twenty feet in diameter, running from the old American dam to join with the new Russian dam.

The two dams had been combined together for added strength, to support the extra head of water required, then roofed over with reinforced concrete.

The effect was to create an enormous turbine chamber between the two dams, equal in size to the Dinorwic hydro electric site in North Wales.

The twelve turbines were spaced equidistantly across the width of the chamber, each set in its own tunnel below the chamber floor; with the appropriate alternator, switch gear and necessary control panels above them, out of the water flow.

* * *

In January 1988 Abdul was given responsibility for the main turbine chamber, and two years later was made chief engineer for the complete power station, the only one in southern Afghanistan.

That night, when the weapons were dropped, Abdul was on duty at the main switch board; with a night staff of six operators and engineers.

About ten thirty that evening he heard a low rumbling sound, and felt the ground quiver underneath his feet.

The pressure gauge showing the water pressure on the dam wall started to vibrate, and both he and his second engineer watched in acute silence, as the gauge rapidly shot upwards, well above the red line indicating the danger mark.

They could see the old American dam vibrating slowly, and both of them prayed to Allah.

The situation remained like that for three and a half minutes, before the gauge slowly dropped back towards the red mark, and the dam stopped vibrating.

After six minutes the gauge was on the red mark, and five seconds after that the initial danger was over.

Abdul turned to his second in command.

"Check everything, and make sure it's safe.

I didn't like the sound of that at all."

They were in the process of checking each turbine individually, when a red warning light started flashing rapidly on the main control panel.

Abdul checked his main computer screen and hurriedly called over.

"Forget that. This is more important."

The screen was showing a series of figures from the stress gauges, set into the concrete of the new dam.

They looked at each other.

Abdul remarked calmly, considering the urgency of the situation,

"Relieve all the night staff.

Tell them to stay away until we advise them that it is safe to return, and get the emergency team here as quickly as possible.

Tell them to keep their mouths shut. I don't intend to end up in Siberia like our Chernobyl friends if Kabul hears about this.

Shut down the four outer turbines at each end of the chamber, and open fully the middle four, to keep the power output up."

Some of the men were told to leave, and other men were told to come in; but they were all told to keep their mouths firmly shut... and Kabul did not find out!

* * *

Ray was following the motorway system towards the west soon after all this happened. He was flying low to avoid the radar, which could pick us up now because we had lost all our absorbent paint.

I felt as if I was walking through a crowded swimming pool with nothing on...

Not there was much to hide mind you!

We crept down as low as we dared, especially during the long detour around the Kandahar base where Michel and his crew were landing.

We were taking no chances.

The Russians were still trigger happy when it came to the Mujahideen freedom fighters...

... They might just think we were one of them, and I didn't fancy a SAM 19 up my backside.

We had the infra red camera on and it gave a clear picture ahead.

The old American road from Girishk to Kandahar was based on the system whereby the shortest distance between two points was a straight line...

And the American engineer who built this one must have had a ninety mile ruler.

It didn't bend at all.

This road now carried all the traffic travelling to the east towards Kandahar. The Russians had built another road alongside it to form the motorway. This road carried the traffic travelling east to west away from Kandahar...

Towards the Helmand river dam at Girishk!

We just followed the road,

It led us straight towards the dam.

Our next port of call to coin a phrase!

* * *

The 'emergency team' had arrived at the dam, and were now very busy under the direction of the Chief Engineer.

The water in the outer tunnels had been diverted to the centre sluice gates, and a huge fountain of water was now surging out at the centre of the dam, to a height of about three hundred feet.

The roaring was tremendous, the ground vibrated under everybody's feet, and the spray blotted out any visibility remaining.

It was like Niagara Falls in the darkness.

A team of men were in the water outlet tunnels of the first four turbines checking the walls.

Another group were in the chamber inspecting the alternators and the electrical control gear...

And the red light on the main computer panel was still flashing!

* * *

"I've got contact with the dam Ray, range ten miles. Get ready."

"Ok, I've got the picture now on the screen."

He now had a clear picture on his left hand VDU screen from the infra red camera. The screen was as clear as daylight, even though it was pitch black outside.

We could see the huge fountain of spray surging out from the base of the dam, and the electrical pylons radiating out from the power station.

The transformers and all the high tension switch gear were about three hundred yards away from the edge of the river, well to the right of the dam.

"All clear ahead, Ray."

Our run in check point was a railway bridge, crossing over the motorway exactly two miles from the dam.

We were flying towards it, with the dam directly ahead on the video screen; one of the visual markers on the bridge, and the other at the base of the dam just to the right of the plume of water.

There was no margin for error here, everything had to be accurate.

As soon as we were over the bridge, I pressed the key on the key board which had already been pre programmed on the run up. Ray immediately pulled back the four throttles, and selected the airbrakes 'out' to slow the aircraft down as fast as possible.

The computer programme selected the under carriage 'down', and the aircraft landed on the motorway, with each of the mainwheels on its appropriate carriageway.

As soon as the wheels touched down, the computer selected our landing parachute out.

Our speed reduced rapidly now, and by the time we were at the slip road to the dam, we could put our nosewheel down onto the ground; so that Ray could steer the aircraft through the power station car park...

And down to the empty water sluice ramp, from the tunnels of turbines one to four, which Abdul had kindly emptied for us...

I didn't fancy a bath yet, that could come later.

Ray turned up the flat concrete ramp leading to the turbine tunnels, towards a flashing white light on the dam wall.

The separation walls between the four water tunnels had been lifted with hydraulic rams, into cavities within the dam, creating a gap about a hundred and twenty feet wide, and about twenty feet in height.

It led straight into the main generating chamber between the two dams!

It was large enough for the Vulcan to taxi through, and when we emerged from the other end of this 'entrance door', we were in the main chamber.

We could see Abdul at the control desk with his microphone.

"Good evening, Zero One. Welcome to Girishk.

Please chop your engines."

We did, because by now we were both very good boys, and always did what we were told!

They dropped the tunnel separation walls back down, re-routed the water, switched on the turbines, connected up the alternators...

And once again we had disappeared from the outside world.

Ray looked down at me from his seat.

"Not bad in the dark, eh!"

Well, I had to give him that one.

"You were a bit close going over that railway bridge.

What the hell would you have done if a train had come along?"

"No problem, dear chap. I'd probably have gone underneath it."

... and I reckon he would have too!

Abdul pressed the flashing red light, then selected page two on his computer.

Our brave heroes back in the Gan tanker now knew that we had arrived at Girishk, and were feeding the pre programmed instructions through the satellite for us.

Abdul looked up at me.

"Mr Barten, we've got the paint men ready, the fuel men ready, and the bomb men ready.

The motorway will be ready for you in two hours.

It will be blocked by an accident thirty minutes after that, so I suggest you both get yourselves ready...

And that's when I had my bath.

* * *

Later on we were both sitting at the control panel watching the re spray job being done.

Ray said to me,

"Do you fancy going out tonight, Peter?"

I looked at him in amazement.

"Where the hell do you think you're going to catch a bus, at this time of night?"

He looked back at me.

"I suppose you're right. The bloody service is dreadful round here.

They keep breaking down.

I think we'll fly out instead. It might be safer."

So we did!

* * *

Abdul and his men were as good as their word. Within two and a half hours they had finished preparing the aircraft, and it was now pointing back the way it had come.

It was time to go.

We looked at the Afghan crew, in their motley collection of clothes and different coloured turbans. They had done well for us.

As we were shaking hands goodbye, Abdul asked me to do them a great favour.

"Mr Barten, please would you let them take a picture of the aeroplane; for their children, their children's children, and all the children after that."

I looked at their hard Pathan faces, hopeful in expectation.

I thought of the security implications, and all our previous instructions on what we had to do...

... And I thought,

What the hell.

What difference would it all make?

I told him to have their cameras ready, he did a final salaam, and we climbed into the cabin.

We went out the same way as we came in, and started the engines on the water sluice ramp outside the dam.

They had fixed up some lights for us, and we could clearly see the car park and the slip road leading to the motorway.

They guided us through the various obstacles, across the car park, along the slip road, and we ended up with our nose wheel in the fast lane of the carriageway leading to Kandahar; the port mainwheel in the slow lane, and the starboard mainwheel in the centre lane of the other carriageway.

They had indeed had their 'accident', as there wasn't a vehicle in sight.

The motorway showed as clear as day on the infra red camera, which was fed through an image intensifier to the head up display unit directly in front of me.

It was just like taking off in the day light. The railway bridge two miles ahead was clear and distinct.

"Everything Ok, Ray?" I asked.

"Yes, you're clear to go."

I gave a little wave to the Afghans, who had collected outside on the hard shoulder, then pushed the four throttles fully forward.

We were heavy that night.

Heavier than we were at the Gan take off.

We had further to go so we were fully loaded with fuel, plus the five bombs.

I was going to let the aircraft roll forward with the engines at full power, until about one hundred miles per hour, then switch in the four afterburners to push it up to its take off speed as fast as possible.

The computer had worked out the best speeds for all this to happen, which were now displayed for me on the head up unit directly in front.

No automatic take off this time. I actually had to work for my meagre wages, and try and to keep the whole lot on the motorway as we shot down it.

The first half of the take off run was slow, but eventually the speed increased, and soon we were bowling down the motorway like a pair of 'ton up' kids...

... Minus the birds unfortunately.

The girders on the railway bridge were individually distinct now.

I had never seen such a clear picture. It must have been due to the clean atmosphere, and lack of smoke fumes.

I could even see two figures sitting on the hard shoulder, underneath the bridge with their backs to the side supports.

Our speed was now approaching the hundred miles an hour point, when I heard a small gasp from Ray, rather like a strangled parrot.

He got out of his seat like a flash of lightning, and climbed up the ladder to where I was sitting.

He pointed wildly to the right... at a string of lights moving towards the bridge, and said hoarsely,

"Peter, for Christ's sake, get a shift on.

There's a train coming."

I could now just see it out of the corner of my eye, chugging around the bend, approaching the bridge.

It was pulling carriages, and was obviously a passenger train.

"It's probably just the three fifteen Kandahar to Herat express," I helpfully remarked to him.

"I don't give a damn what bloody express it is, just get this bloody thing airborne," was his rather offhand reply.

I switched on the afterburners at that moment, and saw the two figures get up... and stand by the road.

They had no doubt seen our take off lights coming towards them, and, thinking we were one of the big juggernaut lorries ploughing around the Afghan motorway, were trying to hitch a lift.

I thought to myself,

"You'd better both get out of the way pretty damn quick after these afterburners cut in, or we'll blow you half way round the world before you know it."

Not only that, they'd have to move damn fast if they wanted to get in the back of us for a lift!

The train was crossing the bridge, and there was now a wide expanse of carriages, full of people ahead of us.

I could see their faces, peering out through the carriage windows in horror at the enormous roaring black monster bearing down on them, now with a two hundred feet solid jet of red flame behind it.

I could now see for myself the reflection of our take off lights in their wide open, fear filled eyes, stretched across the bridge.

It was like a string of Christmas tree lights across a garden wall.

Ray just gave another of his little 'squawks'.

He pointed forward with his shaking finger, his knees trembling.

I could feel them against the side of my seat, and his jaw was sagging hopelessly.

He just managed to get out a pathetic sounding, "Oh my Gawd..."

... And then we shot under the bridge, at approximately one hundred and ninety miles an hour.

We didn't make the 'double ton' unfortunately, as we got airborne just after that.

* * *

The train stopped as soon as it could, and all the passengers and crew got out, pointed towards Mecca and salaamed for the next half an hour after that in gratitude for their great deliverance from the next world.

The two hitch-hikers, still with their very hopeful upturned thumbs, just looked at the roaring flames, as the aircraft turned around to the left.

The young man went into his rucksack, took out a bottle of best Irish whiskey, and they both had a long, long drink.

"Bejesus", he said with his lilting Irish accent.

"Did yez see that, Oi think we'll move on out of this country, for pastures new.

They're all bloody mad round here," and took another drink.

"Too bladdy true, Cobber", said his young female companion.

"Too bladdy true".

They replaced the bottle, picked up their rucksacks, and walked hand in hand towards the distant lights

They had indeed caught the last bus to Kandahar...

...But it had broken down six miles back, and Abdul's men had used it for the road block...

Which is why they were hitching a lift.

But they didn't stand a chance!

They had to walk all the way.

And they were both aiming for Aussie land.

We could have helped them with the afterburners, if they'd only asked!

* * *

I looked at Ray still standing beside the seat.

"Close your mouth, Ray. You look like a pregnant goldfish gasping for air.

There was twenty five feet clearance under that bridge.

I checked with Abdul, and he should know, his brothers were on the construction gang. I didn't want to tell you in case you got worried.

Go and switch on the navigation computer there's a good chap, I might need it in a moment."

I could still feel the vibrations of his quivering legs as he went back down the ladder.

As I said before, Raymond was a smooth operator.

If he says he's going to do something, he'll do it...

Only I gather from his comments immediately afterwards, that he would have preferred to have been in the driving seat when he flew under the bridge, instead of just being a passenger; and that after we landed my lack of parentage would in no way restrict his efforts to reduce the flow of air across my windpipe.

Our left turn took as back towards Girishk, which I could clearly see on the port VDU.

The reservoir created by the new dam spread for twenty five miles upriver, and at its widest point was seven miles across.

"I've got the dam, Peter. I'll feed it up to the head up display for you."

Ray had fully recovered and we were a team once more.

"Thanks, approaching the river now."

The black expanse of water showed up clearly on the screen about one mile ahead, with the dam about five miles away somewhere on my left. When I turned towards it in a minute or so I would be able to see it on the head up display.

"Over the river now, Ray, taking it down."

I flew the aircraft down to about one hundred feet over the water, then turned left towards the dam.

The port wing tip was about fifty feet above the water, and all the air was spilling down from it in spinning vortices. It was causing a wake of phosphorescent water behind us, showing our curved path during the turn.

"Switching on the external ultra violets now, Peter."

I could see the glow of the paint gradually build up to full strength, until each wingtip could be clearly seen from the cockpit window.

The dam was now visible on the head up unit, and I could see the two red warning lights on the towers either side of the central spillway.

They blinked twice, then remained on for our run up. That was Abdul saying goodbye.

I saw the landing lights under the wings flash twice, then remain off.

That was Ray replying.

I took the aircraft very low over the water, at a height of about fifty feet and at a speed of three hundred and sixty miles per hour, aiming straight between the two red lights.

We shot over the dam right in the centre between the two towers.

I pulled the nose up slowly, turned to the right and then headed out to the west.

That was me, saying goodbye to Abdul and his men.

They got their pictures all right.

No problem at all.

The two infra red security cameras, set up at the top of each of the spillway towers by the Government controlling authorities, picked up the Vulcan as soon as it was towed out from the tunnel by one of the heavy goods units;

and followed it all the way around, from the take off point until it disappeared low on the western horizon...

... And then Abdul conveniently 'lost' the cassette film.

Abdul's father and uncle, now two very elderly grey bearded old Pathans, his brothers, his children, his nephews, his nieces and all the other families in Girishk would now be able to sit, sucking away on their hookah pipes for years to come; reflecting with pride on the Afghan labour that had gone into producing the dams, the motorway, the railway and the bridge; and the use they had all been put to with their help...

And Kabul never did find out!

Chapter 17. The Ultimatum

The ultimatum, for that's what it was, had been issued over a month ago at a full session of the United Nations General Assembly.

Never before had all one hundred and fifty nine states been together under one roof, there was always at least one country that, for some reason or other, could not hold session with the others.

This meeting although very important, would only last five minutes, if that.

The President of the assembly, Mr Lee Luanda from the Philippines, specially elected for this extra ordinary meeting, called it to order; and amid hushed tones, the representative of the Islamic Republic of Iran, created in April 1979 by the Ayatollah Ruholla Khomeini, stepped forward to be seated at the front of the vast auditorium, in one of the two chairs positioned there.

The representative of the Republic of Iraq, created in July 1958 when King Faisal the second was assassinated, followed him onto the dais, to sit at the other chair.

At first no decision could be made concerning which representative would be the first to be seated; and the negotiations even for this small event had lasted for three months, with no final conclusion being drawn at the end.

For both representatives it was a matter of pride as to who would be seated first.

It had therefore been decided on a purely unbiased alphabetic basis.

Before that there were the subcommittee negotiations; as to which side of the President the particular representatives would sit. Each wanted to sit by the President's right hand, neither would sit by his left hand.

This lasted longer than the previously mentioned meeting, and could not initially be resolved at all.

It was the representative of Haiti who came up with the present solution, which was acceptable to all concerned including Iran and Iraq, and resulted in Mr Lee Luanda's nomination for this special meeting.

He had lost his left hand during the Second World War, and he had to use a false one!

Protracted negotiations continued thereafter; concerning the shape of the table, the type of chair to use, the colour of material on the chairs... and what was the most important for the Iraqi representative, the heights of the seats of the chairs they had to sit on.

The Iraqi representative was a small man with a short back, whereas the Iranian representative was a tall man, with a long back... who could look down upon him, and this would not do.

Neither side would change their representative, and the problem was only solved by manufacturing special chairs, which were laser controlled by the reflected light from each of their four eyeballs, to ensure that at no time would any one person be higher than the other.

... And while all these various protracted negotiations took place over the long months, the Gulf war had continued, on and on and on and on and on.......

It had taken over two years of hard work by the previous President to organise this meeting, and by the time it was done, he was very thankful to stand down.

The result of all this work culminated on that first day of July 1995 with the new President being sworn in at fifteen minutes to midday. He would take his seat at five minutes to the hour. The Iranian representative would be seated by two minutes to the hour and the Iraqi representative by one minute to.

They were sitting facing each other across a circular white table, rising up and down on their laser controlled hard back chairs, painted to match; awaiting the video screens in front of each of them to come on to display a message to both of them at exactly the same time, at midday according to the new United Nations electronic clock, accurate to the nanosecond.

The sole purpose of all this careful deliberation was to tell each belligerent, at exactly the same time and under equal conditions, the date and time at which the war in the Gulf was to end; with the emphasis on the word 'was'.

No excuse could then be made by either side that they had been disadvantaged by the other.

The ultimatum was that; if by that time, the two belligerents did not return to their previously declared boundaries, as existing at the time when Iraq invaded Iran in September 1980, then the United Nations forces would take the matter to the Security Council; for the decision to enter into a nuclear phase of the war.

There was however a very long argument on both sides as to what these boundaries were.

The original fighting, which commenced in 1980, was over which belligerent had control of the Shatt El Arab waterway, at the head of the Gulf.

Since that day neither side could agree concerning territorial rights and control.

The whole argument was immaterial now, because the waterway had silted up, and only the smallest dhows could negotiate the troubled waters.

The fighting now was purely for fighting's sake.

The members of the General Assembly present that day were representatives of the unofficial 'civil sector' of the United Nations, as no agreement on this policy could be reached between members of the 'official' United Nations.

Apparently they had more important matters of state to attend to...

... Most of them financial!

There had been previous sessions of this General Assembly, especially when the business on the boundary concerning this waterway was being negotiated. Again, initially nothing could be agreed at all, and this was most likely to be the main stumbling block.

It was the Irish representative who came up with a suggestion, based upon the answer achieved regarding Northern Ireland; and that was to create a narrow zone between both countries, which the United Nations would own.

In fact, they would create a new country.

That would make a total now of one hundred and sixty countries in the General Assembly.

The answer was so simple that it was staring them all in the face and nobody had seen it.

As the area had been destroyed completely by war damage for the last fifteen years, it was a wilderness.

The marshes were impassable, the waterway useless and the whole area uninhabited... except for the troops.

These new boundaries were now available for each representative to return with to his native country, for discussion with each Government.

By the date given on the computer, all fighting must cease, and all troops be withdrawn to each country's territories; but most important of all, no troops, personnel or equipment should be in the new buffer country, which was five miles either side of the old Shatt El Arab waterway.

... All of this had been agreed previously.

... All that was required now was the time and date.

At precisely midday the date appeared on their screens.

It to be was 12:00, on the first day of August 1995.

Both representatives must be back at the General Assembly on that day, at that time, to sign the peace treaty.

* * *

As soon as the date was seen by both representatives, a furious row erupted as to who had to make the most concessions in order to achieve this equal status between them.

The meeting was called to order by the new President, and it was clearly pointed out that this was not a negotiating session, but a witnessing session; and that each country now had the necessary information upon which to act... then the meeting was adjourned for one month.

It had lasted exactly fifty seconds,

But it took over an hour to clear the auditorium.

* * *

Mr Lee Luanda was only twenty years of age when the Japanese invaded Manila, where he lived.

He had fought them in the jungles of his homelands for six months before they caught him, and when they did, he wished at the time that they had killed him outright.

They had broken the bones in his legs, from his thighs to his ankles, with their rifle butts; and as he was lying on the floor in agony, they kicked him until he was unconscious,

And when he recovered, they did it again... and again... and again.

Eventually, they tied him up between two trees by his arms, and left him to die...

He refused to.

He was hanging there for over two days, before they cut him down, and threw him on the ground in front of their commanding officer... who ordered that they leave him in front of the house where he had lived all his life, as an example to the other members of the village...

... After they had murdered both his parents.

He knew what it was like to suffer, but like Abdul in Afghanistan, he was tough, and determined, so he survived.

He was a grandfather now.

His children had begat their children, and no doubt theirs would begat others.

He had seen them all grow up to maturity and responsible manhood; but he had also seen them in their teenage phase, when they were all trying to be better than the next man, and tried to score points with fists and arguments.

He had noticed how easy it was for them to get into a fight, but how much more difficult it was to stop them afterwards.

He buried his head in his one remaining hand, left after a soldier had decided to aim a sword stroke through his left wrist, instead of the ropes, when they cut him down from the tree...

* * *

On August the first, at the appointed time and place, exactly the same circumstances prevailed.

The General Assembly ultimatum had been given a month ago.

... And nothing had happened.

The two representatives were then told that a nuclear phase had now developed, and that they were being given warnings of impending strikes by United Nations Forces.

First of all, four atomic weapons would be dropped in the Persian Gulf, followed by strikes on land in each country alternatively; until either they both gave up the fighting, or they were both incapable of any further action.

Both countries had expected the warning shots to be dropped one at a time, with a series of increasingly demanding negotiations for peace, and this would go on and on and on and on...

* * *

How did they pick Bandar Abbas for the first strike on land?

Two names were put into a hat, and Mr Lee Luanda simply picked the first one out with his remaining hand... the one he used to chastise his own children with... and read out with a clear authoritative voice,

"Bandar Abbas"

He then picked out the other paper and said in the same voice,

"Basra"

Not only was Me Lee Luanda tough, he was a very brave man. He accepted his responsibilities.

He knew that when he was offered the Presidency that this was what every one of the one hundred and fifty nine representatives was asking him to do.

So he did it!

There was no riotous discord this time.

Only sadness.

The witnesses all filed out in silence, until only the three of them were left.

The other two looked at each other with hostility in their eyes, the hatred glistening in the laser beams.

Then they got up and left at opposite ends of the room.

* * *

And that was a week ago.

Neither of them expected what Ray and I had done.

They were both calling the United Nation's bluff... and they had both called once too often.

They now knew what to expect, and it was up to the diplomats, politicians and leaders in both countries to do something.

The common soldier, man, woman... and child... had all done their bit over the last fifteen years.

It was time they had a rest.

I looked out of the starboard window, and could see the firestorm still raging in Bandar Abbas.

I said nothing to Ray, but I knew that he could see it as well on the television screen.

He said nothing either.

We were both sticking to our agreement.

* * *

At about the same time Mr Lee Luanda was standing in the vast auditorium in New York, looking around at the empty one hundred and sixty seats.

The additional one was a plain common wooden chair, in front of all the other ones, because that was all the caretaker could find.

He sat down in it, and looked at the two pieces of paper from which he had read those two names one week ago, and quietly spoke to himself.

"Well, little country, I hope you can accomplish what the big ones haven't been able to do."

He sat and reflected for a moment, then get up and limped painfully out of the room, because his own war was still hurting him...

Very painfully.

Both externally, and internally.

Chapter 18. Two Rivers

The Tigris is the northern of the two rivers which border Mesopotamia.

It rises in the mountains of Turkistan and Armenia, then flows south east through some of the most fertile land in the world for about a thousand miles to the city of Qurna, in southern Iraq.

Approximately two hundred miles north of this city is the capital, Baghdad. The ravages of fifteen years of constant war had reduced it from a city to more like a collection of bomb craters, surrounded by heaps of bricks and rubble, in which the present population survived.

The other river is the Euphrates, the largest in western Asia.

It is formed by the union of two others, the Kara Su, with its source in the Dumla Dagh; and the Murad Su, which rises in the Ala Dagh.

The river pierces the Tauras mountains, flows south west until it reaches Aleppo, turns south east, and flows through Syria; eventually joining the Tigris, at the previously mentioned city, Qurna.

The ancient city of Babylon once lay astride this river sixty miles south of Baghdad.

If the hanging gardens were in existence today, they wouldn't have lasted fifteen minutes, let alone fifteen years. They would have been spread across the desert sand, which is all that now remains of the famous Capital of ancient Babylonia...

The two rivers merge together at Qurna, then flow southwards to the head of the Persian Gulf.

The distance that water has to flow is constantly increasing, because of silt deposits from the rivers.

Over the centuries, the area of land has gradually increased.

Previously, the two rivers flowed into the Persian Gulf separately, to the north of the city of Qurna.

Now, once they have merged, they flow a further seventy miles, before they reach the Gulf... give or take a sand bank or two.

This waterway is called the Shatt El Arab.

Because the area is flat and low lying, the silt deposits keep forming unless constant dredging takes place.

For the last fifteen years, every dredger that set out from the port of Basra, which is on the Shatt El Arab, about thirty miles south of Qurna, in an attempt to clear the waterway, just ended up adding to the 'silt', after the Iranians decided that they weren't going to let it clear away.

The end result of all this useless activity was that the Shatt El Arab continued to weave its way to the Persian Gulf at its own speed, in its own time, and didn't give a damn what was going on around it...

Because the two rivers, and the various members of their tributary families, now and in the past, had seen it all before... and they were getting a bit fed up of the whole situation.

* * *

They had seen the ancient Babylonians take over the Sumerians, around two thousand years before Christ.

At that time it was the turn of a keen young man, Kyrash of Ansham, to take over the Babylonians.

He was better known as King Cyrus, the greatest of the Persian kings.

After that it was Mithradates, the first ruler of Parthia, who laid claim to the fertile plain; so he kicked out the Persians.

They got a bit fed up of all this conquering, so they rallied around the Persian banner, and about four hundred years later marched on the Parthians.

Their great leader, Ardashir, the grandson of the Persian chief Sassan, then became king.

This young fellow started the famous Sassanid line of Kings of Persia, until about six hundred and fifty years after Christ...

Then it was the turn of the Arabs, a nomadic race of people who lived in the barren deserts, to the south west of the green and pleasant land.

Not only did they take over the valley between the two rivers, but continued onwards as far west as the river Indus in India; to the north west of the Persian area, well north of Samarkand.

All of what is known today as Saudi Arabia, Egypt, Syria, East Turkey, Libya, Tunisia, Algeria, Morocco, Spain and Portugal...

Because the rise of Islam was vast.

The small trading merchant, born in the town of Mecca, who gave up the family business at the age of forty for a life of prayer and meditation, started the new Muslim religion.

Muhammad's teachings were all written down in a book now known as the Quran, which is as sacred to Muslims as the bible is to Christians; and the five hundred million followers today adhere to the same principles of faith as Muhammad's original followers...

And they still fight each other!

* * *

The rivers by this time were getting a bit war weary, but that wasn't the end of it.

They would have to suffer a bit more.

The Ottoman Empire was expanding.

Suleiman the magnificent, the greatest ruler of the Turkish Ottoman Empire, decided that he would add the green garden to his property, so he took it.

His descendants decided on other suitable properties in the local area, so they took them as well.

The end result being that Iraq and Iran were both members of the powerful Ottoman Empire, until after the First World War; by which time the two rivers were definitely war weary.

They, like everybody else had had enough and were hopeful for a rest...

Which was not to be.

Since then:

King Feisel the second of Iraq was killed at the age of twenty three,

Muhammad Pahlavi, Shah of Persia, had been deposed,

And the present Islamic population of the two republics had been fighting it out for fifteen years, over who controls the river between Qurna and the head of the Persian Gulf.

The longer they took to argue it out, the larger the area grew, because the silt deposits just got bigger and bigger...

* * *

The rivers had therefore not just seen fifteen years of Gulf war.

They had seen nearly four thousand years of continual fighting, and they had both decided that it was time that they did something about it...

And we were on our way to help them!

Chapter 19. Wait At Basra

We didn't speak much on the flight from Girishk to the head of the Gulf. There was a lot to do and many calculations to make.

The rear computer was linked through to 'them' at Gan, and the team there passed us the results which were obtained. They in turn had a separate data link with the main computer in the United Nations building.

Most of the information necessary for a successful outcome was held in their computer memory banks. It had taken nearly a year to get it all, at great risk to the various collectors.

I could see on the port monitor the information which Ray was collecting and storing away on his discs. There was one for each bomb, and a master programme disc to control the complete operation.

This would give us our speeds and heights to fly, and distances from Basra to drop the bombs. The procedure was the same as the Bandar Abbas run; only the dropping parameters were different.

Our main job was to locate the central railway station in Basra as the target point, and leave the rest to the computer.

Ray was pounding away on the keyboard as if he was playing a piano.

I could almost feel the sweat on his brow.

He was hard at it for over an hour with no break, as figure after figure kept pouring into the aircraft.

I had the important job of overall supervision... which was hard work.

My biggest problem was trying to get at an itch right between my shoulder blades. No matter how I contorted myself I just couldn't reach it. I loosened my straps, twisted sideways, and even tried to stand up, but it was still eluding me.

I got it in the end though. Nothing escapes Peter the great when he's in full flood.

It was Ray that gave me the idea. He was still flogging himself to death, playing the flight of the bumble bee on the keyboard, and you could now hear the sweat dropping onto the floor.

I thought to myself that it was a good job he didn't have to write all the information down on paper... when I suddenly got the idea of using a pencil.

I picked mine up between thumb and finger, had just managed to locate the itch with the other end, and was about to scratch, when Ray came on the intercom.

"Peter, can you select the port VDU on page two?"

It was either the message, or the itch... and the itch won.

"In a minute Ray, I'm just doing a fuel check."

It was one of the best scratches that I ever had.

Absolute bliss for two minutes.

On the screen it merely said,

"Stage two confirmed."

* * *

We flew over Shiraz town.

The place was in darkness, a complete blackout. Over to our left, about two hundred miles, was the southern Iranian coastline.

Most of the ports and deep water anchorages destroyed. There was no way that I could see how the Iranian oil was getting out, unless it was by pipeline.

"Start descending for Al Faw, it's selected on the head up unit.

Follow the computer's instructions, and it will lead you right to the mouth of the waterway."

Al Faw was a small port on the exit of the waterway.

I say 'was' because it no longer existed. Ray was using the title purely as a reference point.

Basra was about fifty miles north of this point.

The bombs were going to be dropped every ten miles starting five miles north of the Al Faw reference point, with the last one five miles south of Basra. As before, all we had to do was fly the aircraft, and the computer would do the rest.

There was no interference from anyone in the area, from either side, during our descent and the subsequent run up to the exit of the waterway.

We had timed it so that as we ran up to Basra the sun would be rising behind us, and we would have almost full daylight.

It was time to commence stage two.

"Advise Gan what we're doing, Ray.

We start in ten minutes.

There'll be enough light then."

Gan would be able to follow our progress every inch of the way, and they would see what we could see through the TV camera link via Sky net.

With all the other additional material already collected and confirmed by our on board computer, which they had access to, they could give the final clearance for stage two of the operation...

... Once this stage was over, we could take the Vulcan home to Gan.

Some home that was, especially with Le Boustarde around.

That bloke's a permanent itch that you can't scratch!

Ray started the data link sequence with the Gan tanker, and then we went walkabout. We had been told to fly up the Shatt El Arab from the south, as far as Qurna with all the equipment running, then around specific towns on the return.

The infra red detection cameras, and the sideways looking transmitters and receivers would pick up everything and anybody, in an area five miles either side of the waterway.

It was a wasted country, if you could call it a country...

Take a piece of land one mile square, and fill it with sand and rock.

Add to this four hundred lorries, Landrovers, buses and tanks.

Blow most of them up and set fire to the rest.

When this has been done, tip half of them over onto their sides and backs, and scatter a liberal amount of ammunition boxes, guns and useless stores.

Take any object, building or piece of land over ten feet high, and raze it to the ground with shell and mortar fire, until completely flattened.

Collect most of the bodies, if possible, then bulldoze the trenches flat.

If there are any ships and aircraft in this piece of land, then bombard them until complete destruction takes place, then bombard again until everyone is dead.

Towns, railways, roads, and other means of communication are to be rendered useless.

Oil refineries are to be set on fire after blanket bombing, and then the fires maintained by continual shelling...

And it was like that for every square mile from Al Faw to Qurna.

'They' at Gan saw in on their monitor screens.

The team at the United Nations saw it on their main computer screen.

All the representatives of the other one hundred and fifty nine countries saw it on each of their monitors.

The whole world saw it...

And they all thought the same thing.

What a complete and utter waste.

* * *

We started at the estuary of the waterway, where it entered the Gulf at Ras Al Bishop, and flew up the bank on the left hand side facing upstream.

Al Faw, Ma'amur Dora and Khosrowabad no longer existed.

The Abadan refinery was a mass of flames.

Khorramshahr was just a pile of flattened buildings, and the towns of Abu Al Khasib and Al Ma'qic had been returned to basic desert.

We then went to Basra.

It wasn't a mass of flames yet, but it was later on, when Gan asked us to go back and have another look before we dropped the bombs.

There was a continuous stream of refugees moving across the desert, towards the west, to anywhere, as long as it was towards the west.

No panic, just slow ponderous movements by the weary camels, and laborious plodding from the water buffalo carts.

The people followed in their thousands.

A mass of black stretched from the outskirts of the town, as far as the existing horizon.

It was a slow, tired, line of refugees; not knowing where they were going, only that it had to be west.

There were no trucks, lorries, or cars, because there wasn't any fuel.

If they were lucky they had water to drink.

We both looked at the mass of people as I banked the aircraft around them, and I said to Ray, who was looking out of the front window of the cockpit at the time,

"Send a message to Gan for me.

Make it nice and simple so that even 'they' will understand."

: NO STAGE TWO UNTIL BASRA EVACUATED. CONFIRM PLEASE:

Ray looked at me and nodded his approval.

The message came back immediately.

One word only.

: CONFIRMED:

* * *

We flew around for a while, taking more detailed pictures for analysis back at the UN headquarters; and when they were ready, they asked us to carry out a detailed run south again, on the other side of the waterway.

We flew over the remains of the railway bridge at Al Ma'qic, and followed the river back down to the Gulf once more.

We recorded the ruins of Khorramshahr on the TV cassettes. The infra red receivers indicated not a living soul anywhere in the city. They had either all got the message to get out...

Or they were dead.

The Abadan oil refinery did not exist, and neither did the town.

We could not get good pictures, because of the mass of thick black smoke pouring out of the ground; and the infra red cameras, plus all the detection equipment we carried, was swamped by the intense heat.

But we were all satisfied that nothing could have survived down there.

We continued as far as the estuary, then orbited over the water until we received our next instructions.

Apart from the lines of refugees from Basra, we had not seen a single living thing in the area.

* * *

Then we got an unexpected message from Gan,

: POSSIBLE INFRA RED PICKUP AT KHORRAMSHAR.

RETURN TO INVESTIGATE.

USE CAMERA LINKED UP TO HEAD UP DISPLAY.

ALL INFRA RED SENSORS TO POINT FORWARDS.

AWAIT AND FOLLOW INSTRUCTIONS:

"What do you make of that Ray?"

"Could be a local fire. There's a lot around the Abadan area.

I suggest we skirt around the refinery, and come in from the north east, otherwise the sensors will be swamped by the heat from that inferno and we won't pick up a thing."

Ray put the markers on the screen to a point ten miles north east of Khorramshahr; we flew to the north, and approached the north east suburbs of town with the equipment running as instructed.

The computer was linked directly via Skynet to the main computer in the tanker, so they were able to record everything that we saw and picked up.

The head up display was a mass of red on the left hand side of the glass, from the fire well to port of us.

I turned the contrast control down, to get rid of it all, which would allow me to see any small signal in our immediate area.

There was a very faint horizontal red line, across the right hand side of the screen.

It had been masked by the Abadan heat.

I looked very carefully, to see if this was another fire or hot spot pick up, but it looked different from everything else.

"Ray, can you come up here for a while and have a look at this?"

We both saw the same thing.

It wasn't my eyes deceiving me.

It was a very faint line but definitely there.

... And then it disappeared.

Gan sent instructions on the screen in front of me,

: APPROACH FROM ALL CARDINAL POINTS AND RECORD ON AIRCRAFT COMPUTERS:

"Ok Ray. I'll do the flying bit, you do the recording."

It took about twenty minutes to fly the whole pattern, and on every approach we saw the line on the side of the screen, always horizontal across the bottom of the glass.

We circled round the town for ten minutes before we received the next message

: SELECT CHANNEL 15 ON CAMERA, AND TRY A HOMING ON THE SIGNAL TO ASCERTAIN POSITION:

I did as instructed.

The line was to the left of the head up display, so I flew the aircraft in a gentle left turn to see what happened.

The ruins of the town were just beneath me, and I noticed the left hand edge of the line lift up from the horizontal base of the glass.

It was lying at an angle of about five degrees from the base line, and the more I turned, the more the angle increased.

I kept the turn on until it was almost vertical, then flew the aircraft straight ahead.

It was as if there was a beacon dead ahead of us.

The line began to flicker. The brightness varied as we approached, and then it went out.

I flew on for about fifteen seconds, then turned gently to the right and did another homing run.

The same thing happened again.

It flickered for about ten seconds or so, and then disappeared from the screen.

"Have you got it all Ray?"

"Yes. There's not a lot to go on but it's all on disc.

They should have the same at Gan."

They didn't need any more runs.

They had either got enough data, or had recognised what it was.

The final instruction came on the screen.

: WAIT AT BASRA:

And that's what we did.

* * *

After we arrived there, we flew up and down the refugee track for three hours.

We saw the numbers gradually thin out during the morning. We were determined to stay there until every single person was out of Basra, even if it meant waiting all day if we had to...

But it didn't take that long, and when we saw no more black garments on the road we flew low over the rooftops with the detectors... and after that we went back, and did it again.

By the time they had all left the town was a mass of flames.

They had all set fire to their homes!

* * *

Gan control was satisfied.

The United Nations were satisfied.

Every country watching was satisfied...

And what was more important than that, we were satisfied.

Because nothing was going to be done until that happened, and 'they' knew it.

Mr Lee Luanda knew it too, because he was watching all the time in the empty auditorium at his monitor on the table in front of him, sitting at his official chair.

It wasn't the presidential chair, but the little hard backed wooden chair in front of all the others; because he was the only person that could represent the new country.

He was, at that moment, the official representative of the one hundred and sixtieth country to join the General Assembly; and he had the name in big white lettering, across the front of the table facing the now empty presidential chair.

It said simply,

: Shatt EL Arab:

Mr Lee Luanda signed the paper presented to him. It was witnessed by others then recorded for posterity.

The screen on front of me said simply,

: PROCEED STAGE TWO.

CONFIRMED:

* * *

"Start the spinning Ray.

I'll get into position."

We were starting at the one hundred mile point again. Not because we had to, but it gave us more time for all that had to be done.

All the data was ready for Ray to start the sequencing.

The flight computer was pre programmed with the necessary detail, and by the time we were running in towards the Shatt El Arab, not only had everything been prepared, but it had also been confirmed by Gan and the United Nations scientists.

It did not take them very long to make the final decision, and at one hundred miles from Basra the port screen turned green.

We were flying slowly now as there was no need for any rushing around, at about one thousand feet above the waterway.

The bombs were dropped without any drama, every ten miles, with the last one placed five miles from the outskirts of the town.

It was now just a thick black pall of smoke, and I was grateful that I did not have to go through it.

The job was done now and we could return to Gan, but before we did, there was one more thing we had to do.

We had noticed during our long wait at Basra that on the western side of the town there was a large area, which had obviously been used as a casualty post. There was a makeshift tented encampment with ambulances all around.

It had all the indications of constant usage.

The ambulances could not be used during the exodus, and many of the struggling refugees had been taken from this camp.

This was from where the final ones had walked from... the lucky ones that is!

The rest didn't make it.

We could see the bodies in their thousands, lying on stretchers on the ground across the vast camp.

The red cross and red crescent flags were fluttering weakly in the light wind. The cemetery was just beyond it.

There was no way so many bodies could have been buried individually, so they had all been put into communal graves, some of them not yet covered over.

This was the reason we had criss-crossed the town earlier on, just to make sure nobody was alive...

And I sincerely hoped we were right.

Ray came up front and looked quietly out of the side window.

I closed the throttles and descended to about two hundred feet above the ground, then flew very slowly towards the encampment.

Just before the hospital tent we dipped the starboard wing in a final salute to all the dead, and held it down until we were past.

They were not our enemies, but even if they were, they would still have been given the dignity which those who die for their country deserve.

* * *

The job far which Ray and I had been recruited was now complete.

We had planted the seeds for the United Nations diplomats, and had, previous to this, dropped the first five weapons for their analysis.

It was all up to them now.

I felt weary, then realised that it had been nearly five hours since we departed from Girishk; the majority of the time in the blazing hot sun.

As we flew away from Basra we changed over, and Raymond took control of the aeroplane. He was driving now, and I was the passenger!

We took one last look at the city on the screen.

The rear camera recorded the scene for historians to see forever.

It recorded the view, until the last wisps of smoke disappeared as we got further and further away...

And then it was gone.

"Let's go home, Ray."

He didn't say anything.

He just did it.

Chapter 20. Oasis

Ahmed Ali Khalifa had been sitting in the canteen of the Kuwaiti International railway system, having a final meal before departure.

He was one of the drivers of the large French electro-diesel engines that pulled the long trains from Kuwait City to the surrounding countries.

There was a bit of a flap on apparently.

He had heard about the explosion at Bandar Abbas, and there was some rumour about the trains being used for refugees in Iraq.

The town of Basra was mentioned, but like all rumours it had varied from complete annihilation of the population, to the other extreme of several of them going for a walk around the city walls.

This was very unusual, as the line to Basra, Qurna, Baghdad and beyond had not been used for several years, if it still remained at all.

He had noticed on the controller's board that he was on a freight run to Amman.

He liked this route, as he could normally open the engine to full speed across the desert.

The streamlined passenger trains could get up to approximately two hundred and fifty miles per hour, and it didn't take long to get to Amman at that speed.

The track had been built after the Sheik of Kuwait had been to the July 1989 OPEC meeting at Lyon, in central France, and had seen the new trains which had superseded the TGV Paris to Lyon expresses.

They had cut the time down by half, and that journey now only took an hour.

The greatest reward to the French railway system was the revenue obtained from the London Marseilles holiday route, through the channel tunnel.

There was a regular hourly service from London, bypassing Paris and Lyon to the east, arriving at the south coast of France four hours later.

It now took longer to get across London to Victoria station from the other terminals, than it did for the Channel Tunnel Company trains to reach the entrance to the tunnel...

And British Rail was still trying to get there!

The Sheik had seen the possibilities of using a rail track to the eastern Mediterranean Sea ports for his oil exports when the Gulf had been blocked, and since then the Amman link had been constantly used.

The engineers had built a double track about three hundred yards apart across the Nafud desert, just to the south of the border between Saudi Arabia and Iraq. It was almost a dead straight line, apart from a few minor curves.

His radio pager bleeped in his top pocket. It was time to go.

His control room had sent a tanker train on ahead. He would be fifteen minutes after this, the next to leave.

All his documents were ready, and the engineers had the engine rumbling quietly in the marshalling yard down below.

He climbed up the ladder, and took his seat in front of the array of instruments and gauges, pushed the speed lever forwards, switched on the automatic hydraulic brakes, and the engine moved slowly across the goods yard pulling the freight wagons behind it.

The control lights advised him of his track routing across the sidings complex and within five minutes he was on the northern line to Amman.

The radio bleeped.

It was the control room telling him that he was clear to increase speed.

Freight trains were restricted to one hundred and fifty miles per hour unfortunately, because of the dust thrown up by the slipstream.

He had the speed lever fully forward in the acceleration position. The speedometer gradually crept upwards, and at the designated black mark on the gauge he pulled it back until the speed stabilised itself.

Ahmed had done it all before, and had now settled down into his routine of checking all the instruments, and the necessary communications calls to control. These ensured that he did not fall asleep as he looked at the track ahead.

If he did then the automatic brake system came into operation, which not only stopped the train but closed down the whole track. Offenders received severe repercussions; they tended to lose certain very important parts of their bodies...

So he did not fall asleep at his work!

* * *

Ray saw the cloud of dust and sand thrown up behind the train from twenty miles away.

It was a simple matter to steer towards it, then follow the railway track across the brown desert. The train and the aircraft were the only things moving in the area.

Nobody went into the desert unless they were either crossing it, or getting out of it.

Temperatures soared to an average of one hundred and thirty... in the shade...

And that was in the winter!

We were following the line of the railway track now, two miles behind the train, about three hundred feet above the flat desert.

Ray let the aircraft creep slowly up to the train, then eased the throttles back, until the aircraft was flying at the same speed as the train was travelling along the track.

I had picked it up on the front camera, and had placed the two visual markers on the middle wagon, right in the centre of the train.

It was like hitting a sitting duck, from two feet away, with a gun barrel two feet long.

I put in the appropriate disc, pressed the computer keyboard and started the automatic sequence.

Ray concentrated on the flying.

He had to set the aircraft up exactly above the train, before selecting the auto circuits.

After that his job would be to ensure that they worked correctly.

When the two markers were set up accurately, and the flying parameters were correct, Ray selected the computer into operation.

Nothing happened for ten seconds, while the flying computer and the main computer did a safety check with each other, and then very slowly the aircraft crept downwards to a position fifty feet above the train.

Ray's hands were on the throttles and the little electronic joystick, the movements were barely perceptible.

His concentration was intense now.

But the rear computer did all the work.

The front nose wheel came down first, and locked itself into position. The speed had to be maintained, which meant that Ray had to check all the time that the auto speed control was working.

If not, he was in for some hard work.

When the wheel was down and fully locked, the top half of the port VDU screen turned green to indicate that it was safe to continue.

The computer waited until the speed circuit matched the train speed again, then selected down the tail wheel. The same sequence of operations repeated themselves, until the tail wheel was fully locked down.

When this occurred the whole of the VDU screen turned green...

Both wheels were now ready.

The two computers ensured that all parameters matched, after which the aircraft very slowly crept down towards the flat wagons.

Immediately below the two sets of wheels, in the centre of each wagon, was a depression that exactly matched the shape of the tyres.

The mouldings had taken place earlier during the year.

As the wheels slowly descended, the tyres were fed into these depressions, by wide funnelled guiding ramps.

Up until this point, Ray could have pulled back on the joystick to climb away if he wished, but once the weight of the aircraft pushed downwards, and operated hydraulic locking clamps on the wagon, we were down and locked onto the train.

The two sets of clamps pushed across the top of each depression, and gripped the main metal bogies of each wheel, and as the aircraft thrust deeper into the depressions, the hydraulic pressures increased on the clamps.

At the deepest penetration, with the full weight of the aircraft thrusting downwards into the recesses, the green VDU screen started to flash.

It was only then that Ray pulled gently back on the four throttles, to the idling position, and the train and the aircraft became as one.

The marriage of the two machines had been consummated as planned, approximately one hundred and ten miles west of the city of Kuwait; which was most important, because it was here that the rail track ran across the neutral territory of the At Tawal oasis, situated on the northern border of Saudi Arabia, to the west of the Sheikdom of Kuwait, and south of the Republic of Iraq.

Nobody could then claim that we had violated their territorial rights, and be accused by any other member of the United Nations of direct complicity in our actions.

Ahmed had seen all this happening in the rear view mirror immediately above him, and had seen the sequencing on his computer monitor in front of him.

He saw the green flashing screen, and checked the mileage.

This crew had done well, he thought. They had given him a good twenty miles to go before the junction.

He pressed a key on the keyboard in front of him to tell the crew what he was doing, then pulled back on the speed lever.

He had ample time left.

His real job was for the American space administration, but in between shuttle flights he worked as a relief driver for the rail company.

The main international airport at Kuwait was one of the landing grounds for shuttle operations to the Middle East, but since the Gulf war had intensified, NASA decided that it was too dangerous for the Boeing 747 to land and piggy back each spacecraft back to Kennedy space centre; so they designed the flat bed wagons to take them across the desert to Amman International for recovery.

The next flight was due in three weeks time...

But in the meantime Ahmed had 'borrowed' the wagons for a rush job, which he had been told about, and told to keep quiet about, only two hours ago...

And he knew how to keep his mouth shut when he had to.

At one mile from the junction he was now down to five miles per hour.

He would have to stop before he turned off the main track, otherwise the port wing of the Vulcan was likely to scrape the surface of the ground.

He had previously lost a Hercules propeller, by rushing round too fast, and he was taking no chances this time. He could see the track disappearing into the horizon ahead of him.

Amman was eight hundred miles beyond that.

It was the longest runway in the world, and even then some of them managed to miss it!

The train clattered across the points, then travelled northwards towards the oasis about five miles away. Ray and I just sat up front and watched the passing scenery.

The last time I did that was at night and everything was black. This time it was golden brown.

Life was improving all the time!

The tanker train and the crew had got there fifteen minutes before them. Ahmed could see the refuelling tanks parked up beside the engine repair sheds.

He slowed to a stop three hundred yards before them, and waited until the wide doors were wound fully open. This was the part he liked best.

He reached into his locker, and pulled out a battered old peaked hat which he had pinched from a Kuwaiti bus conductor, and put it smartly on his head.

He had stitched lots of coloured material to the peak, and around the sides.

On the left breast pocket of his shirt he pinned a pair of flying wings that made out of a piece of leather from an old pair of boots, with the inscription 'Royal Tawal Airline' printed across the top.

The chief pilot of the 'airline' was about to make his return to his own personal airport, just ahead of him...

* * *

...He gazed across the cockpit, at the young dark haired stewardess now sitting in the second pilot's seat, and gave her a long slow lingering smile...

She fluttered her eyelashes with acute embarrassment, and in doing so accidently dropped the blue silken front of her veil a quarter of an inch, to reveal the soft luscious flesh of her left cheek...

She quickly returned the material again, but it was too late...

He had seen it... He went wild in expectation of a thousand and one Arabian nights under the desert moon; but at the moment he had work to do...

He pushed the four throttles of his Jumbo Jet forward, and went slowly towards the airport terminal where the waiting multitude, their cameras at the ready, gazed across the tarmac in wonder and admiration at his skills of airmanship...

An enormous crowd of people...

* * *

Comprising at that moment of a dozen rough looking blokes, leaning against the wall of the engine shed, bored to death because they had seen it all before.

Two were picking their noses; another was scratching his backside, and a third was cleaning his greasy fingernails with the big wiggly dagger he carried.

They waited, very patiently, until 'Captain Walter Mitty' finished the little act he went through every time he came here.

* * *

Ahmed slowly entered the engine repair shed with his cargo.

The power of the heavy diesels reverberated loudly around the inside as he crept up towards the far doors.

One of the workmen gave him the thumbs up signal.

The aircraft was now well inside the shed.

He applied the brakes, pulled the engine control lever fully back to idle the powerful diesels, *and with one last lingering look at his beautiful stewardess, now panting heavily with expectation, her soft creamy breasts rising and falling as she did so,* picked up his microphone in front of him and *as she watched him with her large promising blue eyes,* said in his best airline captain's type voice:

: ZERO ONE, WELCOME TO TAWAL OASIS.

PLEASE CHOP YOUR ENGINES:

* * *

Ray pulled the throttles closed, the engines died down, the Arabian crew closed the engine shed doors, we disappeared yet again from the outside world...

And so did Ahmed's stewardess!

I said to Ray when he got down from his seat,

"Not bad for a beginner."

You could see his hair rising.

"Just a word, young sir. We've done four landings now.

How come you're the only one of us that's actually landed on a bloody runway?"

I looked down at a piece of imaginary fluff on my lapel and flicked it off.

"Well, you see it's like this, Ray.

We steelies like to give you young sprogs as much practice as possible."

I could see his thumbs twitch, and his fingers begin to curl so I got out fast. I suddenly remembered that he owed me for the Girishk bridge, so I didn't hang around.

Ahmed pressed the key on his front panel to let Gan know that we had arrived; then went into the cockpit to feed the information that we had recorded on the runs up and down the waterway, onto the main computer discs for them.

He also fed the information from the four discs for each of the bombs to them.

It took about half an hour, then after that his team got to work refuelling and checking the aircraft systems.

The final stage had been delayed for twenty four hours.

We were to remain at the oasis, then carry out a surveillance check down the Gulf, on our way back to Gan...

But that was tomorrow. We were now going to have a well earned rest.

Ahmed went to his cupboard again and pulled out a bottle of whisky and three glasses.

"I thought you chaps weren't allowed to drink alcohol?" I asked him.

He deliberated for a while and said,

"Well, you see, it's like this.

The Saudi Arabians are very strict; the Iraqis are also very strict...

But a little bit more religious tolerance is allowed in Kuwait, so I have decided that now and again I could be a Christian... and we are at the moment in a neutral country, so everything is all right... isn't it?"

I admired his Arabian logic.

So we drank to it.

* * *

We were in the showers afterwards and I was up to my eyes in soapsuds when Ray said to me,

"Do you fancy going out tonight, Peter?"

I stopped what I was doing in amazement.

I couldn't believe it.

There we were stuck in the middle of the desert miles away from anywhere.

That bloke never learnt.

"Don't be so damn stupid.

Where the hell are we going to get the train tickets from?

They closed the bloody station down three years ago."

"I suppose you're right," he said.

"Even if it was open, they'd probably only give out day returns.

We'd still have to come back to this dump afterwards."

I reflected on what we had said in jest, and realised how true it was.

Once 'they' had you in their clutches, it wasn't easy to get out.

At least the Royal Air Force only court martialled us, before chucking us out the back door by the seat of our pants, and the scruff of our necks.

I looked out of the window at the desert stretching away in front of me.

Down by a rock I saw a nasty little black scorpion, with two big ugly brutes each side of it.

They were all looking at me with their evil little eyes, their poisonous tails quivering above them.,

I shuddered to think what they could do to us if they were let loose!

* * *

It was Jim Bowe, back at the tanker, who first saw the infra red signal.

He was the technician responsible for recording and analysing the data as it was picked up from Skynet.

He had done the same as I had done as we approached Abadan, and that was to turn the contrast down on his computer screen; but he did it on the first run up the waterway, as the aircraft was on the northerly heading towards Basra.

Also the equipment that he was using was a lot more sophisticated than the airborne computers we had, and consequently was able to pinpoint something odd very quickly.

He and his team were in an adjacent room to the control room on the tanker, monitoring all the sensors when the screen flared a bright red due to the intense heat from the burning oil at the refinery.

He switched in an automatic contrast control, and he was now able to see the screen better.

The thin red line was very faint at first, but as the aircraft got closer to Khorramshahr it became brighter and more distinct.

The computer enhanced the signal, and it started to show the fluctuations in brightness, then it disappeared rapidly.

Jim knew he was onto something, and quickly realised that it had only been picked up by the forward camera and sensors.

He selected the rear facing camera data and immediately saw the fluctuating line, this time on the left hand side of the screen, and just as bright as when it disappeared before.

That confirmed his suspicion that it must be a signal or beacon, to starboard of the aircraft's position.

"Where's the aircraft now?" he asked quietly.

"About four miles west of the waterway, just passing Khorramshahr.

Have you found something?"

"Maybe...

Put the spectrum analyser on that signal will you, and record what you get.

We'll look at it later."

As the aircraft travelled further northwards the line got fainter, then disappeared altogether.

They continued the monitoring all the way up the waterway, until the aircraft reached Basra.

The 'red line' was the only signal received.

He spoke into the telephone, to Andy in the main control room.

"Can you watch the pictures on your screen for a while. We may have a contact, and we need time to check it out."

"OK, call me if you have anything positive."

They reselected the disc, for the time of response pickup, and put the signal onto their oscilloscope for analysing.

The spectrum analyser indicated that it was definitely a single frequency in the infra red band.

"Well now," Jim said to his other technicians,

"That's very interesting. It can't be a flare or small fire, it's too specific. It must be some form of beacon.

Can you break down the signal for analysis?"

They altered the timebase and frequency bands on the oscilloscope, to steady the signal down. It was flashing across the screen from left to right, like the horizontal hold gone wrong on a television set.

They eventually slowed it down, and then fine tuned it until it was stationary.

"Record that now in case it goes again."

They saved it both on the laser disc and the computer main hard disc, then measured it on the screen with the electronic counters.

It looked like a series of pulses stretched across the screen.

Some of them were rising and falling, and others stayed at the same height.

"This isn't the full signal Jim," one of the technicians said,

"It's only the bit that we have saved at maximum brightness.

We can measure the distances between all the static pulses, and make another waveform to isolate them from the rising pulses...

But it won't tell us what the identification of the beacon is, because the rising pulses are in a constant loop.

I'll get to work doing that bit, if you can get the aircraft to do a full sweep later on."

Jim agreed with the diagnosis so far.

He went through to the control room, and explained to Andy what they had found.

"It's a digital signal of some form, but it can't be identified fully. We need another pass by the Vulcan if possible."

"No problem.

It's on its way back now, and later on you can have a third try as it returns to Basra.

Have a word with Cheltenham, and have them geared up if you think it's important.

Stay with it until you are satisfied.

I need to know exactly what it is, before I decide whether we can ignore it."

Jim was sure that they had something.

He contacted his laboratory at the Cheltenham Communications Centre, via the private Skynet channel, and passed everything through to them.

"There will be more in ten minutes for you, and we'll tune in exactly onto the frequency. You should then have a nice fat signal to chew on."

They were good at the lab.

Whatever it was, they would find out.

On the second run past they received a clear pickup, from the moment the sensors found it on the approach to the town, until it disappeared from the rear camera after departure.

Jim and his team were busy measuring the data, and recording each part of the waveform.

Eventually they had about a minute and a half of varying waveforms, which they could run as a film on the computer.

Andy came into the room.

"I'm holding the aircraft down at the head of the Gulf at the moment. What have you found?"

Jim showed him the film on the main computer screen. It showed the full sequence, which had been picked up on the second run.

"It's definitely an infra red beacon, and it has an identification signal.

You can see the waveforms flashing on and off, in between some of the pulses.

It could be a forward air controller's beacon, for an aircraft strike, that's been left behind by one of the armies during retreat.

Cheltenham will see if that agrees with the waveform. If it is we can forget about it.

I'm just about to get them."

Cheltenham, however, did not agree.

The chief laboratory technician explained why not.

"You see, Jim. You would be correct, but for just one thing.

You can't see it on the equipment at Gan, as it isn't sensitive enough, but the identification is not regular.

If it was an automatic beacon, the time sequence of the flashing pulses would be exact, but there is a small variation in time between sets of identification pulses.

All I can say at the moment is that it is a beacon but not a navigation beacon... If that's any help to you.

I'll keep looking at it and call you later."

Andy looked at Jim.

"We'll get the aircraft to pinpoint it on the ground on the way back.

What channel do you want?"

"Channel 15 is the nearest. Tell them to feed into the head up display, and do a homing run on front sensors only.

We can get an accurate cut off time, and plot the position from that."

* * *

And that's why we got our message from the tanker for the homing procedure.

From what we picked up during that sequence, they found the exact position of the beacon.

It was just inside the north western suburbs of Khorramshahr, not that there was much to see.

The camera films showed a mass of rubble and collapsed buildings. Whatever it was must have been buried weeks ago, by the look of it.

We weren't worried about any of this.

We had crashed out on our bunks in the accommodation train, and were dead to the world.

There was a lot going on whilst we slept.

* * *

The United Nations at New York was carrying out an action which they wanted as many people as possible to know about...

And the controllers at Gan were carrying out actions which they wanted as few people as possible to know about...

And whilst all this was going on,

Ahmed's men played cards all through the night!

Chapter 21. State Of Nirvana

The auditorium at the United Nations building was a lonely place for Mr Luanda to sit.

He could have selected the Philippine Embassy, with other members of his countrymen if he desired. Most of the other representatives had gone to their relative embassies, scattered around New York.

There were a few in the building utilising the communications services provided, but nobody was in the large room with him.

Inwardly, he preferred it like that.

The mantle that he was now bearing was a heavy one.

* * *

The previous month had been relatively simple compared to this.

The general policy, and the procedure followed when dealing with Iran and Iraq, had been a collective one.

All representatives, including him, had agreed on what had to be done.

It was a formality to call out the two names of the cities that had to be destroyed, the order in which it had to be done, and to give the final authority to release the weapons in the Strait of Hormuz; because the decision had been more or less made from the beginning.

His signature on the historical documents presented in front of him was merely an extension of previously agreed policy.

The scientists would use the data collected from the four weapons exploded under the water.

The effect of the quadruple shock waves, integrating through the water, and the cratering on the sea bed would now provide a yardstick, with which to base the distribution of the Basra bombs.

The years of underground nuclear tests in both America and Russia had given them limited information, as no country admitted to having carried out a multiple explosion test, even if they had done so.

In spite of earnest pleadings with the main powers over the last month, none of them said that they had carried such a test, especially on the scale which was required.

... He had to conclude, therefore that the scientist's requests for the Hormuz bombs were justified.

The military could use the four weapon explosions as a safe and efficient way of dealing with the mines lying at random throughout the length and breadth of the Gulf.

A limited attack, using low power weapons, could be analysed, and from the results it would be easy to forecast the time and cost to clear the whole of the Persian Gulf, without interference from any third party.

He had been advised that even if hostilities ceased tomorrow, it would take four and a half years to give complete assurance that all the Gulf mines were cleared.

The time span would be reduced to less than three months by the use of the new bombs. These concentrated on a high blast and shock wave effect, with an 'acceptable' level of radiation for a war time situation.

... He had therefore concluded that the military requests for the four underwater explosions could also be justified.

The fifth nuclear weapon, dropped on Bandar Abbas, was one of the new weapons; and the effects could be examined, and then compared with the computerised model of the proposed Basra explosions.

Final adjustments could be made to the aircraft procedures immediately before release, and he had been told that he could change his mind at any time before this occurred.

He was grateful for that advice.

The 'big stick' policy was a corporate policy, and he was able to justify his decision on that basis.

He would have failed if he had done otherwise.

* * *

But Basra was different.

He suspected that what he was experiencing was the same for all the other members, which is no doubt why they preferred not to be in the auditorium at that moment.

It would be the fear of Mr Luanda asking them for advice and guidance, when it came to him to make his final decision, that kept them all away.

Nobody knew if it was the right thing to do,

And if any of them were asked, they could only reply with some variant of the expression,

"I don't know".

Yes, it was correct to do it...

If it would stop the war...

But that could only be judged after the event occurring.

What about making the decision before the event?

Will we or won't we use the weapons?

Is it the correct thing to do in the circumstances?

Will it, in the long term, save lives and stop the war?

And the same answer came up every time.

"We don't know what will happen."

* * *

They had, therefore, left the final decision to him.

Which is why he was sitting all alone, in the vast auditorium, gazing at the pictures being relayed from the aircraft via Gan.

It was worse than anyone expected. He had seen destruction on a vast scale as a young man, but not like this.

It was complete and utter desecration.

When he saw the masses of refugees he was stunned.

Basra was no longer a name on a piece of paper.

The town was a living thing, and he could see it dying in front of him, its people walking away from it, burning what was most precious of all;

Their home, where generations of them had been born.

* * *

He did not want to stop the overall plan but he could do something to assist.

He picked up the telephone.

"Yes Mr Luanda?"

It was the main communications controller, in direct contact with the Gan tanker.

He responded,

"Please would you convey my wishes to the Gan controller, and ask whether he could delay the dropping of the weapons, until all those people have had a chance to evacuate.

I do not wish to see any panic.

Thank you."

He was a polite man, and he knew that it would be conveyed stronger than he had put it.

The message was duly passed on to Gan.

The controller returned within a minute.

"Mr Luanda, your message has been passed on to the aircraft."

He suspected that they were of the same mind.

* * *

He stayed in the auditorium for the next three hours watching the pictures.

He saw how the aircraft flew around the town, the area to the west and south west. He saw the numbers gradually reduce.

He heard expert opinion from his advisors, and he realised that his decision was correct and humane.

He saw the final stragglers leave the encampment, and noticed how the aircraft had remained to the west of the town, until all were outside the five miles boundary of the country that he now represented.

He watched the final overflying of what was left of the town, and was advised that they were now setting up the airborne computers to plant the weapons.

Within thirty minutes they would commence the sequence to explode them, once he had given the clearance.

The delegation was ready.

They presented the documents for him to approve.

The leader spoke.

"Mr Luanda, I have been asked to convey to you from the other members of the General Assembly; that they all concur with your decision, and wish to express their gratitude.

They all wish to advise you that any decision you make now will have their full support."

He looked up.

The burden had been lifted slightly.

"Thank you Mr Secretary."

The papers were then signed and witnessed by them all; the appropriate message to commence the dropping and detonation sequence was passed on to Gan, and subsequently to the aircraft.

The others had departed, and now he could watch the final phase,

The destruction of his new country.

* * *

The scientists had told him that the strength of each weapon required would need to be two and a half times greater than the Bandar Abbas weapon, and they would need to penetrate to a depth of more than two hundred feet into the bed of the waterway for maximum effect.

They had advised him that the weapons would have serrated teeth of hard steel on the sides of the drums...

That they would be spun backwards very fast...

That they would act as drill bits, bearing deep into the soft earth underneath the waterway...

That they would...

But he was not interested in that any more.

He was still watching the screen in front of him. He saw the aircraft flying towards Basra, then descend towards the ground.

The scientists had not told him about this.

Was this something that they were doing outside his authority?

He picked up the telephone, and was about to press the button to connect him to the controller, when he saw the screen.

He saw the hospital tent.

He saw thousands upon thousands of dead bodies lying on the ground.

He saw the open graves with the bodies lying in the open, unburied.

He was shocked.

He had never seen so many dead people before.

Surely this could not be justified by calling the fighting between two adjacent countries a 'Holy War'.

It was inhumane.

It was worse than that...

It was inhuman!

He looked at the screen again.

It reminded him of the scene he saw in the film 'Gone With The Wind', when the camera panned back and showed the hundreds of dead and wounded soldiers of the Confederate Army, lying all over the ground around the railway track in Atlanta, Georgia.

And then, suddenly, he saw the horizon tilt across the screen, as the aircraft did its final salute.

He watched it for five seconds then saw it return back again.

He saw the camera change to the rear of the aircraft, and watched the capital city of his new country disappear from view, until only the wisps of smoke remained...

And then the screen went blank as the camera was switched off.

He sat in a state of shocked bewilderment.

He couldn't believe what he had just seen.

* * *

The telephone buzzed at his side. It was the controller.

"Mr Luanda. Everything is satisfactory.

We will need your authorization to commence the detonation."

As with the previous detonations, they were asking him to sign the historical documents, which would be retained in the United Nations archives.

This was one of the greatest decisions ever.

Not just the destruction of a city, but the destruction of an entire country...

His new country.

No one had ever been faced with such a task before.

He pressed the button and spoke into his telephone.

"Thank you. Please send in Mr Secretary and the other signatories."

He had a few moments.

It was time to reflect on his own for a while, to consider his responsibilities.

When he was good and ready, he would then see to all the procedures, that the scientists and diplomats wished him to follow.

He sat quietly with his eyes closed, in the peace and silence of the vast auditorium.

He did not hear the door open at the far end of the room, or the footsteps of Mr Hassan Rejad walk down the wide carpeted aisle between the seats and across towards him.

He sensed more than heard the tall figure above him.

Mr Luanda looked up and saw the representative of the Republic of Iran standing over him. His feelings were one of immediate sorrow.

He stood up and took Mr Rejad's outstretched hand and looked into his eyes.

"Mr Rejad. Please accept my sincerest apologies, for what I have had to do to your country.

My deepest sympathies."

There was a pause before Mr Rejad spoke.

"No Mr Luanda.

It is I who come to you, to apologise for what we have forced you to do."

The handshake was more firm, and had more warmth than before.

"I have come to ask of you a great favour.

May we talk?"

They sat in the seats behind the little chair.

"Mr Luanda.

Those bodies.

I ask if you can do for them, what we do for our dead.

You see, as Muslims, we must be buried lying on our right side, facing Mecca within one whole day; and our womenfolk must visit us every Friday for forty days after that, to lay palm leaves on our flat graves."

Mr Luanda nodded.

"Mr Luanda. I must not lose face with the Iraqi representative, which is why I come to you alone.

He must not know of my visit. You must not tell him.

Mr Luanda, today is the sacred Friday, the men are uncovered, and the womenfolk cannot get to them."

Mr Luanda now understood what was being asked.

"Mr Shakir cannot come to see you and ask what I ask.

He cannot lose face either.

He is a very religious man, and is very concerned by what he saw just now."

Mr Luanda looked up at the big man.

Bigger now in all respects than he was before.

"Mr Rejad. Let me assure you, nothing will be done until the Iraqi government can remove those bodies, and the correct religious rites can take place.

You have my word."

The tall Iranian looked down at Mr Luanda, and suddenly realised that he was in fact looking up at a great man.

"Thank you, Mr Luanda."

Lee Luanda smiled at him.

"No, Mr Rejad. Thank you for telling me."

He lifted the telephone, pressed the button and spoke to the controller.

"You may send in Mr Secretary now please"

By the time the signatories had arrived, Mr Rejad had departed, and the film on the screen had been wound back to show the encampment.

They stood in silence looking at it.

It was Mr Luanda who spoke.

"I wonder how long it would take the official United Nations, with our assistance, to help the Iraqis?"

There was a slight pause before the secretary replied.

"We estimate about twenty four hours, Mr President."

Mr Luanda rose slowly from his hard wooden chair, took his stick, and looked at the delegates.

"Then I think I will return tomorrow.

Please send my compliments to Mr Shakir when you see him."

He walked slowly up the aisle.

Up the broad carpet which Mr Rejad had walked before, as he left the auditorium.

***

Mr Luanda was a Buddhist.

He had not fully appreciated the sacred Friday, or its significance.

His own search was for Nirvana; a condition where all the deeds of a previous existence have perished, been forgiven, and supreme peace is attained.

Mr Rejad had shown him the way, and he was following in his footsteps.

The delegation watched him, as he slowly ascended the aisle, and departed from the auditorium.

Today they would evacuate Basra completely.

Tomorrow...

They would destroy it.

Chapter 22. Micro Jets

The laboratory technicians at Cheltenham Communications Centre got to work on the Khorramshahr signal as soon as they received it from Gan.

The team that investigated it had spent hours looking at all the information that they had managed to obtain from various sources throughout the past years over the airwaves; ranging from the Moscow taxi service to the obscene CB messages by unprofessionals buying the gear for Christmas presents, then discarding it after they realised that they would have to buy batteries to keep them working.

They had ascertained three points very rapidly:

The waveform was made up of two signals; as yet unidentified,

The flashing identification was regular and was a Morse code signal; which one of their operators was working on now,

And what was the most important factor of all,

It was definitely not an automatic beacon.

The only logical alternative solution was, therefore; that the flashing Morse identification must be non automatic...

It had to be manually switched.

The team were rapidly coming to the conclusion that there may be a person underneath the rubble at Khorramshahr...

It was their job to give a reasonable judgement to this effect, before any positive information one way or the other was passed to the Gan controller.

A full investigation had to be conducted; otherwise a conclusive decision would not be able to be made.

* * *

It was the radio operator who reported his findings first, which confirmed the suspicion that it was a person who was doing the coding.

His experience in this matter was based on at least twenty five years of listening to other peoples 'fists',

"It is definitely Morse code being transmitted very slowly, by someone who knows the letters of the code, but as yet, does not know the sounds.

He or she is therefore not a radio operator.

He or she can hear or see what is being transmitted.

You can tell by the fact that the signal is nice and clipped; therefore the beacon is linked to a noise indicator.

The sequence of dots and dashes is as follows;

Dot , Dash, Dash, Dot, Dash, Dash, Dash;

But there is no variation in between the dots and dashes to indicate what the specific letters are.

The sender is either extremely weak, or has an injured hand, because the identification signal is very, very slow."

* * *

It took longer to identify the beacon.

It was not a piece of discarded military equipment, but a hand held infra red controller for a laser disc video recorder of Japanese manufacture.

The firm were immediately contacted, and it was soon possible to obtain one of the same controllers for a comparison to be made.

The waveforms matched exactly; and it was soon found that the static pulse sequence of the signal increased the brightness of the television screen to maximum, and the pulsed sequence operated the circuit for the volume control.

The operator's diagnosis was, to say, right on the button.

"We have got a very intelligent person here gentlemen," the chief investigator declared to his team.

"The control unit has been directed vertically upwards to act as a pinpoint beacon,

The brightness has been put on maximum, to allow our radioactive sensors to pick up any reflected radiation from the screen, and he is using the sound of the set to obtain an accurate Morse identification signal.

I suggest we tell Gan control our findings and advise them that we are informing the Foreign Office to see if we have any special forces in the area."

They sent a 'certain office' in Whitehall a complete list of all the combinations that the coding could be.

'Certain people' spent about two hours on it, before they came up with something fairly definite.

* * *

The message was sent by telex to Cheltenham and Gan:

: THERE IS A HIGH PROBABILITY THAT THE PERSON WHO TRANSMITTED THE MESSAGE IS FREDERICK ARTHUR WATT, HER MAJESTY'S SPECIAL ENVOY WHO WENT MISSING FOUR YEARS AGO WHILST ON A PEACE MISSION TO TEHERAN.

LAST SEEN AND HEARD TWO YEARS AGO WHEN A LASER DISC RECORDING WAS SENT TO THE BRITISH EMBASSY IN RIYADH DICTATING TERMS FOR HIS RELEASE.

EARNEST ENDEAVOURS FOR HIS REPATRIATION ARE REQUESTED.

REGRET IT IS NOT POSSIBLE TO DELAY DETONATION:

Andy looked at the telex. The Cheltenham and Whitehall teams had both done a professional investigative job.

It was up to them now.

He looked at the clock on the control room wall. It had been set to show the time before weapon detonation. There were twelve hours to go before the explosion, with no chance of delaying it.

He wasted no time.

"Get the Bear ready for a long trip, and wake up Michel and his crew.

Get him in here fast; he's got some work ahead of him.

What forces have we got in the area for a rescue attempt?"

They looked at the display board with all the shipping and forces in their current positions. All had been pulled out of the Gulf and were now in the Indian Ocean returning to Gan.

There was nothing at all at the northern end of the Persian Gulf to effect a rescue.

It wasn't just a case of walking in and saying, "Hello, old boy, How are you?"

It was more likely to be a shooting match with a number of fanatics flinging small lead projectiles in your direction, and screaming insults at the same time.

"Andy, we've got the commando ship, Bulldog, en route to Colombo for rest and recovery.

Number Six Airborne Para Commando Group's on board. That's a possibility.

If we can get a small team up to Khorramshahr, they could do something positive. They're a hard bunch of characters, that know what needs to be done.

Give me a quarter of an hour with Michel and I'll work something out."

The distances were enormous to travel in the time available.

To have any chance on the ground, the team would need at least two and a half hours to get in, pick up the man and somehow get out of the area.

The flood plain of the river was such that it would be difficult to go south or southwest unless they had a boat, and that would be too slow.

If they went north by land, that would be going back into Iranian hands again.

He put the electronic map of the Khorramshahr region on his screen for a detailed look.

The main roadway and railway communications came in from the north. This was the main source of overland military communication for heavy forces into the town, and would have been maintained to a reasonable standard, in spite of the war.

He pulled out the reconnaissance photographs and went over them with a three dimensional viewer.

"John, look at this.

I think we can get them out by air, if we use the disused airfield ten miles north of the town."

They both checked the runways.

It was a double runway airfield, crossing at right angles with each other. The surfaces had been shattered by bombs, but the taxiway adjacent to the road leading south to the town was intact for more than half its length.

The bombers had concentrated on the runway, and only random bombs had struck the taxiway.

"If the team can get to that point, we can pick them up with the Vulcan.

It can get off in that distance with the afterburners no problem at all, so work back from there."

Michel joined them, looked at the map and shook his head,

"I can't get them there in time. It is too far. The wind is against.

I lose time landing at Colombo.

It cannot be done."

He gazed downwards, and they could both see his Russian brain working overtime.

"How many micro jets do we have at Gan?"

Andy looked at the technical board.

"Two usable, both ready for loading."

"Ok, this is what we do.

We do a carrier pickup at sea.

Four people only will transfer to the Bear, with the micro jets.

We fly towards Masira. Peter and Ray fly high level, very fast to meet us.

Transfer the four commandos to the Vulcan, then they transit fast, back to Khorramshahr.

Parachute descent into the area. Estimate descent time about three hours before the detonation.

We continue as back up aircraft if needed, and refuel at Masira."

They fed the plan into the computer and tested it. With the forecast winds, and estimated carrier position, it was possible to do it.

Michel would have to be airborne as soon as they could manage to get the micro jets loaded.

The other bits of the planning could be done by Gan whilst they were airborne.

Andy agreed that it was possible, so they got on with it.

* * *

It is surprising the reserves of strength that individuals find when they are required.

The word got round the tankers, and everybody was there preparing Michel's aircraft.

It took an hour of concentrated hard work to get the jets slung under the fuselage in two cradles, mounted in the forward and rear bomb bays. They would by piloted by Piotr and Ivan.

All four of the crew could fly the micros, it was their means of escape in emergencies; there was an incentive to learn to fly them.

It was better to be scared to death, than be in a position where you could never be scared at all!

The ground crew pulled the bomber across the drawbridge, and down to the runway, whilst Michel and the engineer tested engines and equipment.

No time was wasted.

The tug cast off the tow bar as soon as it got on the runway, and Michel opened up the huge turboprops to full power.

It's always a slow start for heavy aircraft to get airborne, and this was no exception. It took the whole of the runway before the wheels lifted slowly off the concrete.

It managed to get into the air just before the edge of the road crossing the end of the runway, leading down to the rocks by the beach.

Andy looked at John.

"Jeezus, that was a bit close. We must have overloaded it."

John grinned.

"No, that's only Michel's bit of Russian drama.

He used to be an actor before joining the Soviet Air Force.

He's only playing to the crowd.

He had stacks of room to take off."

They watched the Bear turn to the north east and climb out towards Colombo. Both went back to the control room.

There were a few important messages to be sent to various people.

* * *

The United Nations commando carrier was about fifty miles out from Colombo when the request arrived at the communications centre.

The Captain was roused, and after reading the signal, called in the Regiment Commander.

"They want four men who have been in the area before, and know what to look for.

I know all your men are good but they want the best.

Who do you suggest?"

Bill Carter was selected first. He would lead the group.

Captain by rank, and had been in the regiment on active service all over the Gulf for four years.

His number two was Lieutenant David O'Mara.

He made his name undercover in Northern Ireland, during the final three years of the campaign.

Les Wilson came next.

Two years in one of the Iraqi units, on desert patrols against the rebel suicide squads. He spoke Arabic like a native.

Jock Campbell, the fourth in the team, came from the Gorbals district of Glasgow.

He was a tough nut to crack. He spat sulphuric acid and was as hard as nails. If he went down he'd take a whole regiment with him.

People only spoke to him if he smiled... and that was very rare.

The Colonel spoke to them quietly in the ward room.

They had a job to do.

There was no moaning about being pulled out from their rest and recovery. No groaning and wingeing about why they had been selected.

They got the weapons, equipment and ammunition ready.

The parachutes that they needed were already in the Bear. The transfer would take place within the hour.

They had all done this sort of thing before, and by the time the Bear was overhead the carrier, all four were waiting patiently on the flight deck.

* * *

Michel opened both the bomb doors together, and lowered the cradles into the airflow underneath the fuselage.

He was flying at two thousand feet above the ground, at about one hundred and fifty knots.

The front of the cradle, into which the nose of the micro jet fitted, had a blue flashing beacon for the pilots to aim for on their return.

To help them see the fuselage in the dark, the silver paint would be illuminated by the ultra violet lights.

It would be no joke for the jets to accidentally home in on the engine nacelles...

They would be chopped to bits by the propellers.

The return procedure was to fly up underneath the fuselage, and slowly lift up and forwards, keeping clear of the downwash of the propellers.

"Start engines."

The little engines soon burst into life.

"Alpha ready."

"Bravo ready."

Michel ensured that all the systems were working safely in both the jets. The data link with each one showed up clearly on the screen in front of him.

He flew towards the carrier, which now had its lighting on.

It looked like a Christmas tree. There would be no problem landing on it.

When the computer got them all lined up, the clamps released automatically, and the two jets dropped downwards.

The leading microjet curved down into a smooth approach, straight towards the deck and engaged the arrester cable.

The carrier groundcrew opened the Perspex cockpit hatch to let Bill Carter get in, then pushed it to the steam catapult.

Ivan circled around the carrier once, then landed on the rear deck... as Piotr was catapulted off the front.

It was a quick operation and worked very efficiently.

On the return to the Bear, the micro jet eased slowly up towards the cradle; and stabilised underneath it, fifty feet below the fuselage.

Piotr could see the blue light, and lined the laser pick up towards it.

The on board computer did the rest.

He kept his hands and feet on the controls in case of a quick pull away, but that had not been required in all his approaches. The little jet eased up and forwards, and engaged smoothly into the front cradle.

The wing clamps operated, and both aircraft were mated.

He looked upwards into the bomb bay, to make sure all was satisfactory, then closed down his engine. The cradle then retracted, the wings folded underneath, and the bomb doors closed.

It was now safe to get out.

"Nice to see you again Bill," he said,

"See you later."

The sequence was repeated until all four were on board.

It took only twenty minutes to get them up from the carrier, and then they were heading northwest for the next rendezvous with the Vulcan.

* * *

Andy got the message on the screen from Michel.

"John, let Ahmed know they're on their way, then he can give our two willing heroes the good news.

It's time they saw some real action.

All they've done so far is sit on their fat backsides, flying around first class.

A few bullets up their rear ends will soon wake them up.

You take first watch. I'll take the exciting bit, and watch them both sweat..."

John grinned.

"I might even stay up and watch myself.

I wouldn't miss this for all the tea in China."

Then he sat down at the screen and typed out a whole load of instructions on the keyboard.

It was going to make interesting reading at Al Tawal.

Oh, to be a fly on the wall when they got this lot!

Chapter 23. Outriggers

As soon as 'Captain' Ahmed had shut off his engines in the power unit, after arriving in the engine shed, his team of men got to work on the aircraft.

The engine was uncoupled from the flat wagons, and used to move the tanker train into the shed, and the fuel transferred into the Vulcan.

They filled the forward fuselage tanks first, then filled the wing tanks from the centre of the aircraft outwards, which ensured that it did not tip over.

When fully loaded with fuel it settled lower on the wagon, and gave the appearance of sinking into the ground.

It looked very strange to see it with no supports under the wings; one gust of wind and it was bound to tip over, and dig into the ground during the take off.

"Don't worry Mr Barten" said Ahmed encouragingly,

"We put outriggers on for you. It's just like a child riding his first bicycle.

We bolt onto the mountings where the external tanks are fitted, and when you get airborne, just drop them into the desert.

Our magpie team will soon find them.

They have a nose for picking things up, especially when there's a thick bundle of dollars tied around each axle."

The team were wheeling the outriggers underneath the aircraft as he spoke.

They had obviously done it before with other types of aircraft. The top of the main strut was lifted up and bolted on under the wing, then electrically checked for continuity.

When that was done, the four large low pressure wheels were rolled underneath, and lined up with guide lines beside the track.

Between the strut hanging down from the wing, and a support in the centre of the wheel axle, a hydraulic ram was fitted.

This extended in length, under hydraulic pressure from a ground power unit, and connected wing and wheels together.

Steel pins were then inserted, to form a complete undercarriage unit.

Side supports were added, to take the sideways pressures during turns whilst on the track and any cross wind forces,

And when both wings were supported, the aircraft was resting on four sets of undercarriage, all with equal strength and loadings.

* * *

"We used to put the outriggers on first, before loading the fuel, when we started doing this a couple of years ago.

Then we found the reason why big holes appeared in the top of the wings... as the weight of the fuel increased during refuelling, it pushed the undercarriage main struts right through the metal surfaces.

It was very embarrassing," Ahmed confessed.

"We are getting better now.

Tomorrow I will tell you how you get airborne, but now we rest."

Within two hours they had all finished, and had retired to their accommodation train to start their game of cards.

They all sat around a small table, covering up their individual cards with their huge hands held close to their chests, their eyes flashing around seeking clues from the other players...

* * *

The Vulcan was now ready for takeoff, but that wouldn't take place until tomorrow.

It may only take two hours for a machine to recover, but it takes much more for a human body to service itself.

As they were playing the first hand of poker, we crashed out at the back of the train in the sleeper van, dead to the world.

And apparently we stayed that way until early the next morning.

* * *

It took about twelve hours to service our clapped out old bodies; and whilst that was going on the United Nations were assisting the Iraqis to remove the bodies, which had passed all hope of recovery, from Basra.

Kuwaiti International Railways provided a constant supply of suitable carriages and wagons, under the auspices of the Red Cross and Red Crescent, from a point ten miles west of the city to Qurna and Baghdad.

The trains travelled all night until the encampment was pronounced clear.

This occurred around midnight.

The United Nations Assembly then took an unprecedented step in the Gulf war, by announcing exactly what they were going to do and when.

The element of shock surprise had gone, but I understood from what I heard later that this was no longer an issue.

The bombs were definitely going to be detonated at midday the following day.

This was the information that Ahmed told us, before we sank into the black abyss.

To eliminate any panic, it was also announced that the international railway system would run expresses to Amman on a continual half hourly service through the night, and flights could take off from Kuwait City International Airport unhindered from either side.

A twenty four hour truce had been arranged by the United Nations, and it was working...

And we slept on.

The United Nations were also allowed to patrol through the new country of Shatt El Arab to ensure that no fighting was taking place, and that all troops were out of the area.

Not that they would stay in any case unless they were mad!

One does not calmly walk around the garden, looking at the flowers, when the seeds are poisonous!

They checked the main cities as far as was possible; Basra, Abadan and Khorramshahr, and any minor settlement if it had survived the war.

Nothing that lived was in the area.

Even the desert mice had got the message and had cleared out fast.

The United Nations then patrolled as far north as Qurna.

An orderly evacuation had taken place there. Nothing was broken. Nothing was ransacked. Nothing was looted.

The city was a silent as a tomb.

With a bit of luck the population could soon return in their dribs and drabs, as returning people tended to do after a disaster, but in reasonable safety.

The Iranian and Iraqi navies were invited to move further south down the Persian Gulf, through the gaps in the minefields, which they both knew about; and to escort the Kuwaiti tankers and other shipping, which had accumulated at the head of the Gulf over the years, due to the blockade.

It was amazing how quickly this was achieved, which only went to prove that it was not just the mines which caused the blockade, but the fear of them.

Both navies produced a five mile wide clear lane within four hours of being asked, and the majority of the shipping was led through this, and hugged the southern Iranian coast all the way down the Gulf, until they were through the Strait of Hormuz into the Gulf of Oman.

It took about a day altogether to get most of the shipping out, or into safe berths at various ports down the Gulf, but it was better than joining their sister ships on the sea bed...

And still we slept.

There was a continuous flow of information on world radio and television media, in all languages, directed to the immediate area at the head of the Gulf.

For what started out as a very secret operation... for which we both received bent noses, they could not have told more people on the planet if they tried.

They even sent people round making sure that they had all received the messages.

By the time they were finished, everybody knew what was happening, and everybody knew what the result was going to be.

It was just like a general election. Everybody wanted it over and done with, then they could get back to the important things in life like football, the TV and a pint in the evenings.

It would take more than a war to change some people's way of life apparently!

***

When down broke the following morning, the country of Shatt El Arab was deserted, and awaiting the next stage; which Mr Lee Luanda had yet to authorise.

A few hours before this, in the accommodation train at the Tawal oasis, there was a huge pile of dollars in front of one smiling poker player, his broad white teeth gleaming in a wide crescent grin; and nothing at all in front of the other crinkly chipped faces.

The game came to its natural conclusion.

It was time for breakfast.

It was two thirty in the morning when Ahmed came in to my room with the message. I was in the middle of a great dream...

A crafty weekend in Paris, with a hot blonde, and she was paying for everything...

... When the piercing white light of his torch nearly blew my eyelids apart.

"For gawd's sake Ahmed, put that ruddy torch out.

Just switch on the room light will you and cut the dramatics.

What the hell do you want?"

"I have a long message from the men at Gan, who wish you and Mr Preston to get off your asses, and into your aluminium horse pretty damn quick."

I took the telex from him and nearly died of shock.

I know I wasn't getting paid much for this job, but I didn't fancy a bullet up the backside for my meagre pittance.

"You'd better get Mr Preston up, and rouse your boys.

We're lifting off the track in one hour.

You can tell us how to get airborne over breakfast."

The message was plain enough. It gave the bare essentials of the plan, and told us that all the details were already preloaded into the main computer and flight computer.

All we had to do was follow the instructions.

Ray's comment was to the effect that... if the ruddy aircraft was as good as they ruddy well made it out to be, why couldn't the ruddy thing fly by itself, and leave ruddy people alone in their ruddy beds, in the ruddy morning...

I think he ran out of 'ruddies' by the time he finished.

I was desperately trying to remember how my dream ended.

I wished now that I hadn't.

It was another of life's great disappointments!

* * *

The computers were all linked up apparently, and would continue to do so all through the transit, right up to the moment when Ray would take over for the flight refuelling stage, and the transfer from the Bear.

The rendezvous over the Indian Ocean could take place anywhere along track.

The sooner we could get airborne, the sooner the transfer could take place, and the longer the team would have on the ground.

"Get everybody's skates on Ahmed.

This looks urgent."

They didn't hang around.

He told them what was going on, and we were almost thrown into the cabin.

Talk about, 'mind your fingers, and the cabin door going thump behind you...'

We got the impression that we both had the plague or something.

Ahmed told us about the take off procedure during the pull out from the engine shed.

It was well proven, and had been used many times during the past year; particularly at the western end of the track, to remove the various hostages from the area when they had been rescued.

The aircraft used there was an 'invisible Hercules', which regularly used Ahmed's team.

The key to the whole operation was the power unit.

It had two electric motors, which received their electric current from superconducting alternators powered by the huge diesels.

The current generated was enormous, due to the low resistance wiring, and produced a gradual well controlled output from a simple microprocessor circuit, which Ahmed operated in the cabin with his computer.

By linking this with the main aircraft computer, the throttles could control both the engine power units and the four aircraft engines, to accelerate down the track until take-off speed was reached.

The clamps were released just before this, and the aircraft could then lift off the wagons.

If we couldn't make it in the first eight hundred miles, he could turn around at the other end, and we could try again all the way back!

Ahmed was in the power unit with his assistant, who monitored the aircraft for him.

The gang wound back the doors of the shed, and he moved slowly forward to the track leading to the junction. He then stopped outside the doors, to allow the team to get on board the engine.

I could see them all crowding into the small cabin of the engine, and crushing against the rear looking window.

Soon there was a mass of black hair, beards and grinning teeth stretched across the full width of the glass, as they all peered out at the aircraft.

They would have a ringside view of the take off, and a worm's eye view as it lifted away.

There were just the two wagons coupled to the engine, with the Vulcan on top, and when they were all on board the engine we moved slowly away, the outriggers running smoothly on the roads astride the track.

Ahmed was in charge of the proceedings until the main line.

When he was lined up at that point, Ray would take over with the aircraft computer.

Kuwaiti control was monitoring our progress via the data link, and had cancelled the through trains until we were away.

He travelled very slowly, and was careful not to tip the wings over at the curves of the junction, as they would easily rip off the outriggers, and within fifteen minutes of leaving the sheds we were facing down the main line for Amman.

We could always catch one of the Amman International jumbo jets home if we couldn't make it!

"Ok to start engines, Peter."

I pressed the engine start buttons at the side of my seat.

All four wound up, and soon I had control of them plus the two in the power unit. I could feel them purring away below me.

Ahmed was satisfied, and connected his computer to ours.

"Ok, Ray?"

"Yes, go ahead."

I pushed the throttles forward slowly, and felt the electric motors bite.

They weren't harsh but were very definite. You knew by the continuous pull that they were doing the major portion of the initial work getting the Vulcan moving.

Within ten seconds we were at one hundred miles per hour, and very soon after that the needles were approaching one hundred and fifty.

I decided that I had better catch up quickly, or else my mind would still be back at the oasis.

I pressed the joystick forward, and noticed the nose of the aircraft tip forward as the elevators reacted.

"Everything OK, Peter?"

Ray had felt the movement.

"Yes, just getting the feel of it. Everything's fine."

Ahmed had noticed it too, but he wasn't too concerned.

All of them had a little twitch at this point just to test the system.

Stupid pilots.

You'd think they'd never taken off on a railway wagon before.

All they wanted was a nice big lump of concrete to do it on.

Spoilt they were. All of them.

Spoilt!

The speed soon reached one hundred and eighty miles per hour, and the port VDU turned amber.

This told me that both the clamps had withdrawn from the undercarriage bogies, and the wheels were now free.

I eased gently back on the joystick, and we were immediately airborne.

It was exactly as if we were flying off a runway, only a lot smoother.

I lifted it gently away, and selected the nose and tailwheel up. There was the usual 'clump' as they merged in with the fuselage.

I pressed the transmit button and spoke to Ahmed.

"Where do you want the outriggers dropped?"

As he pressed his button to reply, the sound of great cheering came over the air from his team crowded in the small confines of his cabin.

"Please to drop them ten miles ahead in the soft sand by the wadi, and we will stop on the side track and collect them."

"What's all the hilarity and cheering for?"

Back came his reply to a backcloth of great Arabic singing, shouts of delight, whoopings and roarings.

It was like a circus down there,

"We have won a bet with one of the gang.

He said that you didn't stand a chance getting airborne.

He said that you were going to crash and get blown up.

He said that you had better make peace with your maker, as you were going to meet him pretty damn soon.

The rest of us thought you might get into the air, but weren't too sure if you would or not, so we had a little bet on it.

We are very happy now that you didn't crash and kill yourselves, because we have won back all the money that we lost in the card game..."

The rest of his message was drowned out by an enormous bout of loud cheering and backslapping.

So, that was their little game was it?

Right...

I'd soon sort them out, I thought.

"Nice charming bunch of friends you've got there Peter.

Are you going to prove to them that we're still alive then?"

"Too right mate.

Let's get rid of these wheels first, and call in on them on the way back."

We found the wadi without any problem. It showed up clearly on the camera and the head up display.

There was a side track that looped around, and eventually joined up with the main eastbound track. It was here that they intended crossing over for the return trip.

I put the two visual markers onto an area close to the track, and at the right moment the computer blew the explosive bolts.

They both dropped away at the same time, and at a point one hundred feet below the wings a parachute deployed from each strut, big enough to cushion the impact.

We could see them drop in the wadi, not more than fifty yards from the sidetrack. It was a good shot, and both could be seen from the train with no problem at all.

It would be a case of 'who ran the fastest' got the money the 'firstest'.

... But before that, we had a call to make!

"Turning back now Ray.

See if you can pick up the engine on the camera for me will you?"

"My pleasure."

I still had the camera linked up with the head up display.

When it locked onto the train, the display would give me indications; as if we were on a bomb run...

And we were good at bombing!

It would take us right to the front of the engine if I followed it, and I intended doing just that.

"You have it now Peter, just follow the little blue cross, and do exactly as it tells you."

He came up to the front, and stood beside the seat for a look, as I dropped the aircraft down towards the railway line ahead.

We turned towards the train; and I took it very low and very, very fast... along the track.

They'd find out that we were alive all right!

* * *

The two rails were flashing under the nose of the Vulcan.

If we were any lower we would have needed tickets.

I could see the engine directly in front of us at roughly the same level.

"Landing lights on please Ray."

"Splendid idea," he said, as he bent over to select the switch.

We were now about half a mile from the engine.

I could see the lights of the cabin very clearly now.

I pressed the UHF radio transmit button and spoke with a very worried voice...

"Ahmed, this is Zero One calling, we have a problem with the engines:

It could be that we took in some sand during the take off,

We are crash landing on the railway track ahead of us,

We have our landing lights on...

So if you can see us, come and give assistance as soon as you can.

Over and out."

... And then I switched on the four afterburners, and pushed the throttles fully forward to give me maximum power.

* * *

They all stopped shouting when they heard the message, and were peering ahead out of the front widow looking for the lights.

They all saw them at the same time.

We were now only four hundred yards from the train, travelling straight at them like a bat out of hell; low and fast, with the landing lights full on, and a stream of red flames pouring out the back end of each engine.

They must have thought that their end had come.

During the mighty evacuation from the train cabin, there was a mighty evacuation from the lower colon...

It took the fans nearly half an hour to clear the air. It must have been like the cow shed at farmer Jones's natural fertilizer farm...

I pressed the transmit button.

"Ahmed, that's just to let you know that we're both still alive and kicking.

You can all collect your winnings now.

Have a good day."

Ahmed couldn't answer the call.

He was too busy stuffing neat whisky down his throat with his shaky hand.

His hat had fallen onto the floor so he leaned over backwards to pick it up...

... But a soft smooth hand got there first. He looked up at the velvet skin of his gorgeous stewardess...

"I've come to look after you," she purred.

She lifted up his battered old hat, placed it on his head, and gently wiped his fevered brow with a piece of black satin from the hem of her dress, her lips close to his ear.

She then sat down in the second pilot's seat again, and crossed her legs, displaying at least half an inch of her right ankle as she did so, from beneath the long black dress...

She lowered her veil slightly and winked at him...

"Strewth, this is getting serious," he thought.

"I'm going to have to get rid of her, but maybe not just yet.

I've still got another one thousand Arabian nights under the desert moon left..."

But at the success rate Ahmed was getting, it was going to take him years!

* * *

They didn't even bother with the fifty dollars tied on each of the outriggers after that low pass.

They had a lot of difficulty trying to walk properly, let alone run.

As far as I know, the money's still there...

Assuming some stupid camel hasn't eaten it!

We were to return to Tawal again within two months on another mission, but at the moment we let the aircraft climb on its heading for our rendezvous with Michel.

Ray was already in contact with him on page two on the communications circuit, and was receiving the fine details of the operation.

It was due to take place at six o clock, with thirty minutes allowed for fuel and personnel transfer, and a return trip of just over two hours.

If we'd already had that modification with the shock waves, that we observed during the Bandar Abbas explosion, we could have cut the time down by a third.

We must have looked like a comet, as we streaked across the eastern sky with the afterburners on.

I don't think the three Kings of Orient or the shepherds would have mistaken us for the Christmas Star though.

It was hardly a mission of peace...

More like a mission of pieces!

Chapter 24. Overflights

It was pleasant just to sit quietly in the front seat for a few minutes away from all the frenzied activity going on all around us. I had selected the hydrogen peroxide injectors to the engines to give us added power, and climbed up to ninety thousand feet.

From the cockpit it looked as if we were suspended in black space with the stars above us, the lights of the villages below, and the flares of the oil rigs scattered across the Saudi Arabian desert. The horizon merged with the blackness of the ground and could not be seen.

I was in a complete globe of pinpricks of light, set in a backcloth of darkness.

The only way I knew that the sky was above us was by the aircraft's instruments, but also by the fact that the stars were there in their billions.

The Milky Way was as clear as a phosphorescent sheet across the surface of the ocean, after a ship has passed.

I could see the three main planets in their orbits around the sun.

Mercury across to my right, the brightness of Venus ahead of me, and the faint reddish tinge of Mars just discernible to the left.

The Moon, around which I had done the illegal barrel roll with my Tornado companions the other evening, spread a silver glow around us all.

There was no noise except the swishing of the air over the top of the cabin roof. The roaring of the four engines was miles behind trying to catch us up at the speed of sound. We were in front of the combined shock wave by at least three times that speed .

There are few moments of pure bliss in one's life, and this was one of them. I could see how the Russian and American astronauts became addicted to space flight.

Apart from the gravity that I felt, this was the next best thing.

I spent the next ten minutes in perfect peace and tranquillity, shared only by the stars around me.

* * *

"It's going to be a long trip by the looks of it, Peter.

The information from Gan control is still flooding in.

I'll take the first half of the flight and do the refuelling and the transfer, then you can take over after the parachute drop at Khorramshahr."

I was now well and truly brought down to earth again.

Moments of pleasure rarely last long enough to enjoy fully.

"Ok, Ray, up you come."

We did the swap over, and I sat in front of the computer at the rear station and looked at all the 'bumph' from our glorious leaders; sitting in their armchairs, drinking French coffees in their salubrious surroundings.

It took me thirty minutes to read everything.

"They were crafty enough not to tell us any of this before we took off," I said quietly.

"They knew what they were doing," Ray replied.

"Maybe they thought that we might have a spot of bother with the aircraft, and not be able to get airborne or something. It's been done before you know, and in their eyes we're only new boys to the game."

"I suppose you're right.

They're sending in a United Nations patrol to have a look first, but only told them to have a general look around.

There's a message here to the effect that they have not told the United Nations officially that there may be someone down there, in case the detonation is delayed again.

It could be that we're on our own with this one."

It was true.

The message had been sent to Andy in the tanker; that nothing official could be presented to the authorities at the Security Council about the coded beacon.

Nobody would have believed them in the first instance,

Saying that it was ridiculous that such a low powered unit could be picked up by an aircraft;

That it was a figment of somebody's imagination,

And that it was merely a ploy to delay the final detonation further.

* * *

The Iranians would insist in sending in a team to verify this specific accusation of hostage taking.

The Iraqis would also insist on sending in their representatives, with the object of ensuring that it was correct; for another session of mudslinging, and the whole shooting match would start all over again.

The only effective way to deal with it was as they did to get the bombs out from Teheran those many years ago, and that was to quietly send in a small team to have a look around.

If nobody was there, the aircraft would pick them up from the disused airfield as planned, and if there was anyone then they would deal with the situation as circumstances dictated.

* * *

"I like this bit where it says that the Aircraft Commander can use his own discretion when in the combat area.

Does that mean we can sod off now?"

"I hardly think they expect that from one of the chosen few, and remember, if you did, you'd lose out on your next unemployment benefit giro cheque, and that's the last thing you want.

It would take you months before you got another one.

You know the way the DHSS works."

He was right...

'They' knew how to trap you, and ensnare you into the system forever!

It was about an hour to go to the rendezvous.

I switched to the wide range screen to show the Indian Ocean sector that we were in.

The infra red signals from the big bird satellite were superimposed with the information from our own triple inertia navigation system, and I could see our position to the west of India, heading south east.

Michel's aircraft was clearly positioned over the ocean, to the south west of the tip of India, heading north west.

The Gan computer was working out the intercept course for each aircraft, and feeding the information to both of the computers, which eventually controlled each flight control computer.

As far as we were concerned, they could get on with it... but we would make sure that it was correct.

The artificial intelligence of these 'brains' was not yet at the stage where fear and the sheer panic of possible collision, with its impending doom, would grip the control stick and pull like hell to get out of the way of a hundred tons of metal... coming towards you at a combined speed of a couple of thousand miles per hour.

That simple pleasure could be left to the human being at the sharp end.

I would trust the computers so far, but where my skin was involved, I was going to keep it in one piece, and make sure all the other bits and pieces stayed inside it.

"When we get closer, Ray, I'll take you behind Michel.

We'll do the transfer as you refuel, to save a bit of time.

They're doing six trips with the micro jets; Four with the men, and another two with the equipment and medical supplies.

We're going to Socotra afterwards, if we pick anybody up, or on to Gan if we don't."

I was reading the latest information to Ray as it came through to us. We could then discuss the operation, and plan our little campaign as we saw it from our point of view.

It was all right sending instructions from thousands of miles away, on what could be probable, but nobody could know what would happen until we got in there.

We intended to exercise our discretion in the field all right, and make sure that we didn't drop in the cow muck!

I asked Gan to send me the signals picked up by the TV camera of the immediate area in Khorramshahr, where the beacon was detected.

It was stored on the laser disc, and would provide a good view for Bill and his team when they transferred across. They could work out where to land with their chutes, and the best means of approach once they were down.

They also had an added bonus; a complete overview of the whole operation from above.

From the aircraft computer!

It could tell them exactly where they were, where they had to go, and what was going on around them.

It was like having a second pair of eyes each.

The communication radios each of them would carry were linked into the data base via Skynet.

They would each have a readout on its liquid crystal display, for the distance and direction to travel from any position within one thousand metres from the beacon, to the exact location of the transmitter.

It was accurate to within half a meter and could operate in pitch blackness.

They had been designed originally to pick up the survival beacons on bodies underwater, in the ships which had been sunk in the Gulf, and were very successful.

I would be able to update the position of the beacon even if it was being moved, by asking them to point the instruments in various directions.

The triangulation of the signals received would not only tell me which room the beacon was in, but in which corner, and whether it was on the floor or on the ceiling...

Rather like the television detection vans prowling around the streets looking for licence evaders...

Only much more accurate.

There was a message on the screen.

: GREETINGS FROM THE RUSSIAN BEAR:

I sent one back.

: GREETINGS FROM THE VILLAGE BLACKSMITH:

* * *

The Vulcan had been named after the Roman God of fire, who was identified with the Greek God Hephaestus, who became the divine blacksmith and patron of all craftsmen.

Bandar Abbas had been the first strike on the anvil of the Gods, Basra was to follow shortly.

* * *

"Fifteen minutes to go, Ray. You can slow down a bit and start descending.

We'll link up at ten thousand feet.

I'll feed that into the Gan computer and let it work out the link up procedures."

Ray pulled back on the throttles, and almost glided down the atmosphere, similar to a shuttle re-entry from orbit.

Michel was doing the same from his height of forty thousand feet.

It had to be a low altitude transfer because of the oxygen and pressurisation problems.

We had to take the passengers out of the microjet into the bomb bay, and it would take too long to pressurise and unpressurise both the Vulcan bomb bay and the two bomb bays in the Bear.

We could do transfers if necessary at the Bear's present altitude, but time was against us. The quickest it could be done, as worked out by the Gan computer, was twenty five minutes at ten thousand feet.

They got the timing wrong by half a minute,

They didn't know about the extra bottle of vodka which we loaded on board...

So much for the power of the computer!

***

I could see us turning around behind the Bear on the computer screen display.

Michel had closed down the two inner engines, and turned the propellers to the fully feathered position, in order to cut down on the turbulence for the micro jets as they both shuttled across.

The computers took us to a point about a mile behind, then Ray took over.

"I've got it Peter. It's all lit up like a Christmas tree.

Only the fairy is missing.

It's a pity Le Boustarde's mates aren't here. We could have stuffed them on a prop each.

Can you take the bomb bay position now?"

"Ok. Going aft."

This was what Ray had done at Cheltenham, to look for the damage to the rudder. I put on the radio mike, opened the rear bulkhead door, and crawled across over the nosewheel bay to the front bomb bay compartment, where the docking cradle was positioned.

I clipped my harness onto the nylon safety line, and took up position beside the barrier stretched across the width of the bomb bay, in front of the bomb doors.

The hydraulic control panel was situated here and I could control everything on the spot.

"Camera on Peter, give a little wave."

Ray had switched on the internal television camera, and could see what was going on in the bomb bay from the pilot's seat, by the picture displayed on the port VDU of his instrument panel.

"Where are you now Ray?" I asked.

"Two hundred yards, closing up. I'll call you when in contact."

I could wait until he was taking fuel on board, before opening the bomb doors.

I was not going to risk unnecessary damage to my body until the last possible moment...

It must be the natural cowardice in me. I was born with a yellow streak down my back, and I had no desire to look at a rectangular black hole, two feet in front of my boots, with ten thousand feet of nothing below.

I also had this intense fear of heights!

The time passed too quickly for my liking.

"When you're ready Peter. Your customers are waiting."

The dreaded moment had came.

I opened the doors and the noise was frightening. The blast of the engines was enormous, and the air flooded into the bay like a tornado.

When the doors slid fully into the side chambers, I was going to drop the cradle into the slipstream.

The powerful hydraulic rams pushed the front nose of the cradle downwards into the maelstrom, and the change was immediate. The noise was still there but the turbulence had gone. The slipstream had been deflected downwards, leaving a clear patch of air behind the shield, which could easily be negotiated by the micro jets.

I switched on the blue strobe light at the front end of the cradle and we were ready.

"Call them across Ray. Everything satisfactory."

We saved time by not cooling the microjet engines to fully cold, before pulling them into the bomb bay. Ivan and Piotr just switched off the engines and folded the wings, then I pulled them up and closed the bomb doors.

Bill came across first, with Ivan flying.

It was the first time I had met both of them, and it was a new experience to meet fellow colleagues, standing on a bomb door ten thousand feet above the Indian Ocean, in the wee small hours of the morning, freezing with cold.

The passing of the personal compliments was, to say the least, short and sweet.

The introductions could come later in the warmth and safety of the cabin. I pointed forwards and shouted to Bill,

"Under the barrier and through the bulkhead door."

He gave a 'thumbs up', and crawled under the safety barrier and over the nosewheel bay.

"The first is on board Ray, coming forward."

"Thanks, I can see him all right. He's in the cabin now. Ok for number two."

The sequence was repeated until the four of them were on board.

The last two shuttles brought the parachutes, equipment and supplies across...

And the extra bottle of Russian medicine, courtesy of the Leningrad distillery.

***

I had a personal chat with Ivan, pilot to pilot, before he left, concerning a bit of serious bird watching in a little dacha to the south of Moscow next time we were there.

Let's face it, it's very important to keep up to date in these matters.

These refresher courses were essential parts of our personal training, to keep abreast of affairs, and to be aware of the latest equipment available to us, in order to achieve our objectives successfully.

The addresses were exchanged and the dates arranged!

All the equipment was now on board and stored in the cabin. Ivan closed the hatch of the microjet and I pushed the cradle downwards into the slipstream for his departure.

He started his engine, gave a 'thumbs up', then I pressed the button to release the wing clamps. The aircraft dropped down out of the range of the bomb bay lights, and disappeared into the blackness.

I was back in the cabin within five minutes.

Ray was still on station behind the Bear, but had completed his refuelling well before the final transfer.

"The microjet is on board now Peter. All OK with you?"

I looked at Bill. He nodded.

"Clear to climb Ray. Up you go."

I keyed out a message for Gan control, which Michel would pick up as well.

: TRANSFER COMPLETE. ESTIMATE KHORAMMSHAHR NINE FIFTEEN:

The message from Gan said,

: GOOD LUCK. INSTRUCTIONS TO FOLLOW:

The message from Michel said,

: BON VOYAGE:

I just keyed out a simple

: THANKS:

* * *

"Ray, I've set the computers for the disused airfield north of Khorramshahr. That's your aiming point.

We'll get some pictures of the local area first before we go down to lower altitude.

Follow the flight indicators.

I'll show Bill the latest photographs of the town."

I set up the laser disc on one of the screens at the rear table, and they examined in detail the area around the position of the beacon.

I had marked it with a cross for them to see.

"Strewth," Bill said to the others,

"It hasn't changed much since last month. It was a mess then and it's a mess now."

"Isn't that the old Hilton over there?" asked one of them.

"We could use that clear bit there for landing on..."

"That looks like an old transport dump..."

... and so it went on for a good hour of the flight.

I had a word with Bill and David about how they wanted to be dropped.

"I can put you right on the doorstep if you want. The computer will calculate the dropping point for the free fall, and you can do the rest.

How do you want it?"

Bill looked at the screen and pointed to a clear patch about four hundred yards from the beacon's position.

"There appears to be a landing point there which looks good.

We don't want to go too close just in case there's a bit of opposition.

If you can get us down to twenty five thousand feet, and out for a fall to two thousand feet, we can find that with no bother at all."

We would be coming in from the north, so we looked at close up pictures of the track which they would follow during their descent. They each made notes, which they could memorise later, but the key navigation point for them was the rail track, and the main railway station in the centre of the town.

Although it had been bombed to an unusable state, it was still clear on the screen. We decided that that would be the track to follow.

I get it all up on the flight computer and picked the disused airfield as the first reference point.

We now knew what we were doing for the first time. Up until then it had all been guesswork.

I took the four hand held radios and showed them how they worked.

They plugged into the main communications computer, by a flying lead, and were individually programmed.

When the transmit button was pressed each could be identified, and information sent to it by a radio link.

Each one of them could find out where the other was; they could talk to anyone, including the Gan controllers if necessary, and they could receive any information they wished on the display.

I clipped a programmed module into each of the radios, which converted them into infra red detectors.

I spoke to Bill and Dave.

"As soon as you land, point the front end towards the beacon, and I can get an accurate position.

It would be better if I could get a ninety degree cut, so can you have two landing areas?"

They looked at the screen again. It was not possible because of the debris, therefore the team would have to split up after landing, reconnoitre, then join up at the beacon position after I had recalculated everything for them.

We continued in this fashion throughout the complete return journey, and virtually rehearsed the operation on the computer screen.

"How will you get out?" I asked.

It was David who told me.

"We will find a truck or something. It shouldn't be too difficult.

There are a lot lying around, we know for a fact that some were dumped 'conveniently', when the occupants went to ground, until things quietened down enough for a disappearing act.

Well take the road to the north; it seems clear."

He pointed onto the screen.

"We take this road out of the town, follow the railway track up to this point here, then there's a narrow side road from the main road to the edge of the airfield.

You wait at this end of the peritrack, where the side road meets the boundary wire, and we'll find you.

You're big enough to see."

Bill nodded in agreement then asked me.

"How long will you wait?"

I looked at the screen, and switched on the wide range to show the whole of the area. I pointed out the airfield, and traced a track to the north.

"I'll hear the countdown from Gan as the detonation sequence starts.

I can stay until zero minus five minutes, then I have to go.

If you're around at that time I can delay a bit, but not by much.

After zero minus two don't worry if we've gone, because you'll soon catch us up.

In fact, you might overtake us...

I'll wait as long as I can."

There was a muttering of appreciation from them all, including Jock.

At least they weren't going to be left on their own.

If they were, it would have been too late anyway.

'Twenty minutes to go Peter. I'll turn and descend at the airfield, and we can have a look around before they go."

They got their equipment ready.

Each had a heavy insulated black coverall in flameproof cotton, over which they had their harness and belts.

The weapons and ammunition were placed into a special container, which was belted onto their chests by quick release straps.

It made them look pigeon-chested, but during free fall it added stability in two ways; It kept their centre of gravity low whilst in the spread-eagle position, and also acted as an aerodynamic shield as they descended through the air.

The parachutes were fully flyable wings, and as long as they had room to stand up after landing, that was all the landing space they required.

The goggles they used were moulded in unbreakable clear plastic, and fitted onto the helmet.

The oxygen bottle was strapped across their shoulders, which allowed them to use it on the ground in gas or heavy smoky atmospheres.

The parachute harness fitted over all this, and could be detached instantly on arrival.

When fully fitted out, and all equipment on, there was not a single colour to be seen except black. It was like the first Henry Ford car. You could have any colour you liked as long as it was black!

I looked around the four of them. They all double checked their equipment and when each was ready they gave a thumbs up to Bill.

He spoke over his radio mike.

"We're ready when you are, Peter."

I checked each one of them and they all nodded.

"How are you doing Ray?"

"Fifteen minutes to go."

... And then my communications screen started to flash bright red, filling the whole cabin with an eerie glow.

* * *

Andy had been at the main computer screen in the control room at Gan from the moment we took off at the Tawal oasis.

He had monitored the flight down across the Indian Ocean, and checked the flight computers for the intercept with the Bear.

Just before this occurred the green telephone on his table buzzed.

He picked it up and heard the static from the satellite system, as it connected through to a certain Ministry of Defence room in London. A voice spoke hurried instructions then rang off.

"What was all that about?" John asked him.

"They're sending in another United Nations patrol as soon as possible, to look over the area where the beacon is, but it's only a quick look for any bodies which may be alive.

They've been at it too long already. They should have found something by now.

I get the impression that nobody believes us. There's no official search going on."

"It's a good job we found out then, otherwise nothing would have been done."

They watched the transfer take place between the two aircraft, then sent a message to Michel to proceed to the island of Masira, refuel, then carry on further north to support the Vulcan as necessary.

He could see both aircraft proceeding on their separate tracks, north westerly towards their separate destinations.

The Vulcan was about fifteen minutes short of the disused airfield when the phone rang again.

Andy answered it... it was the top man in the organisation!

Andy listened to the message and said only two words,

"Yes Sir,"

Then slowly replaced the receiver and looked quietly at the screen.

"Is that what I think it is?" said John.

Andy nodded.

"They've scrubbed the operation."

The only sound in the control room was the fan in the computer console.

Andy sighed heavily.

"Apparently the Foreign Secretary got to hear of it somehow, and decided to review the request for the repatriation of Mr Watt; on the grounds that it was highly improbable that it could be him.

Therefore, the official line is... that the beacon is a discarded piece of military hardware, of no importance at all."

John looked at Andy long and hard before he replied.

"He's chickened out, hasn't he?

He doesn't want any embarrassment with the Teheran Government if we're right.

What's the Ministry of Defence doing about it?"

"Nothing." Replied Andy.

"They can't do anything. It's all officially closed.

Even our man has his hands tied.

It's all 'off' as from ten minutes ago.

Where is Peter now?"

They looked at the screen.

The computer counters showed fifteen minutes to the turning point for the run into Khorramshahr.

* * *

Andy thought long and hard, and tried to put himself in the aircraft.

How would he have carried on, after an order to abandon the operation had been received from official sources?

He only had a few minutes left, and if Peter did not respond correctly, it would all be over for good; and Mr Watt, if he was down there, would be lost.

He typed out his message on the keyboard, looked at it on the screen, then pushed the button to send it out to the aircraft.

He spoke to himself,

"Come on Peter, use your noodle."

* * *

I pressed the key to show page two on the communications screen.

We all saw the message.

: **FROM GAN CONTROLLER TO VULCAN CAPTAIN. OPERATION IS CANCELLED.**

YOU ARE TO RETURN TO GAN. PLEASE ACKNOWLEDGE THIS MESSAGE:

Nobody said anything.

I looked around the cabin at them. They all looked at me without saying a word.

"How far to the turning point Ray?"

"Fourteen minutes"

"I want it in ten.

Move yourself"

He was ahead of me. The aircraft leapt forwards as the afterburners cut in. The four passengers had to hang on as the acceleration built up.

I turned to Bill.

"Are you all ready for a free fall in that gear of yours?

It's going to be very cold and it's a longer drop than planned for."

I looked at the external temperature gauge. It was showing minus sixty degrees.

"We've all dropped from high altitude before, Peter.

Just get us within twenty miles and we'll do the rest."

"Ok, I'll do my best to twist their arms.

In the meantime, I must officially point out to you, as the Captain of this aircraft... if we should have any form of emergency, I will be relying on each of you to escape from the cabin through this exit door; which you operate by that lever down there...

... After I remove the safety lock, with this switch here."

I then flicked a little switch beside the door lever, and the exit light turned green.

Bill looked closely at the lever.

"Please be careful Bill.

The slightest movement of that lever in either direction will open the emergency door in the floor, and anyone crouching low beside it is very likely to be sucked out, with the sudden decompression of the aircraft cabin."

It was obvious to me that they were all very concerned by what I said, in the way they all huddled together for comfort, close to the front of the emergency exit... with Bill's hand covering the lever in case anyone touched it!

I returned to my seat and strapped myself in tightly, then typed out a message to Gan.

: YOUR MESSAGE ACKNOWLEDGED. REQUEST REASON:

* * *

Andy first of all saw the speed of the Vulcan increase dramatically on the computer readouts.

"He's catching on. Get ready with that phone.

We're going to need it soon, if I'm correct."

John got a connection with MOD in London, and held it with the duty operator.

Then the message from the aircraft came through and showed up on Andy's screen.

"Good, he's delaying his turn back to Gan, until he reaches the airfield.

That will bring him nicely towards Khorramshahr, on his return heading."

He typed out,

: ACTING SUB LIEUTENANT CARLOS DA QUERRA, LEADER OF AN ARGENTINIAN PATROL OF THE OFFICIAL UNITED NATIONS PEACEKEEPING FORCE REPORTS NOTHING IN THE AREA OF THE BEACON, AND HAS CALLED OFF THE SEARCH.

OPERATION CANCELLED AS A RESULT OF THIS.

ANDY:

* * *

I read it out to them all on the intercom.

Nobody said anything. We couldn't believe it.

Les sat down on the floor and held his head in his hands. I could feel the hard glare of Jock's eyes boring into my skull.

Bill looked at me long and hard. He found a piece of paper, and wrote on it a message for my attention. It said.

"Les lost his brother at Bluff Cove."

I turned to the screen. I had to do something fast.

Come on Barten. Think.

The original message.

The discretion in the field.

Do something...

Make it legal before you push them out, and get crucified for doing it against orders.

"Ten minutes Peter, then the turn."

I could only send one message, and it had to be the correct one.

There would be no second chance.

I typed out on the keyboard, then transmitted it to Gan.

: FROM VULCAN COMMANDER TO GAN CONTROL.

REQUEST AUTHORITY FOR OVERFLIGHTS, TO FIND AND PICK UP THE BEACON, WITH INFRA RED DETECTORS:

* * *

Andy got the message, grabbed the phone and got through to his commander.

"Sir, the aircraft captain is requesting authority for overflights, to pick up the beacon with his infra red detectors.

May I suggest that we consider it, in case the beacon is still transmitting?"

There was a short pause at the other end of the line.

"Yes. I think we will. Tell him to proceed."

"Thank you, Sir," and he went to put the phone down...

"One more thing, Andy,"

"Yes Sir?"

"Tell him to make use of the most accurate equipment we have available, to ascertain the exact position of the beacon; and to ensure that the aircraft picks it up, before returning to base.

Do you understand?"

"Yes Sir. Thank you."

He keyed out to the aircraft.

: REQUEST GRANTED. SUGGEST MINIMUM OF FOUR OVERFLIGHTS.

DEPLOY AND RETRIEVE INFRA RED DETECTORS AT YOUR DISCRETION.

GOOD LUCK, ANDY:

* * *

"Ok Ray, depressurise the aircraft cabin as soon as you can.

All oxygen masks switched on.

Get ready Bill."

We felt very uncomfortable as the cabin reduced its internal pressure, from a comfortable fifteen thousand feet normal altitude, to a debilitating ninety thousand feet.

I reckoned that we could stand about thirty seconds of this low pressure, before any bends or adverse effects began.

Nobody could speak. We were too busy gulping down oxygen.

I gave all four a 'thumbs up', they acknowledged, then I blew the door open with the emergency hydraulic system.

They went head first into the slipstream, adopted the freefall position, and down they went.

The door shut and we started repressurising.

It all took less than fifteen seconds.

I watched them falling down with the rear view camera. I tried to imagine the chill factor of those four blokes falling through very cold air, at about one hundred and twenty miles per hour, as they reached terminal velocity.

Free falling from ninety thousand feet certainly sorted out the men from the boys!

They had grouped together and held hands forming a star. I could hear them talking to each other over the radio.

Something about freezing something off brass monkeys...

I timed the descent, and worked out that it would be about eight minutes of free fall. We recorded them every single second of that drop.

As they got lower I could hear them planning the forward motion of their flight, and when they got into warmer air, they split up and flew in pairs towards their landing spots by the railway station.

They were flying right down the track, towards the centre of the town.

I called Bill on the radio.

"Landbase Leader from Zero One. Any problems?"

I could hear them check in with him individually before he replied.

"All Ok, Zero One. I'll check in on the ground. Thank you."

I had to zoom lens the camera as they got lower down, and then the parachutes deployed at around two and a half thousand feet as planned.

They flew horizontally, using the hot air thermals of the desert, in line astern across the town; then circled around the landing area, searching out their own spots.

I could see the weapons containers, dropped on long nylon ropes below them, hit the ground first.

And about ten minutes after leaving the aircraft, each of the four had landed in the clear patch, about four hundred yards from the estimated beacon position.

* * *

They were each carrying the most accurate pieces of equipment available to me, capable of detecting the infra red video recorder control unit; and I had to get them to within one thousand feet of the beacon's position for them to work...

Therefore, they had to parachute down, to correctly deploy the detectors.

When they found the beacon and picked it up, if by any chance Mr Watt was still holding onto it, then all to the good...

They would have to bring him back to the aircraft as well.

I sent my next message to Gan.

: FIRST FOUR OVERFLIGHTS SATISFACTORY. CONTINUING NORTH-SOUTH TRACKING:

Andy sent me my final clearance for the operation.

: **WELL DONE. REMAIN IN THE AREA UNTIL BEACON PICKED UP TO YOUR SATISFACTION:**

That's what we always intended to do... but it was nice to have it officially approved!

* * *

Andy picked up the phone and waited for the connection.

"They're down now Sir."

"Thank you Andy. A first class job.

I'll advise the Defence Secretary. Call me with any results."

Andy replaced the receiver for the last time, and watched the Vulcan as it flew north and then south, communicating with the team on the ground.

"I think these two will fit nicely into our organisation.

I hate to admit it but Le Boustarde chose well when he dragged both of them out of the gutter.

Let's hope they find Mr Watt alive. He's down there somewhere."

He was.

But he wasn't all they found!

Chapter 25. Cellar Life

As soon as they landed split up into their pairs.

Bill and Les opened the weapons containers and clipped the Israeli made Uzi sub machine guns onto the front of their harnesses. Each also had a Browning nine millimetre pistol, and a selection of wire fragmentation grenades and stun grenades.

They put on a number of other explosives, including ring charges and timed grenades. The former would be handy if they had to get through concrete or brick walls; the latter very useful for lying around, causing nervous bangs for the unexpected.

David and Jock had a similar box of surprises, including extra amatol and percussion caps. Not that they were expecting any trouble, but if it did come their way, they intended giving as good as they got.

"Landbase Leader to Zero One, splitting up now.

Check detectors."

Bill transmitted to the aircraft, then they both crouched low and slipped to the left, along the side of one of the collapsed buildings on the street.

They kept their masks on, because they both knew the wretched smell of a dead city and had no desire to be nauseated.

They took careful paths, keeping advantage of all available cover. The last thing they wanted was a surprise shot in their direction. They travelled for about two hundred yards, then stopped beside the junction of two broad roads.

"Landbase Two, check in."

"We're in position three hundred yards north of you. Scanning now."

Bill did the same with his radio detector. He pointed it ahead of him then slowly scanned full left, then full right, and back again for two minutes.

He waited until the aircraft called him.

"Landbase Unit from Zero One. Accurate position is now on your readouts.

Proceed to within fifty yards, then repeat the scan.

Position is indicated by a collapsed building.

Can see you on camera. No hostiles observed."

"Close in all units," Bill transmitted.

There was no need for the 'with care'.

That was automatically assumed.

They went slowly and under cover. They could see the building ahead; it had been an apartment block, but had collapsed, probably due to intense shell fire.

Layer upon layer of concrete slabs formed a mountain of rubble and dust, surrounded by dereliction and ruin. The entire area was quiet. Not even a dog barked.

Bill checked it over with his binoculars for any signs of life or lookouts. It appeared dead.

They crept closer, until the second scanning point was reached.

"Landbase One from Landbase Two. We've found a Landrover hidden under a tarpaulin. Probably boobied. Will check it later.

Moving up. Will call in position."

Bill looked at Les. They touched visors and he spoke.

"Move over further to the left and check the other side."

Les nodded and crept away.

"Landbase Two scanning now."

Bill repeated the scanning sequence, then waited for the reply.

"Landbase Unit, repeat scan. Point downwards."

Bill was thinking rapidly. It had to be a cellar.

After the scanning session he called David up.

"Landbase Two, check for an entry by that Landrover."

The aircraft called him on the radio.

"Landbase Leader. It's fifteen feet underground, and sixty five yards from you; the heading is shown on the readers.

Coding has stopped, but still transmitting on both channels."

It was Les who found the way in.

He knew about pot holing in Derbyshire, and rock climbing in Wales; and he recognised the evidence of boot scrapes, when bodies slide across rubble and loose stones.

The others had checked all around the building, and agreed that this was the only way in.

"I'll go first," said Jock.

You didn't argue with Jock. Not even Bill.

So Jock went first.

* * *

He adjusted his eyes to the gloom, and crept slowly through the gaps in the concrete slabs.

He took his helmet and goggles off, and listened first of all without the hearing equipment. It was quiet. Then with the headphones; each earpiece contained a small amplifier for a directional microphone.

He checked around the area, moving forward slowly as he did so.

He found himself crawling across a carpet about four feet in width. He checked across the pattern, and recognised that it was for a corridor.

The most recent scrapes made by the previous 'guests' were not covered up by fallen dust, so he followed them along the carpet.

The headroom was about three feet at this point, and made crawling easier now.

There was nothing heard in the earphones, so he went up in the direction his readout indicated.

As he got closer to the beacon the counters reduced in distance, but the heading indication remained the same. He was crawling directly towards it.

The counters were reading twenty five yards, when he came to a corner. Jock took out a fibre optic tube, and carefully bent it around the corner for a good look, before proceeding further.

The corridor led into a chamber, with a steel door set into a wall.

Nobody was around. He checked with the directional microphone, but nothing was heard, so he crawled around the corner slowly and had a careful look.

The corridor led into what was once the bar of a hotel. There was broken glass all around.

The steel door must lead to the cellar. He crawled quietly to the door, and checked with a stethoscope for voices.

There were definitely low murmurings on the other side of the door. That was the evidence he wanted.

He retraced his steps back to the entrance and told the others what he had found.

Bill and Dave talked quietly together for a while to draw up an attack plan.

"Les, go with Jock and listen to what they're saying.

I want the room layout, how many there are, and what they're doing."

Both crept along the corridor to the cellar door, and set up a listening station.

"Dave, you check out that Landrover for a quick departure."

Dave disappeared around the corner. The vehicle had been left under the tarpaulin, and covered with loose dust and rocks as camouflage.

* * *

Lieutenant David O'Mara had not lived and survived undercover in Northern Ireland for three years by doing stupid things; so he ignored the option of pulling back the tarpaulin sheets, jumping into a strange Landrover, starting the engine and driving away; because if he had done so, the grenade which he found lying under a concrete block, with the pin tied to the corner of the tarpaulin, would certainly have given him a headache.

If that didn't catch him out, the eight ounces of plastic explosive under the bonnet catch would have done so.

He had to crawl on his back underneath the front wheels with his torch, to see the detonator wires tied to the front headlight cables.

He'd seen that trick in Lebanon. The plastic grenade under each seat was obviously a bluff, so he looked further afield after dealing with them.

Altogether he picked up six little surprises.

After fifteen minutes he was almost sure he'd found them all, but not quite.

There was something else around. He could almost smell it. His dog would have done so, and Dave had the same instinct.

He crouched low, and looked at the seat cushion on the driving seat. There was a different coloured thread along one edge.

The crafty little devils, he thought.

He very carefully lifted the driver's cushion out, and laid it on the ground beside the vehicle, then gently slit the new stitching with his knife...

He cut all round the flat top of the cushion, and peeled back the plastic material.

Underneath there was a circular black plate resting on the rubber foam.

"Well, well, well," he said to himself, as he took it by the edges and laid it on the ground.

"That would have made my eyes water."

He did the same with the other seat, and removed the pressure operated explosive device from the soft foam base.

"Somebody here doesn't like us, that's for certain."

Those were the last two.

He was now sure of it. He pushed the vehicle back to where the entrance was, and made sure it was ready to start.

All the ignition wires were secure, and the engine would fire when he wanted it to.

He crawled through the hole, and joined the others beside the door.

* * *

Bill was waiting for him at the corner with all the equipment, looking at a plan of the room which Les and Jock had drawn, by poking the fibre optic tube through the keyhole.

"Look at this Dave. There are four of them.

Two asleep and two on guard, with Kalashnikovs ready, primed for trouble.

The room is square, with only one door in and out.

There must be a hatch in the floor somewhere, but we can't see it from the door.

This is the plan. We take out the two guards, and speak to the two sleepers.

That's the room layout there.

Watch it when you go in. There's a pile of rubble just where you're going to roll.

You go right, and I go left.

Go along to Jock, and he'll let you see through the wire.

Les says we have forty minutes. There's a squad coming into the town, to get them out before the detonation.

We'll have to be away by then!"

Bill then got on with preparing the ring charges. They were going to use two, one either side of the door.

They would be held hard up against the wall, about four feet from the floor by long pieces of wood; and when they exploded, not only would they make two holes big enough for Bill and Dave to dive through, but the blast and the rubble flying into the room would certainly fill the pants of anybody inside.

Dave inspected the room with the optical binoculars coupled up to the fibre wire. He had a good look around, and knew exactly what to do when he got in.

He saw the rubble on the floor, and decided to go further to the right; this would take him closer to the wall, which he preferred.

He handed them back to Jock, and nodded.

Les spoke to him.

"After you've gone in, I'll put on the high intensive strobe for two seconds to blind them, then normal light for you both to see what you're doing.

I'll use the left hand hole to draw any fire."

Dave nodded then returned to where Bill was.

"We just take the Uzi machine guns, and the Browning pistol.

Les and Jock can cover from the outside."

They checked each other for oxygen and mask connections, then tapped the microphones to check them. Both put their thumbs up.

There were no risks taken at this point.

If there was a radio inside the cellar, they could easily be picked up.

The weapons were checked and put on 'safety'. They would be put to 'fire' as they want through the wall.

Both were ready.

Les and Jock came back to them, and got their machine guns ready.

Bill and Dave would stay low on the floor, and the other two would then take out anyone who would be foolish enough to stay upright.

"Ok, Les. Place the charges, then give us ten seconds on the timers."

Les took them both, and fixed them on the wall either side of the door with plastic charge; then leant a heavy wooden beam against both of them, to direct the majority of the blast inwards.

He checked that both firing circuits were armed, then looked back.

Bill gave thumbs up, so he set each arming circuit to fire in ten seconds, then ran back behind the corner.

The explosions occurred within two seconds of each other.

The first blew a hole about two feet diameter on the right hand side of the door, and filled the cellar with blast waves and flying bricks.

The second did the same, but also added to the concussion and disruption of the occupants inside.

* * *

The human frame needs a finite time to adjust after a severe shock, and during this time Bill and Dave ran across the corridor and dived through the two holes.

Les followed with the strobe light, and flooded the cellar with high intensity flashes of very strong white light for about two seconds, followed by a normal white light.

Jock got up to the right hand hole, and covered the inside with his machine gun.

Bill and Dave rolled over the floor in a forward roll, and took up a firing position, pointing to the two guards who were severely disrupted by the blast waves.

The more experienced one immediately recognised what was happening, and instinctively pulled the trigger of his Kalashnikov, firing wildly in the general direction of the strobe which had blinded him.

The stream of bullets smashed into the ceiling and wall without causing any damage.

He only managed to fire a half second burst, before his head was blown off by Bill firing from his right, and Dave from his left. He was thrown backwards against the wall, and a jet of blood from his carotid artery sprayed over the paintwork.

The second guard didn't even know what day of the week it was.

He had been blinded by the flying dust, and was groping around in the middle of the room when Dave took him out with a half second burst which nearly split him in half.

The shots echoed around the cellar, and Bill and Dave stayed where they were on the floor until the sound died down.

The two guerrillas asleep on the mattresses, lying on the floor, were in a greater state of confusion than their dead colleagues.

Les shouted in Arabic,

"Don't move.

Don't move or you're dead."

They didn't move!

They probably couldn't.

But they still didn't move.

* * *

Bill and Dave crawled quickly over to them, stuffed the muzzles of the machine guns under their chins, and forced their heads back hard against the floor.

Bill spoke into his microphone to Jock.

"Come in Jock and open the door."

He came through the hole, picked up the key from the nail, turned the lock, and opened the door for Les.

"Why couldn't they have hung the key outside?" he said quietly.

"It would have saved all this bother."

Les walked across and looked at the two Arabs.

He and Jock were old hands at this game. He said to Bill.

"We question your man first, then the one Dave has."

"Ok. Go ahead."

Les knelt down beside them both and lit a cigarette. He blew the smoke into the Arab's face, and said in Arabic.

"Where's the other door?"

The man said nothing.

Les said it louder, so that the second man could hear.

"I'll give you five seconds, then we blow your head off. Where's the other door?"

The man said a few words in Arabic.

"What did he say?" Asked Bill.

"In simple English... you would have to be hermaphroditic to perform this impossible act."

Bill pushed harder with his gun.

"Tell him he's got three seconds."

Les stood up, drew a long drag on his cigarette, and gently flicked the ash onto the floor.

He said softly, but loud enough for the second man to hear.

"My friend says that you are to tell us within three seconds."

The Arab repeated his swearing, then spat in Bill's face.

Bill pulled the trigger, and the whole of the Arab's head and brains spread over the wall behind.

At the same time, Les jumped down and grabbed the other man by the throat, and yelled into his face as loud as possible,

"Tell us where that door is."

Then he dragged him upright, and slammed him hard against the wall, hitting the back of his head as he did so.

There was an incoherent jabber of Arabic, as the shock of all this expressed itself in a panicked outburst of screaming.

When it died down, Les said quietly in English,

"He's all yours, Jock."

Jock moved up swiftly, and grabbed the collar of the man's shirt with his left hand. He held the Browning pistol in his right, pointing to the floor.

Les picked up the cigarette, inspected the end which was alight then took another drag.

He looked the man in the eye. He was close to breaking but not quite.

There was still a bit of resentment present.

"Make it three, Jock," he said quietly in English.

"After I do the shouting bit."

"With pleasure."

Les then said quietly in Arabic,

"Where's the door?"

The man stared at him with panic in his eyes, and hysterically shook his head sideways.

Les then looked at Jock, and said fast and very loud in Arabic,

"Kill him now."

Jock fired three times.

* * *

The first bullet hit between the man's ankles, and spread concrete chippings into both his legs.

The second hit the brick wall between his lower legs, and brick chippings cut into his trousers.

The third hit the wall between his thighs above kneecap level.

Then Jock rammed the gun hard into the young man's groin. The Arab gasped with combined shock and pain and bent forwards.

Jock pushed his head back against the wall, and forced him upwards, so that he was standing on his toes.

"My friend has one bullet left," Les said in Arabic.

There was now real fear in the young man's eyes...

He could see his chances of contributing to his country's population requirements dwindling rapidly.

He was close to breaking point.

"Push the muzzle in just a bit harder please, Jock. We're almost there."

The man's eyes watered as the pain suddenly increased. His head fell forwards and stayed there.

Les lifted it up.

"Where's the door?"

The man pointed to a pile of bricks and concrete slabs piled up in the corner.

"It's over there. Under the concrete" he replied weakly in Arabic.

Les said to Dave,

"Wander across to that pile of bricks in the corner, and do your disinterested act, then come back."

He then said to him in Arabic,

"The little man says it's over there in the corner, but I don't believe him.

He's lying through his teeth."

The man looked up in panic and watched Dave casually wander over, kick a few stones, then spend about thirty seconds looking around the rubbles and lifting the odd brick now and again.

Les could see him becoming desperate.

He said to Jock,

"When I nudge you, look nasty at him and twist your gun muzzle hard a few times; then throw him over there."

Dave had finished his 'inspection' and wandered back, shrugging his shoulders as he did so.

Les turned and slapped the man's face hard a few times, and said loudly to him,

"You lying little sod."

Then he turned to Jock, and said quietly in Arabic as he walked away, nudging him as he did so.

"Shoot him."

Jock put on one of his nasty grimaces right in front of the man's face, and scared the living daylights out of him.

He pushed up hard with his left arm, and slid him up the wall as far as he could.

At the same time he twisted the muzzle of the gun very hard, continuously, until the man screamed his way up to full arms length.

Jock then threw him over the room, into the pile of rubble.

There then followed an hysterical thirty seconds of activity, as the concrete was pushed aside, and bricks thrown across the room; until a wooden hatch was opened, to reveal a flight of steps leading downwards.

The young man collapsed on the floor in front of it, gasping for breath.

* * *

He was allowed five seconds to recover, before Jock picked him up and rammed the pistol hard behind his right earhole.

He was then pushed ahead of them down the steps, into the corridor of an under cellar.

Jock covered himself behind the man's body but it was unnecessary. There was nobody there.

It just went for twenty feet, then ended in a brick wall.

They walked slowly up to it, checking for trip wires and mines, but it was clean all the way from the hatch to the wall.

"Ok, Bill. It's all clear," Jock called back, still holding the Arab in front of him.

The others came down the steps, and switched on the portable lights which they had brought from the top room.

They looked around and saw four doors.

Two pairs of two, set opposite each other across the corridor.

Bill said quietly to Les,

"Ask our friend what's in each of these."

Les gripped the man's collar as he did so. He looked shocked at the reply, and stared at Bill before he spoke again.

"I'll ask you this once and once only. Are those doors booby trapped?"

The man shook his head.

"Right, you open one... slowly."

He said to Bill,

"There's four altogether.

Two American, one French, and one British."

Bill quietly said.

"Good God almighty."

Jock led the Arab forwards to the first door, which opened without any force or unexpected results.

Bill looked in carefully, then slowly slid around the door keeping close to the wall.

He was only in a few seconds, then he came out holding his mouth with his hand, leant against the wall and was violently sick.

Dave quickly put his oxygen mask on and went in.

There was a body stretched out full length, face downwards on top of the bed, handcuffed to the bed head.

The fingernails of one of the hands had been torn off, as the poor fellow had tried to scratch a message on the wall.

Dave went closer to see what it said.

There were three letters, clearly visible, etched in darkened blood:

USA

He looked closer.

In front was a faint letter 'S' and behind a faint letter 'N':

SUSAN

He looked at the body. It had obviously been dead for about two weeks, and had decomposed beyond recognition.

He closed his eyes and backed out the way he came in, then slammed the door shut.

As soon as he was in the corridor he ripped off his mask and grabbed the Arab by the throat, bunched his fist, and held his arm up above his shoulder ready to strike hard.

The 'natural man' in him wanted to hit and hit and hit until the Arab was unconscious. The 'disciplined soldier' in him said 'no'.

His face was black with fury, and his fist was quivering with the exertion of restraint.

Bill came up to him and put his hand on his shoulder.

"Don't lower yourself to his level, Dave.

The little bastard's not worth it."

Dave looked at the Arab long and hard, let him go, then crossed over the corridor to the wooden door and punched it as hard as he could.

His fury was spent.

* * *

Les had checked the room opposite and came up to Bill, tapped him on the shoulder and pointed inwards.

"It's our man I think. In there."

Bill walked slowly through the door, stood still and looked at the figure on the bed.

He saw a gaunt skeleton of a man.

The hair and beard were long and grey. The cheek bones protruded through thin flesh, and the ribs were showing through his chest.

He was holding onto a video recorder control unit in both of his thin hands, pointing it straight upwards, with his two thumbs pressed on the buttons.

Bill walked slowly across and looked down at the man's face.

The eyes slowly opened and stared weakly up at him. A gentle smile slowly appeared across the man's face as he saw Bill Carter, and he said very faintly, almost unheard,

"Thank you, Lord."

Bill knelt closer, and spoke quietly to him,

"Mr Watt?"

The man nodded.

Bill patted his shoulder.

"You're Ok now, Mr Watt.

My name's Bill Carter, United Nations.

We've come to get you out."

He took the controller gently from the man's hands, and pointed it towards a battery operated video recorder in the corner. The contrast and the brightness were both fully on.

He pressed the buttons, and saw the screen flash in front of him.

He then held it in his left hand, and sent a series of dots and dashes with his right index finger...

* * *

"Landbase Leader from Zero One.

Reading you loud and clear."

... Bill continued to transmit his Morse to the aircraft.

"Landbase Leader, Zero One. I don't think I'll pass on your message.

The Foreign Office wouldn't appreciate it.

Some of them couldn't do it, and the rest probably are...

I will advise Gan regarding Mr Watt.

Pass your estimate for pick up when you can."

* * *

They were busy during the following ten minutes.

Les had fixed up a glucose drip above the bed, which could be replaced throughout the return journey.

He washed Mr Watt's face and constantly wet his lips.

Bill and Dave wrapped him up in blankets, to cocoon him for the journey. He would need protection as he was still very weak.

He was then strapped securely to the bed frame, which was going to act as a stretcher. It would eventually be tied onto the Landrover outside, and that was their means of transport to the airfield.

If they could pick up another one to carry the other equipment, that would be even better. It shouldn't be too difficult to find one.

They took the head and foot off the bed, then carried Mr Watt up the steps to the top room.

Les stayed with him to reassure him, and change the glucose bottles. They wanted a bit more strength in his body before departing.

The shock of the journey could affect him for the worse.

Dave came up to Bill afterwards and showed him three dog tags.

"I picked them from the other bodies.

The other American was handcuffed to his bed like the first, and the French lady had dehydrated.

She was lying on the floor."

Bill took the three tags in his hand and looked at them.

"I'd better pass the names to Gan."

He took out his radio, spoke to the aircraft, and read the details directly from the tags for the United Nations and Red Cross to act upon.

Jock came forward, still holding the Arab,

"Shall I deal with this little booger now?"

Bill looked at Dave before he answered,

"Bring him in here Jock."

He walked into Mr Watt's room and laid a blanket on the floor.

"Lie him on that please Jock, facing the video recorder."

Jock pushed him down onto the blanket, stood back and covered him with the Browning pistol.

Bill took another blanket and spread it over the Arab, leaving his arms free. He bent down, put the controller into his hands, and carefully placed one finger each onto the contrast button and the brightness button.

He looked down at him, then they both left the room locking it behind them.

They walked up the steps followed by Dave, closed the hatch in the floor, and covered it with the heavy slabs of concrete.

It took them about five minutes to make a good job of it.

There were a few more lumps lying around, which they added to the pile,

When they finished, Bill sat down and admitted to Dave,

"I must be getting soft. I decided to give him the same chance as Mr Watt had.

I'm getting too old for this game."

Dave sniffed.

"You must be. I was going to put him in with the first American we saw.

It's time you packed this job in mate. You're getting past it."

* * *

"Landbase Leader from Zero One. There's a patrol coming in from the east towards the town.

It could be a pick up relief unit. I suggest you head west through the town, then north."

"Thank you Zero One, leaving now."

He said to Les,

"Is Mr Watt ready?"

"Yes. We just throw away the empty glucose bottles, and push in the tube for a replacement.

It's fixed up on the frame above him."

"Ok. Let's get him on the vehicle."

They each took a corner of the bed, and carried him through the steel door to the low corridor outside. It wasn't easy getting through the slabs of concrete, but because they were lying horizontal some of them could be shifted with a bit of heavy leverage.

It took over a quarter of an hour to get him to the Landrover, and when they did, they were exhausted.

"Get it over the passenger's seat, and tie it on tightly at the front to the radiator grille, and to the top of the rear seat."

When they had finished, Mr Watt was lying comfortably on his mattress, lashed to his bed frame, which was firmly secured to the Landrover.

As long as they didn't turn over, he would be quite safe.

If they did turn over, then it wouldn't matter anyway, because they wouldn't be going anywhere.

"Get the weapon packs Jock. We might need them."

"Landbase Leader from Zero One. Suggest you get your skates on.

They're rolling into the town."

Bill took out his radio and transmitted to the aircraft,

"One minute, then we're off. What's the opposition?"

"Standby"

Jock returned and threw the two packs into the back of the vehicle, Dave was at the front sitting on the bonnet next to Mr Watt's head with his machine gun and spare ammunition magazines.

Bill was driving, and both Les and Jock were behind the rear seats.

"Ok. Let's move it," said Bill, as he started the engine and set off up the road.

"Landbase Unit, opposition as follows:

One scout Landrover with two people on board, in front of two others with general purpose machine guns.

Four hundred yards behind these are two Vixen armoured guns with supporting Landrovers, two in front and two behind.

You're going north, by the way. You're going to cross over their path in one mile if you don't turn."

"I can't go west. The whole area is impassable. It's just a mass of ruins.

We'll have to make a run for it. See if you can head them off will you?"

"Ok. Keep on that road. Don't move off it.

It takes you straight out of the town."

They went as fast as they could.

The vehicle could only do forty miles per hour, and it seemed to drag along the road.

They saw the Vulcan well to the right, swooping in low across the desert.

It seemed to be following the same road as the patrol and coming up fast behind it. They could hear the popping sound of guns firing.

It could only be the ground patrol as they knew the aircraft had no weapons.

If only it had a cannon sticking out of the front, instead of a flight refuelling probe, it could have caused some damage and a few cracked heads.

It was down very low now, and stirring up a lot of dust behind it.

They lost sight of it as it dropped down below the level of the buildings; and a lot of them were only two or three storeys high...

The next thing they all saw was a roaring triangle, climbing vertically upwards, about a quarter of a mile to their right; with plumes of black smoke pouring out of the engines, stirring up tons of dust and sand around the patrol.

It rocketed upwards, and even at that distance they could feel the blasts from the engines.

"Landbase Leader from Zero One. Move yourselves will you.

Those sods are shooting real bullets at us.

I can cover you some of the time but they're getting through as we climb away.

They know we're here now so they're ready for us.

Keep straight on through the dust."

Bill gunned the engine, and entered the minor sandstorm.

As they came up to the crossroads, Dave shouted out loud so that they could all hear.

"One Landrover.

On the right.

Twenty yards.

Open fire."

He started firing his Uzi in that direction...

They had met the patrol.

Chapter 26. 23c/5672/89

David had seen a pair of headlamps through the dust storm, and recognised it as the scout Landrover.

He aimed high, and brought the muzzle of the machine gun lower as he fired. The two guerrillas on board met a hail of bullets and were killed instantly.

The windscreen disintegrated, and flying glass embedded itself into their bodies as they slumped forwards. The driver fell out of the side of the vehicle, which began to veer across the road towards a ditch.

"Bill, slow down.

Jock, get that Landrover.

Les, come with me."

Dave was obviously exercising command, and was controlling this little operation. You had to be fast when you were out as a team of four, or you could be dead just as quick.

When it was safe to jump, all three got out and raced to their various points.

Jock had the shortest distance to run.

He Jumped into the slow moving vehicle, and yanked on the handbrake. It was easy to climb into the driving seat after that, and get full control of the vehicle.

He threw the body of the other occupant out into the ditch, then drew up alongside Bill.

"Move the weapons packs into that one Jock, and you can follow up the rear end and cover us."

He left Bill his Uzi with two full magazines, and the first aid gear for Mr Watt.

"Get going, Bill. We'll catch you up later."

He was half way back to the others when he heard the noise of an intense fire fight, coming out of the dust clouds.

Dave and Les had ran up the road towards the other Landrovers, and were going to hit them hard before they knew what was going on.

They would have heard the initial burst of firing from Dave's weapon, and would now be on the lookout. If they were foolish, they would have put their headlights on, to see their way forward through the dust.

Both of them had done exactly that, which was to their downfall.

The first Landrover was threading its way slowly through the concrete rubble and bricks littering the road. Dave and Les saw it at the same time and fired simultaneously.

The crossfire of bullets knocked the machine gunner off the vehicle before he managed a shot in return.

Their fire was then directed towards the driver, the passenger, the tyres, the exhaust system and the petrol tank, in that order.

The object was twofold; to knock it out, and to block the road.

The petrol eventually seeped out, and the tank caught fire with a whoomph.

The occupants of the second Landrover saw this, and immediately all three fired in its general direction.

Dave and Les could not be seen, but the whole area was covered in bullets to flush them out.

* * *

The 7.6mm general purpose machine gun, with belt feed on a pintle mounting, can knock holes through four inch brick walls when it's used in anger; and this one was furious.

The bullets were of the hard nosed variety, and were cutting swathes of concrete chippings from the walls around Dave and Les.

There was no respite.

* * *

They had both expected this, and had both gone to ground well away from the burning Landrover.

As the bullets moved on to another part of the wall, each of them moved forward until they could see the gun.

That's when Jock arrived.

Dave heard his voice in the earpieces set into his GRP helmet.

"Stand by for grenades on your left.

Five seconds from now."

They both counted down, then directed their Uzis towards the machine gun.

Jock had better be right, or they were both dead.

There were two explosions just to the left of the vehicle, and another two in the front.

Jock came tearing through the dust, and hit the ground behind a low wall, twenty five yards from them, on their left hand side.

He was firing at the tyres, which disintegrated into strips of burning rubber as the red hot bullets hit home.

Les took out the machine gunner, and Dave killed the other two through the windscreen.

He ran forwards, firing from his hip, right up to the front of the Landrover, and made sure all three were dead.

The other two gave him covering fire until he reached the front of the vehicle.

He then jumped into the back of it, turned the machine gun around on its pivot, and aimed it down the road in the direction of the oncoming patrol.

"Reloading," shouted Les.

"Over here," shouted Jock.

Les threw him two magazines from his weapons bag.

"Get ready, They're almost here."

The powerful roar of the Vixen's diesel engine could now be heard through the dust.

As soon as Dave saw it, he opened fire and kept his finger on the trigger.

Jock and Les would hit the six heavy tyres and try to blow them out; he was trying to break the armour plated glass, set in the hardened aluminium turret, through which the driver was looking.

If he didn't manage it, the stream of bullets hitting the window in front of the driver's nose would probably be enough to scare him off the road.

At least it should have done... but not this time.

The car came straight for them.

Dave shouted into his microphone,

"Hit the window, hard."

The other two changed their aim from the tyres to the centre of the armoured glass, and let rip with the Uzis.

Both had a full magazine on continuous fire, and there finally comes a point in the laws of physics when the force applied to a crystallised structure must eventually break it down.

The combined force of the two handheld machine guns, and the one pivot mounted general purpose machine gun exploded the armoured glass in the front of the vehicle. The driver's face disappeared immediately, and bullets ricocheted around the inside of the cabin like red hot hornets.

They set fire to the percussion caps and ammunition inside the cabin, and a series of explosions added to the general mayhem...

But not before the machine gunner had managed to point the Vixen's internal machine gun in the direction of the Landrover.

He was killed immediately afterwards by one of the ricochets,

But his death grip held onto the trigger.

* * *

Dave was virtually cut in half as the bullets smashed into his body.

He was thrown backwards over the bonnet of the Landrover, and fell into the road just in front of the burning tyres.

The armoured car continued on its path, sprayed with bullets from the Uzis, until it hit the rear of the Landrover.

The Vixen bounced up and crashed on top of it, pushing the Landrover forward over Dave's shattered body, before it fell over onto its side.

The petrol tank of the Landrover exploded, and engulfed both vehicles in a sheet of red flame.

The ammunition inside the car now caught fire, and the resultant explosion blew the turret with its 76 mm armour piercing gun across the road.

The whole area was now a mass of flames.

Jock and Les had to retreat from the intense heat, and regrouped fifty yards away.

Jock was holding onto Les, who wanted to go back.

"Don't be bloody stupid Les.

He's dead."

His arm was punched hard and he let go. Les turned to face him and shouted in his face,

"You don't know that, do you.

You can't be sure, can you.

That's my mate you're talking about. I want to be sure he's dead.

He's not burning to death if I'm around."

Jock looked at him.

"Ok, Les," was all he said.

Les edged forwards against the heat, until he could see Dave's body through the flames; and with tears in his eyes, shot him twice through the head.

He must have already been dead in that lot, but Les was now reassured that he would not suffer the agonies of a burning death.

He got back and said to Jock.

"Do the same for me will you, if you have to?"

Jock nodded.

"Let's go then. Get moving."

They ran back to the scout car, which had been left with its engine running, and raced up the road after Bill.

Les took one final look back at the funeral pyre, saluted, then reloaded the guns.

* * *

Lieutenant David O'Mara had been killed outright by the first burst of machine gun bullets from the armoured car, so he did not suffer at all.

The Landrover, from which he fell and was crushed when the heavier vehicle landed on top of it, was reference number 23c/5672/89, purchased at Aldergrove near Belfast, at an army surplus sale after the Northern Irish conflict had resolved itself.

It had been bought by a Lebanese gentleman who was on holiday in the Republic in the south, and had crossed over the border for a day visit.

In addition to this vehicle, he and his colleagues of various nationalities purchased a considerable amount of equipment that particular day.

He also placed a number of lucrative contracts for specialised military items, which provided employment and income for a considerable number of people, for a considerable amount of time.

The official military procurement offices for the two belligerents had been closed down many years before that day, but it had not made one jot of difference.

Instead of direct purchasing from suppliers and manufacturers, all that happened was that the series of agencies and middlemen increased in number accordingly. In fact, it became easier for the belligerents to buy arms and equipment, because there was no need for them to run the gauntlet of the arms blockade themselves.

They just sat at home and let other people do it for them.

The saddest thing about the death of David O'Mara is the fact that he was probably killed by some of the very equipment that he had used himself, during his three years of undercover activities in the province.

Whilst others were laughing all the way to the bank, with the proceeds from their many and varied dealings in the international black market arms trade, the current account of Lieutenant David O'Mara was closed for ever at about ten thirty five, on a Saturday morning in August 1995, at the cross roads in Khorramshahr.

He died as he wished to be remembered,

A professional soldier to the very end.

Chapter 27. Landrovers

Les passed the news to Bill via the short wave radio.

There was a pause of about thirty seconds before anything else was said.

"Zero One from Landbase Leader. We've lost number two.

Please advise Gan control."

"Ok Bill. Sorry mate, we did our best for you."

"No, it's nobody's fault. It's something we all live with."

The two Landrovers made slow progress through the town. The streets were littered with fallen buildings and concrete slabs.

It took about half an hour to get out of the north eastern suburbs of the town, but eventually they reached the road that would link up with the main northerly road leading to the airfield.

They received instructions from the aircraft as to which road to take. It would have taken twice as long otherwise.

"Landbase Leader, Zero One. The patrol has backtracked down the road.

It can't get past the burning car, and it is now on the airport road in the town centre, travelling north.

Get a shift on Bill. They're going faster than you.

Carry on up that road. The main junction is about a mile ahead. Turn left.

Go for half a mile, then right onto the narrow track for the airfield.

I'll keep a watch on them, and land on the peritrack when you're past the junction, but move yourselves."

When Les and Jock eventually got out of the town they could see Bill about a quarter of a mile ahead of them travelling fast, trailing a cloud of dust and sand behind him.

He wasn't wasting any time.

They didn't have much to waste as it was.

It wasn't a case of getting to the junction first. They had to get to the aircraft, and away before that armoured car get in range with its 78mm gun.

A couple of shells into the wing of the Vulcan, and it would be November the fifth, two months earlier than it was due.

Bill was about a quarter of a mile from the junction, when the two Landrovers leading the patrol emerged from the suburbs. The armoured car was immediately behind them.

They had about two miles to go before the junction, but Bill's dust trail was easily picked up by the binocular visual rangefinder in the turret of the car.

They fired as soon as they could.

The first shell fell short and to the rear, the second one closed up, and the third exploded close enough to cause serious damage to the Landrover.

Bill had his Uzi machine gun jammed into the shoulder of his right arm, with straps attached so that he could fire and drive at the same time.

His right arm and shoulder were severely hit, breaking the upper forearm and shoulder blade. The Uzi fell into the road and bounced into a ditch at the side of the road...

... A shell splinter penetrated the right hand side of his GRP helmet and broke his lower jawbone.

That was bad enough, but the most serious problem occurred when the engine misfired, then stopped altogether.

A large splinter had cut through the metal sides of the Landrover and smashed the distributor cap off its mountings. The vehicle slowed down, even though Bill was pressing hard on the accelerator pedal.

He managed to keep it in the centre of the road and came to a stop, two hundred yards from the junction.

Les saw the shell explode, raced up to the side of the stationery vehicle, and stopped beside it.

He saw the condition that Bill was in, checked that Mr Watt was still alive, then lifted Bill over the driver's seat to sit him up in one of the back seats.

"Jock, get behind and push me with that Landrover.

Stop wasting time.

You should be here by now."

Jock was looking to his right, and pointed towards the patrol.

"Look over there Les.

There's no point in rushing now."

Les looked up and saw the Vulcan.

"Bloody hell", was all he could say .

They both watched in stunned silence as the aircraft fell out of the sky.

It was about two hundred feet above the ground, immediately above the armoured car and the Landrovers, in a high nose up attitude, descending fast.

The two Landrovers were firing their machines guns at it as it came down...

... They saw it bounce on the road, about a hundred feet in front of them, and thump onto the ground, ripping up swathes of stones and sand.

Black smoke and flames were erupting from it as it did so.

Les and Jock watched as a fireball shot upwards, and the black smoke billowed into the air, taking dust and sand from the desert floor with it.

"Christ Almighty. What a bloody mess this has turned out to be." Les said to no one in particular, and rested his head on his arms crossed on the steering wheel.

Jock just looked across the desert scrub, and said nothing.

There was nothing he could say!

* * *

I could see that they were going to have trouble even before the patrol got out of the town. The time and distances were against them.

"Ray, put a video map of the area into the computer, and work out how much time they've got will you.

From what I can see, they're not going to make it.

I don't think they'll get anywhere near the airfield.

That armoured car is going to start firing as soon as it sees them."

Ray carried out some calculations which confirmed what I thought.

"They don't stand a cat in hells chance Peter.

They won't even make the junction.

They're in range as soon as the patrol gets out of the town, and six shells will do it.

They've had it."

We had no weapons or bombs that we could drop, and I couldn't do my previous time delaying dust cloud again, they would just go around it on the desert. The surface was sun baked hard.

As soon as I went away to land at the airfield, they could just cut across and intercept us at the peritrack.

Even we would be in range.

I knew how to take them out though, to give us all a bit more time.

"Ray, feed both cameras into the computer, and give me the rear picture on the left hand screen, so that I can see where the armoured car is.

If we can take that out, we can get the Landrovers later."

As he did so I circled round and lined up on the road, about three miles behind the patrol.

We fed instructions into the computer, so that we would be above them as they emerged from the suburbs. We had to assume that they would travel at roughly the same speed as they were doing now.

"Put it all up on the head up display, put one of the visual markers on the armoured car, and the other one hundred feet in front, then strap yourself in tight."

There were two Landrovers just in front of the car, and another two about four hundred yards behind.

That would reduced the number of weapons being fired at us by about half, and if they didn't notice us until the last thing it would reduce it ever further.

I had the speeds and markers now to tell me what to do, and I came up behind them about five hundred feet above the ground.

The computer told me that we would reach them just after the built up area. That was the best that we could achieve, but it had to do.

They might be able to get some rounds off if they were quick, but it was a risk we had to take.

I flew the aircraft level, and watched the bombing markers tell me the minor adjustments to take to land the aircraft immediately ahead of them; then I put the engine power switches to the 'emergency power' position.

This would give me a further ten percent of thrust from each of the jets, as I pushed the throttles forward to full power. It came in handy on occasions, to escape from radar guided missiles, fired in anger from fighter aircraft.

At the present weight of the aircraft, it almost gave me a thrust to weight ratio of about two to one; in other words, I could take off vertically if necessary.

"One mile to go Peter. I'm strapped in ready.

Engines selected?"

"Yes, all at emergency power.

Standby, going down now."

* * *

My old flying instructor had told me how to drop the Vulcan out of the sky, then recover at a lower altitude, by using the big wing area as an airbrake.

I had used the technique to land on a tanker in the ocean, and was using the same system now, but this time I wasn't using ground effect.

I was going to drop down, then stop the descent with the engines, and land on the road ahead of the Vixen armoured car; with the intention of blowing it out of the area, or into the next country!

I chopped the four throttles, punched the undercarriage button to select the wheels down, rammed the airbrakes out to the maximum drag position with the hydraulic rams, and pulled the nose back to a high attitude position, which the computer had calculated.

The aircraft went down like a brick, and at two hundred feet above the ground I saw the armoured gun right behind the tail of the aircraft on the camera screen in front of me.

The Landrovers had seen me coming, and were now firing at the wing; raking the guns across the width of the aircraft.

They couldn't miss a target as huge as we were.

I could hear the bullets thudding into the wings, and decided that maybe Mr and Mrs Barten's eldest lad was more stupid than he was made out to be.

I looked at the radio altimeter to get an accurate height reading, switched the afterburners 'ON', then pushed the throttles as fast as possible to the fully forward position.

The resultant explosion of power and thrust from the engines virtually stopped the aircraft in flight.

We almost hovered above the ground, before the mainwheels touched down either side of the roadway.

I had misjudged it slightly, and we landed on the desert surface just a shade harder than I had intended.

* * *

Sometimes I tell the odd white lie.

This was one of them.

I didn't misjudge is slightly, I misjudged it quite a lot.

We hit the desert surface a lot harder than I intended, and we thumped into the ground.

Either the ground vibrated up and down, or else my eyeballs did!

It was one hell of an arrival.

A 'false teeth rattler'; but we landed exactly where we wanted.

* * *

The flames and powerful jets of air from the engines engulfed the two Landrovers and the armoured car.

Not only did it blow them all off the road, but it threw the Landrovers fifty feet backwards, turned the armoured car over onto its side, and set fire to the rubber wheels.

That was the initial result.

We then bounced forwards to land straight ahead, and I slipped the wheel brakes to move along the road at about twenty miles an hour.

We had to keep rolling slowly, or else the tyres would plough their way into the ground; and then we would never get out.

The afterburners kept the fires going, and the red hot stones and sand from the desert surface were flung backwards to keep the other two Landrovers from catching up.

I had managed to give Bill, Les and Jock a breathing space.

Ray selected the front camera onto the two Landrovers where they had stopped.

The close up showed them looking in our direction.

"For God's sake Peter, tell them to get moving will you.

They're both sitting there watching us doing nothing."

I had been on the proper speaking course for Officers and Gentlemen, and had been tutored in the delicate art of tact and diplomacy; so I recalled the sum total of my knowledge, and pressed the radio transmit button, to advise them as to their next immediate actions.

* * *

Les was looking at the fire ball when his radio burst into life.

"Landbase Unit from Zero One.

Get a bloody move on will you, and shift your backsides, and get the bloody hell out of it.

I'm not staying here all bloody day, waiting for you three stupid burglars, sitting on your fat backsides sunbathing, so bloody well get the hell out of there."

At least... that was the general text of the message.

The actual language I used was a bit stronger!

It did the trick.

They moved, and they moved fast.

Jock got behind the dead Landrover with his, and gunned them both down the road to the junction.

"Zero One. The front Landrover's no use.

 We'll have to push it to the airfield."

I called back.

"Negative. Stay on the road.

We'll pick it up in the bomb bay with the microjet cradle."

They were at the junction now, travelling north.

"Ray, get to the bomb bay and open up ready for them. Select bomb bay camera on.

Drop the cradle and clamp the Landrover when it's in position.

Shift yourself, were nearly on top of them."

Ray moved fast.

He was there within ten seconds.

I had the bomb bay doors open for him, and could see him on the television screen lowering the cradle until it was scraping the road surface.

"Les, move across to the left will you, and let me past.

Stop hogging the bloody centre lane."

He steered the Landrover to the left, then I pushed past him and got the nosewheel in front of the two Landrovers.

Ray was hanging upside down from the bomb bay opening, with his head and shoulders out, shouting his head off and waving them into the cradle.

Les steered the front Landrover underneath it, and Jock rammed it as hard as he could into the front shield.

Ray pressed the hydraulic control button for the wing clamps. They thumped down onto the sides of the Landrover, almost bursting the tyres as they did so; then gripped the metal sides and crushed their way into the steel, forming a strong grip.

I now had the Landrover well and truly attached to the aircraft.

"Get him on board Ray. Move yourself.

Those Landrovers behind us are coming up either side on the wing tips.

Tell Les to do something about them fast."

Ray jumped down onto the bonnet of the Landrover, and helped Les cut the ropes holding the bed stretcher on the top.

He pointed left and right and shouted to him.

There was one on the starboard wing tip, with two people in it. The gunner was firing his machine gun upwards into the wing, and shooting hell out of the metal surface.

Ray could see chunks of aluminium splattering all over the place.

The other Landrover on the port wing tip only had one person in it and no gun.

The mainwheel tyres were hurling stones and rocks backwards and upwards, as they dug deep groves in the surface.

The noise underneath was ear-splitting. Les shouted to Jock and pointed to the starboard side.

"Get the gunner."

Jock looked to his right, pulled back slightly, then drove hard through the stones being thrown up behind the tyres, and bounced across the grooves.

He had ducked down under the dash board for protection, which was just as well. The windscreen disintegrated, and the Landrover was showered with rocks. He would have been stoned to death if he had stayed upright.

The gunner and driver were not expecting him to come behind the wheel. They were taking the long way round the front of the wheel, to get out of the rubbish, and Jock hit them hard.

His Uzi was difficult to aim accurately, so he kept his finger on the trigger until he ran out of ammunition. He killed the gunner which was the main thing, but had missed the driver.

He was lucky.

He had seen Jock coming out of the stones, and had been quick enough to duck down out of the way. When he looked up again, he saw Jock turning back again to get on board the aircraft.

The driver was a suicidal guerrilla, and intended to stop the aircraft.

He screamed at the top of his voice, and aimed straight for the front of the mainwheel, to smash his Landrover into the tyres.

Jock heard this and looked across.

He recognised the death scream; he had heard it before, when they had crashed fully laden ammunition lorries into hotels in Beirut, so he turned his vehicle in towards the undercarriage wheel to act as a barrier.

Both Landrovers smashed together with bang, and then bounced apart. Jock turned the steering wheel again and crashed into the other one, and repeated it in an attempt to move it away.

He heard a voice in the earpiece of his helmet.

"Jock, get back on board, we're going."

He could see the aircraft moving away slowly, then heard an enormous explosion from above him. He looked up automatically and saw pieces of metal shoot out the front of the air intake.

The gunner had managed to hit the outer engine, and it had blown up inside the wing.

He couldn't hear the other Landrover coming at him because of the afterburners roaring away, and the noise of the engine exploding, and he got hit on the front offside wing.

His vehicle caught the two outside tyres of the mainwheel as they were rotating at speed, and both Landrovers were thrown up into the air by the turning force.

The rear tyre blew out with a terrific bang, hurling chunks of hard rubber all around him.

Jock was thrown out of the seat, and he hit the underside of the wing.

He took the full force of the impact on his back and shoulders, which stunned him for a second or two, and then with horror he realised that he was falling downwards, headfirst into the wheels.

The aircraft was still accelerating at the time, and as he fell, the undercarriage strut moved forwards towards his falling body.

All that Jock could see was an enormous black metal object coming at him, which thumped him hard on the chest.

He grabbed at it as if it were they only thing in the world which could save him.

A drowning man will clutch at straws in desperation, and Jock was desperate!

He held on hard, but the strut got narrower as he slid down the red hydraulic fluid which covered it. The axle of the wheels was only eighteen inches below him, and on each side were the wheels ready to churn him into mincemeat.

He flailed his legs about, trying to catch onto something and gripped as hard as he could. He slid a further twelve inches before his left boot caught on one of the cross levers of the undercarriage system. This gave him something to aim for now with his other foot, and he got that stuck in under the hydraulic jack which operated the release mechanism.

His helmet was now resting on the axle, and every time the aircraft bounced on and off the ground he saw stars.

He managed to lift his head back a few inches, by hunching his shoulders a bit and pulling up with his legs; and when he stopped slipping downwards he was locked into a position, upside down, hanging on for grim death, two inches above the wheels throwing out rubber, rocks and stones all across his back and helmet.

He burrowed his face visor into the strut for protection, and it was another four seconds before he realised that it was not hydraulic fluid that he was slipping on.

The other driver had been thrown forwards under the undercarriage wheels, and during the loudest part of his scream he was crushed to death.

His blood had sprayed upwards and backwards, covering the wheels, undercarriage jacks and main strut with gore, which resembled red hydraulic fluid.

"Jock, get back on board will you for God's sake.

We're getting airborne now."

He could still hear Les shouting, but daren't take his hand away to press his radio transmit button in case he slipped down.

Jock was on board, all right, but certainly not in the first class seats!

* * *

The other Landrover came at them from the front of the port undercarriage. Les spoke to Bill, who was in a bad way lying across the rear seats.

"Can you manage that one Bill?"

His jaw hurt badly so he just nodded, and pointed to his pistol.

Les reached down and took it out of the quick release clip, and put it into his left hand.

He shouted in his ear,

"Just keep him off for a few seconds, while we get Mr Watt inside."

Bill took up a comfortable position and aimed at the driver.

It was not as easy as he had thought.

He was being bounced around the Landrover, as the aircraft accelerated.

He was also fighting off waves of pain from his arm, jaw and shoulder, and the other driver was ducking and weaving around the Landrover dashboard.

He fired single rounds every time the vehicle came close enough, but there was no indication as to where they struck.

The driver was clever. He could see that Bill was wounded badly, and was drawing his fire until the pistol was empty. It didn't take long. Bill only had four rounds left, and when this was fired, the pistol could not reload.

The driver saw this, turned the Landrover steering wheel rapidly to the right, and drove onto the road behind them.

He could now drive a bit faster and catch them up. He could see Les pushing the bottom of the bed frame into the bomb bay, so he had to act fast.

He pulled out his Wesley revolver, took aim with his right hand extended, whilst controlling the Landrover with his left.

Bill had anticipated this and had got the toolbox ready.

The first missile he threw was the empty 9mm pistol, followed immediately by a hammer.

Both smashed through the windscreen, and hit the Arab in the stomach. The force of the missiles at a speed of about fifty miles an hour knocked his breath away. They would have killed him if they had hit his head.

He tucked the gun into his belt, got down below the dash board and pulled a tool bag from underneath the passenger seat.

By wedging it behind the brake pedal, he managed to force the accelerator flat onto the floor with the weight of the bag. He could now lie under the dashboard, and look out of the side of the Landrover without having to think about the engine.

His vehicle was now going flat out, but the Vulcan was accelerating away from him. It was too far for an accurate shot, but he intended to try.

The number four engine exploded just before he pulled his revolver out of his belt.

The aircraft lurched in front of him, swung to the side of the road, and then came back to the middle again. It did this a few times, swinging right and left until control was regained.

It was during this time that he made up lost ground.

He noticed that he had crept closer, until he was only six feet behind the Landrover in front. It looked good, but he was not in luck.

That was the closest that he managed to get, and was now falling back as the aircraft accelerated away.

He could kiss goodbye to his last chance to hit the man on the stretcher.

* * *

The driver however, was Major Seyed Ali Hassad of the regular Iranian army.

He was attached to the guerrilla patrol as an official observer, during the twenty four hour cease fire, and had also been drawn into this incident by the mere fact that he happened to be present at the wrong time.

But he was not a man to sit back and watch, as he had been in the war from the very onset, as a regular soldier on all fronts, and had been trained in desert warfare, paratrooping and commando operations.

He was the Iranian equivalent of the four soldiers against whom he was in combat.

He had noticed that these were no ordinary soldiers, and had been bright enough to let the other guerrillas take the brunt of the initial fighting, waiting in the background for the final kill, and he was determined to do it.

* * *

He carefully judged the distance that he was from the rear of the Landrover in front of him; and before Bill could do anything about it, he leapt up onto the passenger seat of his vehicle, pushed himself forward onto the bonnet, and took two strong running steps towards the front radiator grille.

He hurled himself as hard as he could into a forward dive, and leapt across the seven feet separating the two Landrovers.

He almost made it.

His face and chest hit the tailgate door at the back of the vehicle, breaking two teeth and smashing his top lip in the process.

He fell downwards and hit his forehead very hard on the metal handgrip, bolted onto the rear of the door.

His immediate instinct was to bring both hands up to protect his broken face, and the natural desire for survival made him grab onto the handle with both hands. He hung there for a moment, shaking his head, trying to clear away the fainting spasms he was going through.

Bill tried to get over the back seat to push him off, but he couldn't get up; he was too weak from his previous exertions. He picked up a heavy spanner in his left hand, ready for him when he climbed over the back. He slowly got up and moved backwards over the seat, towards the tailgate.

When Seyed Hassad recovered himself, he realised the extremely awkward situation that he had got himself into.

He looked back over his shoulder, and saw his own Landrover's front offside wheel, now eight feet away, directly behind him.

If he let go he would be run over by his own vehicle.

He looked forwards and upwards over the tailgate, and saw Bill trying to get to him.

He looked downwards, and saw the roadway below him moving backwards faster and faster, ripping the front material from his trousers, and scraping the skin off his legs into the bargain.

The toecaps of his army boots bounced up and down as he was dragged along the road, and were beginning to cut into his feet.

He also had only two bullets left in his revolver, and somehow he had to overcome the remaining soldiers in front of him, and an undisclosed number of soldiers and aircrew in the aircraft.

On the whole, it was not exactly an enviable position to be in.

He straightened his legs to protect the front of his kneecaps, and decided that discretion was the better part of valour.

He therefore made a very senior executive management decision, and decided that somehow or other he was going to get the hell out of it, or whatever the equivalent is in Arabic.

He was just working out how to get into a side rolling position, to evade the following Landrover, when he heard a shout in English above him.

He looked up and saw the others, hanging on to various parts of the aircraft and the Landrover.

He could only assume that some unpleasant situation was about to occur, feared the worse and closed his eyes.

He wondered whether to recite part of the Quran, just in case, but he didn't have time.

***

I saw Ray shout to Les about the two Landrovers coming in at us from the wingtips; then saw him bend down to cut the ropes holding the bed frame, on the picture from the television camera pointing down at them, at the rear of the bomb bay.

I could now concentrate on getting the aircraft airborne again. I had kept the afterburners on, to give me as much power as possible.

I was going to need it, to drag the wheels out of the grooves they were making at both sides of the road.

Most of the surface was hard packed earth and flat.

The main trouble was the loose stones, that I could feel hitting the underside of the aircraft. It was like driving across a recently gravelled road, and having all the loose gravel hit the underside of your car.

I had to accept any damage caused to the undercarriage, and hoped that the steel stone guards at the front of the wheels would deflect the larger rocks away from the tyres.

I decided that it was time that we got airborne, and away from this place.

"Ray, warn the others, and get everybody on board as soon as they can.

I'm leaving now, and anyone who wants to come with me can do so if they wish."

I could see an increase in the already high frenzy of activity under the aircraft.

I pushed the throttles up to full power, and felt the aircraft bite against the drag of the desert surface, and gradually accelerate away.

The road was dead straight ahead, so that was no problem, but it was slow to get going.

I could hear gunfire to my right, and looked over my shoulder. We were like sitting ducks unless Les and Jock did something fast.

I looked at the airspeed, and died a million deaths when I saw it was still only fifty miles per hour. I needed at least a hundred and thirty to get us into the air.

It was like driving a fully loaded double decker bus, up a very steep hill, and waiting to get to the flat bit at the top so you could increase speed enough to get into second gear.

If I wasn't so panic stricken I would have started a crossword.

There would be enough time to finish it... even the times crossword!

Very, very slowly the speed increased.

Talk about a burn up...

I was nearly touching sixty, when disaster with a capital 'D' arrived.

The number four engine blew up, and disintegrated into a pile of turbine blades and flame tubes.

* * *

The aircraft nose shot across to the right hand side of the road, as the full power of the two engines on the left hand side of the aircraft won the battle of supremacy over the remaining single one on the right hand side.

I now had a choice of four decisions to take:

Carry on as I was, and go round and round in circles on the desert surface,

Shut down the number three engine, in case that had been damaged as well, and still go round and round, but in smaller circles,

Pull back the power on number one engine, to balance off the power, and hope that we had enough thrust from the remaining two engines to get airborne,

Or hand in my notice and go home to Lincoln!

I desperately wanted to go home, but as the only transport I had was the gradually diminishing aircraft that I happened to be sitting in at the time, and as Lincoln was a long way off to my left, even I knew that the first two decisions were out of the question; so I had to pull back the power on engine one.

Such is the process of decision making, to a highly tuned brain like as what I possessed!

I did manage to control the swing to the right, as soon as the power on number one was pulled back; but I really needed five pair of hands, in the one and a half seconds I had to juggle everything that had to be done.

There was the warning to Ray and the others,

Whilst I had to switch off all the fuel to the engine on fire, fill the stainless steel containment tube with foam, and hope that the explosion hadn't ruptured it, and blown broken metal into number three.

There was the throttle to pull back on number one...

And the afterburners to switch off...

And whilst all this was going on, my feet were trying to stop the sideways desire of the aircraft to head off into the desert, by applying the brakes on the opposite side of the aircraft...

Until I had a spare hand to press the little button which could give me power to steer the nosewheel left and right.

Add to this a sudden desire on my part to wallpaper the cockpit in self adhesive wallpaper in my spare time, and it's little wonder that our speed only reduced by ten miles per hour.

At least I had regained an element of control.

We managed to stay on the road.

It took a long time, but eventually we got up to ninety miles an hour. At this speed the elevators began to have some effect, as the airflow rushed under the wing, and I pushed the joystick forwards very fast.

The effect was instantaneous.

The elevators instantly hammered down into the airflow, and acted like flaps in the takeoff position.

The back of the aircraft lifted, and reduced the drag on the main wheels from the desert, and we increased acceleration.

* * *

The message from Ray sounded urgent.

"Peter, Are you there?"

"Yes. What do you want? I'm a bit busy."

"Don't raise the undercarriage.

Jock's hanging onto the starboard main jack.

He's in trouble."

Charming. That's all I needed.

What a fiasco this was turning out to be.

"Ok. Tell him to hang on. We'll get him in when we're airborne.

... If we get airborne."

* * *

Jock's trouble was nothing to the trouble that I was looking at.

There's a railway track, which runs parallel with the main north-south road from Khorramshahr, used to take the oil and exports from Teheran to the docks on the waterway.

It crosses over the road on occasions, which generally speaking is no bother. You just rattle across the rails.

Unfortunately, some previous traveller had tried a chicken run with a train, on the level crossing that we were now approaching.

And had lost.

There was a wrecked freight train lying on the road ahead of me!

The engine was on its side, right across the road, on top of an army truck; and the wagons stretched for about two hundred yards on our left hand side.

I had to use the number one engine now, or we would be well and truly in the mire.

"Ray. Look ahead and tell the others to hang on tight.

It could be a bumpy ride."

I saw Ray look underneath the aircraft around the shield, and he had kittens on the spot. I saw him shout to Les and Bill and then hang on to the bed frame with one hand, and an internal spar with the other.

He shut his eyes for additional strength.

I was doing my one handed wallpapering act again, trying to keep the aircraft straight, as we increased speed from ninety miles an hour up to about one hundred and ten.

There was a strong tendency to swing to the right, as the power of the engine bit, and it was one almighty job to keep it on the road.

At a distance of about three hundred feet from the crashed train, and at the speed of one hundred and fifteen miles per hour, it was obvious even to me that we weren't going to get airborne before we reached the train.

I waited until the last possible moment, and pulled back fast on the joystick, to bring the nose up as quickly as I could.

There was nothing else I could do.

As soon as the Vulcan was in the air, I then pushed forwards just as fast, and brought the right wing up, before the excessive power on the left hand side tipped the wing tip into the ground.

It was terrible.

The tail of the Vulcan hit the front main bogies of the diesel engine, and ten feet of fuselage ripped off from behind the fin, and crashed onto the road on the other side of the crossing.

I had over corrected with my sideways movement on the joystick, and the right wing came up too far.

That was not the problem.

It was the left wing going downwards that had the trouble.

The portside undercarriage ripped through the side of a freight wagon and took the roof off, which hit underneath the wing, and stuck itself neatly into one of the wing fuel tanks; and the wingtip sliced itself off, as it hit the steel bumpers of a wagon that had reared up on top of the wagon in front of it.

Not a very inspiring take off to say the least.

We crabbed sideways across the desert, at about fifty feet altitude, with what remained of the port wingtip ploughing deep channels of sand and dirt as it bounced along, with the starboard wing pointing high up into the air.

The speed had to increase somehow, so I switched on the one remaining afterburner and hoped for the best.

It kicked in and lifted the port wing up fast, nearly too fast.

I rammed the rudder as hard as I could over to the left hand side, and pushed the joystick further over in the same direction...

And watched the speed increase bit by bit, and the altitude climb slowly upwards, as the port wing tip rose away from the desert.

We flew along like that, crabbing sideways to the right, with the starboard wing higher than the port wing for nearly two minutes, until we reached a height of five hundred feet.

It was only then that I had the courage to move any of my muscles, to unwind my arms and legs again into some semblance of normality.

I also started to breathe again.

I found that it helped!

* * *

I was under less pressure now. It took a further two minutes to settle the aircraft down to reasonable power ratings on the three engines, and I flew at the same height over the desert.

I was still heading north and decided not to turn until I knew what was happening underneath me.

"Ray, how are you all doing?"

There was activity on the screen so I knew they were still around.

"We've survived no thanks to you.

What the hell was that about?

Les fell off the Landrover bonnet. It's a good job he fell backwards and not sideways.

Jock's still with us, thank God.

Bill's on his last legs I'm afraid and we have another passenger in addition to Mr Watt."

"I'm not in the mood for riddles. What the hell are you an about?"

"There's a bloke hanging on to the back of the Landrover handle grip, splayed out flat in the slipstream like a horizontal skydiver."

That was it.

I'd had enough of today.

Jock was on the starboard undercarriage.

Half a train was embedded in the fuselage behind the port undercarriage.

I had lost the back end of the fuselage.

We were leaking fuel like a sieve.

The number four engine was in little bits.

We were heading north into bandit territory... and now I had a bloke hanging underneath the ruddy bomb doors, at the back end of a Landrover.

"Ray. I'm going home.

Tell everyone that's hanging around my aeroplane to hang on a bit longer will you."

I turned slowly to the right, and gradually picked up a southerly heading back towards somewhere.

I didn't care where. Just anywhere else!

When I was a bit happier I pressed a few buttons, so that I could speak directly to the control centre at Gan.

They didn't believe me at first.

They insisted that it was a joke, but when I relayed the pictures to them they suddenly took notice and acted.

We got our instructions within two minutes after that.

Michel and his rescue cavalry were despatched to us immediately.

We were going to Socotra.

* * *

Our additional passenger, Major Seyed Hassad didn't have the necessary time to work out his side roll. Even if he had managed to think it out, it would have been too late to act.

He suddenly felt the nosewheel lift sharply off the ground, and he lifted up with it, still hanging onto the aluminium handle.

He looked down and saw the road flashing underneath him in a fast blur, then felt the aircraft tip over and hit the train.

That was when he started reciting the Quran.

He chanted as the aeroplane scraped across the desert, leaving a trail of dust behind it, and continued as he felt and saw the flames of the afterburner kick the aircraft upwards, and tip the wings over.

He died nearly five times altogether during the incident, and still couldn't believe that he was alive when the aircraft settled down on a northerly heading.

He knew where they were going. He just had to look downwards at the desert five hundred feet below him to know where he was.

He splayed his legs out wide, to give some stability, and used his parachutist reflexes to stop himself spinning over onto his back. That would be the end. He couldn't possibly hold on if that happened.

He looked down again, and closed his eyes at the thought of the big drop below him. His chances of survival were nil, and his choices were limited.

He could either kill himself or be killed. Some choice, he thought.

He looked over the tail gate. They were still trying to pull the bed frame into the bomb bay.

It was too wide to pull through the gaps in the safety rail which stretched across the aircraft, and they were attempting to lift it over with great difficulty.

It was the opportunity that he was waiting for.

He was very careful with his next movement, as it was imperative that he did not spin around and fall before he fired.

It wouldn't matter afterwards. He would be a double martyr if he killed the hostage on the bed frame.

He slowly released the grip on his right hand until it was free, and he had his full weight on his left grip. His toes were acting as mini elevators in the slipstream rushing underneath him.

He could not have held on if he had not been shielded by the Landrover.

He kept his right hand and arm as close to his body as he could, and edged it down to the revolver in his belt.

He moved his toes every time he felt a sideways movement, and managed to remain horizontal. He was breathing normally now, and felt quite relaxed at the thought of finally achieving success.

He got the gun out, and repeated his careful movements until he could see the chamber in front of his eyes. The two cartridges were next in the firing line.

It would have been a shame if he pulled the trigger onto a blank shell.

Professionals don't do stupid things like that.

He cocked the gun, raised it up, and rested his wrist on the top of the tailgate, with the butt over the lip.

He saw the hostage in his sights, and pulled the trigger...

* * *

There was a black object immediately in front of him, and he felt an agonising pain in his wrist as something hard crashed down upon it, smashing it into the top of the tail gate.

He felt the bones in his wrist crunch, as they splintered inside the flesh, and fought off waves of nausea and pain, as he screamed out loud in agony.

That was his way of increasing his pain threshold, so that he could endure it a bit more, and hope that he didn't faint.

He gripped harder with his left hand now, and it was pure will power that kept his body attached to the Landrover. His useless right hand dropped the gun inside the back of the vehicle, and his arm flopped down below him.

A small oscillation set up, which was automatically corrected by instant reflex action, as his brain moved his left leg down a bit into the slipstream, to balance off the initial spin.

He hung there, closed his eyes to the pain, and gritted his teeth.

It took about a minute to recover, and when he looked up again he was staring into a round black hole, in the centre of the muzzle of his own revolver.

He had failed.

* * *

Bill Carter had heard and recognised the click of the gun cocking.

He could recognise that sound in his sleep, in the middle of a clap of thunder.

He did once and it had saved his life.

He had the heavy spanner ready, and painfully raised himself over the back of the seat. The gun was already there on the tailgate, and he saw the pressure increase on the trigger finger.

He threw himself towards the gun, crying out in pain as he did so, and brought the spanner down heavily on the man's wrist.

The gun fired, and he felt a dull thud as the bullet entered his chest wall, and ripped away the lower lobe of his right lung.

He stopped his forward momentum, reared up in agony above the seat, then fell in a crumpled heap on the floor, just in front of the tail gate.

There was no feeling in his chest at that moment. He coughed up blood for a few seconds, then heard his breath rasping, as he struggled to breathe.

He saw the revolver, picked it up in his left hand, leant over the back of the Landrover and looked at the man hanging there.

He recognised the uniform, the rank, the person that he was, and instantly realised that this was a professional soldier like himself, and not a guerrilla fanatic.

He cocked the gun and held it four inches from the top of the man's head…

But he could not pull the trigger.

It was different in a firefight.

You did it to survive.

The major raised his head and looked at him.

Bill was now feeling red hot metal inside his lungs.

He was in agony.

He pulled the revolver back towards him, to check that there were two bullets in the chamber.

One for the major and one for himself.

He broke the weapon in half on the floor and emptied the cartridges.

Five spent ones fell on the floor, and one live round.

He lifted it up and looked at it.

He coughed in agony, and spat blood for about a minute.

He looked down at major Hassad, then looked at the bullet. The man was going to fall anyway. All he had to do was smash his other wrist, then shoot himself.

The pain was now intense inside his chest. He was biting his lip, drawing blood with his teeth.

He picked up the spanner and lifted it up high.

* * *

Bill Carter wasn't going soft.

He didn't like murder; because in his eyes at that moment, that's what it would have been. The man deserved a quick death, not a terrifying fall to the ground.

He couldn't do it.

They looked at each other, and Bill willed the man to fall.

They met eye to eye, and it was then that Bill picked up the revolver, put the live bullet in the chamber, closed the gun up and ran the side of the revolver against the back of the rear seat.

The chamber spun round a few times then slowed down and came to rest. The live bullet was somewhere in the firing line, but neither of them knew where.

He looked down and the man nodded at him, and said a few words of prayer. Bill put the muzzle to the man's forehead and pulled the trigger...

The firing pin clicked onto an empty chamber.

It was an unknown factor as to whether the major was relieved or not. He probably would have preferred a quick death, and yet he was happy to be alive a bit longer.

He looked up, and saw Bill put the gun to his temple, and again had double feelings when the click sounded.

He wanted the quick death for himself, and yet wanted the man in the Landrover to die.

He looked down now and saw the desert far below him.

The aircraft was turning around to another heading.

He looked across to his right and saw the wing drop downwards in the turn, and recognised the ground features. They were about twenty five miles north of Khorramshahr, obviously turning south.

He wanted to die on his homeland if possible, and waited for the next bullet.

The gun was right in front of his nose when it went 'click' for the third time.

He only had one more chance.

He watched with hope as the man in black held the gun up to his forehead, sweating with the red hot searing agony of a bullet on fire inside his chest, and burning the inside of his body.

The hope that it would be another blank...

He watched him pull the trigger.

* * *

The recoil of the gun as it fired threw the gun out from Bill Carter's already dead hand. The relief from pain was immediate and Bill was no longer in agony.

Major Hassad's hopes for an equivalent quick release had faded away with that final bullet.

He looked down at the flat countryside below him, then looked ahead at his wrist clenched tight on the handle.

He decided to have one last try.

If he could get into the Landrover, he could climb into the bomb bay, then he could cause irreparable damage to the aircraft. He concentrated his strength in his left arm and wrist muscles, and pulled himself forwards.

It was an enormous effort.

The perspiration flowed down the front of his shirt, as he gradually pulled his face up against the tailgate.

He locked his chin against the bunched up fingers of his fist, and slowly pulled his legs forward until they were bent beneath him.

He moved his right leg towards the towing bracket on the bumper, rested his foot on the flat angle iron, then pushed himself upwards over the tailgate, and fell on top of Bill Carter's dead body.

The feat was superhuman to say the least.

He shook his left arm in front of him to restore the blood circulation, then rested his chest on the tailgate looking over at the ground far below.

His breathing was fast and heavy. and he stayed there until he started to recover from the ordeal.

He sensed something was wrong.

He looked around sharply and saw two figures standing in the bomb bay looking down at him. One was dressed in aircrew coveralls, speaking into a headset, and the other was dressed in black, pointing a 9mm Browning pistol in his direction.

So near and yet so far.

Maybe he had been too hopeful.

He turned away from them and stared out ahead of him towards the far horizon. A little smile appeared at the corner of his mouth as he looked around.

There weren't many people who had sat in the back of a British made Landrover, hanging underneath the wings of a British made Vulcan bomber, looking at the countryside of his native land from a height of five hundred feet.

He looked across to the port undercarriage, and saw the roof of an Iranian freight wagon embedded in the underside of the wing.

Immediately in front of him, the metal skin and framework of the back end of the fuselage was being ripped off by the slipstream, and falling away to earth.

He saw gallons of fuel pouring out, from the hundreds of bullet holes that his comrades had shot into the wings; and over on the starboard undercarriage, he saw a man in black hanging upside down on to the main bogie strut.

He just shook his head and remarked to himself in Arabic,

"They're mad. The British are all bloody mad."

He rested his chest for the final time on the tailgate, watching his country pass beneath him.

For him it was the finest country in the world and he didn't mind dying for it.

He just waited there patiently for the final bullet in the back of his head.

Chapter 28. Praying To Mecca

Ray and Les had been struggling with the heavy bed frame, trying to get it into the bomb bay, when the first shot from Major Hassad fired.

Les looked back and saw Bill, with the spanner in his hand, hanging over the back seat.

"Pull like hell Ray, get Mr Watt into the cabin.

Bill can deal with him. I'll come back for him later."

They got him onto the floor over the nosewheel bay, and cut him from the frame work. Les checked his pulse and stuck a new bag onto his drip.

Ray had opened the door in the adjoining bulkhead ready for them, and they gently carried him through into the relative quietness of the cabin, and strapped him down on the bunk. Les did the first aid act again, and said quietly,

"Are you Ok, Mr Watt?"

The man looked up, smiled and nodded.

He beckoned Les closer with a weak hand movement. Les bent forward and listened to the faint voice.

"An exciting journey."

Well, at least somebody was happy about it. I suppose anything's exciting after you've been cooped up alone for four years or so in a cell!

"Peter, we're going to get Jock and Bill now.

Go easy on the speed and check the fuel. You're draining away tons underneath the wings."

I was able to tell him what Gan were planning with Michel, and how we were getting to Socotra.

"Ok. I'll be back in ten minutes to sort it out for you.

Take it easy with the power or you'll set us alight at the back end."

They both went back towards the bomb bay, and that's when they heard the second shot.

Les went off like a rocket, unclipping his Browning at the same time.

When Ray caught him up he stood beside Les, and watched as Major Hassad made his superb effort for survival. Even Les was respectful for what he saw.

He knew the strength and will power that was required, and just stood there watching with the gun in his hand. Ray spoke into the radio headset.

"Peter. Bill's dead. It looks as if he shot himself.

He must have been in a bad way to do that.

The passenger is climbing aboard the Landrover now.

Les is going to deal with him. He won't get on board."

"Ok Ray. Then get Jock into the wing as soon as you can."

Les told Ray quietly after he finished.

"If Bill hadn't done it to himself, Jock or I would have had to.

He hadn't a chance and he knew it."

"What are you going to do with him?" Ray said, pointing to the figure looking out of the back of the Landrover.

"Kill him." was Les's reply.

"No prisoners Les?"

He looked at Ray.

"Nobody would take me prisoner," he said, "and he's one like me.

This aircraft wouldn't exist in five minutes time if he came on board.

He dies Ray, and he knows it.

He's ready now."

Les looked down into the Landrover, transferred his pistol into his left hand, saluted Captain William Carter with his right hand for five seconds, then pressed the wing clamp release button on the hydraulic control panel in front of him.

The Landrover dropped down into the slipstream beneath the front protection shield, and tumbled over and over, throwing out tools, debris, seat covers and the two bodies in the back.

The doors twisted back and ripped off their hinges, and the bonnet smashed itself back over the front seats, blew off, then fluttered down after the heavy main body chassis plunged to earth engine downwards.

The dead body of Bill Carter flailed its arms and legs as it rotated round and round, throwing off loose articles of clothing and equipment.

It twisted over and over as it fell, and soon disappeared from their view. They lost sight of it as it plunged through a cloud; but it was the body of Major Hassad that transfixed both of them.

They followed it all the way down the five hundred and fifty feet of airspace, until it hit the ground.

* * *

As soon as the Landrover fell away, Major Hassad rolled into a tight ball to protect himself from the initial blast of the slipstream.

As soon as he was free from all the other debris, he shot his arms and legs out in free fall parachutist's fashion, arched his back, and slowly rolled over until he was falling face down, under full control.

They watched him adjust the position of his arms and legs to turn through the air, and point in a south westerly heading. He was using the ground features on the desert surface below to navigate by.

At about two hundred feet above the ground, when he was lined up exactly, he extended his two arms fully forward, as if he was in a high dive, and lowered his head.

His speed increased rapidly at this point, and Major Hassad hit the surface of the desert in an almost vertical attitude.

He died just as he had finished the words of his final prayer.

He had managed to turn just in time, and at the last moment had raised his arms and bowed towards the exact position of the Kaabah stone in the Holy City of Mecca, nearly one thousand miles away.

He hit the ground at about one hundred and twenty miles per hour, and joined the rest at the souls of his fallen comrades who were all waiting for him.

* * *

"Good God," was all Les could say.

"Why didn't you shoot him?" Ray asked.

"Anything would have been better than that."

Les looked down at the pistol in his hand for a moment, then threw it through the bomb door exit and watched it tumbling downwards.

"I couldn't Ray. I ran out of ammunition after the fire fight in Khorramshahr."

He pressed the 'UP' button to raise the cradle, then the 'CLOSE' button to slide in the bomb doors.

"Let's go and get Jock, shall we?"

They walked down to the middle of the bomb bay, and Ray opened a servicing hatch that led into the engine bay. Both engines were contained within a stainless steel tube, which stopped bits of metal flying around the wing in the case of an engine failure.

The number four tube was completely distorted and bent in its mountings, but it had stopped any further damage to the aircraft. Les and Ray crawled under the narrow gap between the bottom of the tube, and the main servicing doors on the under surface of the wing.

"Don't worry Les," Ray consoled the worried figure,

"They're both locked. They won't open."

Then he crossed his fingers, and hoped they wouldn't!

The hatch to the main tank area in the wings unfastened just as easily as the bomb bay hatch, and it was a simple job to crawl between the self sealing rubber fuel tanks; except for the fact that they were leaking gallons of fuel like kitchen colanders, and they were both slopping along in two inches of fuel along the inside base of the wing.

Ray shouted loudly to Les.

"This is an oxygen mask job Les. Make sure yours is switched on.

Don't touch your eyes and don't use your radio."

They crawled along the middle of the wing, through a third hatchway, which opened into the undercarriage bay where Jock was.

Les leant over to look downwards and saw the slipstream blowing against Jock's back, pinning him to the undercarriage strut. His feet were entangled in one of the cross hydraulic jacks.

They both climbed through the hatch, and stood on top of the undercarriage main bogie support. The ground looked hundreds of miles below them.

"This is no problem Ray. It's as easy as falling off a log. Leave it to me."

"With pleasure mate, he's all yours!"

He turned a bright shade of green as Les climbed down the undercarriage, stood on the front set of wheels, and shielded the slipstream from Jock's back.

Then they had a small conversation, whilst the aircraft wing swung up and down in the strong thermal up currents of air from the desert below them.

"Where the bloody hell have you been?

I've been hanging around here for hours waiting for you,

Now get me out of this stupid position will you?"

"You got yourself into it, you get yourself out of it; or shut your face, and let a man get on with a man's work."

"Don't you bloody well argue with me mate, or you'll catch one."

"Oh yeh. You and who's army?"

"I don't need an army to deal with a little Welsh squirt like you.

Bloody Welshman.

Go on, get back to your sheep farming and pheasant plucking."

"Bloody Scotsman.

You couldn't catch a cold, let alone an aircraft, or a number five bus.

You're about as useful as a lead balloon."

"Will you two stop arguing and move yourselves..."

Ray in his desperation had climbed down the back of the undercarriage strut, with his eyes closed, to shut them both up.

"Now shift your damn backsides, and get back into the bloody wing will you?"

They both looked at him in amazement.

"Bloody aircrew," was all Les said, then heaved Jock's shoulders upwards.

Ray unentangled Jock's feet from the hydraulic jack, to the tune of pure Glaswegian, reflecting on the parentage of the Welsh gentleman who was causing this extreme discomfort.

The aircraft wing continued to swing up and down, adding a bit of sideways motion to the proceedings.

Ray then climbed up into the bay, grabbed hold of jock's feet and pulled, while Les pushed up from the bottom,

Jock continued in his homily concerning the limited usefulness of Welsh race.

"I think we ought to drop the ungrateful bar steward right now" Les said to Ray.

"Ok..."

And Ray released his grip for about a micro second!

The lanquage was dreadful from the inverted one.

Les nearly fell off, as he creased up laughing, and had to hang onto Jock; which made the situation worse.

The aircraft lurched sideways at this point, which swung Jock's body to the side of the undercarriage strut then back again towards the hard metal.

The famous Scotsman bounced a few times, before Les decided to catch him again.

"That'll teach you not to tangle with us mate.

Next time it's overboard, so button your lip."

He cursed them every inch of the way up, expanding Ray's knowledge of ancient British Anglo Saxon, Scottish flavour of course.

He only shut up when they tied an oxygen mask over his mouth, and ripped off the microphone; and even then they could see him mouthing away behind the plastic face plate, shaking his fist at them.

"I think he's better now Ray, he's back to his usual miserable bloody self.

We'll leave him to find his own way back."

... So they left Jock cursing and blinding everyone and everything, as he crawled back to the fuselage.

He didn't shut up until we reached Socotra, and that was about four hours later.

We left the Oxygen mask tied on to cover his face.

It acted both as a noise filter, and volume control!

* * *

Back in the cabin Les was attending to Mr Watt before we set course for Socotra.

That was as soon as we got Jock off the mainwheel.

He had changed the drip again, and it was obvious that he was improving as every minute passed. It was the morale factor of being free again.

Les was washing his face when Mr Watt beckoned him closer, so that he could speak to him.

His words were indistinct but they sounded like "En Vlow."

Les searched his Arabic memory, but it didn't make sense.

He knelt down beside Mr Watt and asked him to repeat it until he understood.

"En Vlope, En Vlope."

He turned to Ray who was at the main computer at the time.

"Ray, do you know anything about an envelope for Mr Watt?"

He shook his head.

Mr Watt held Les's arm and shook it gently and pointed to his bony chest.

"Pock ket."

Les understood, and looked in the top pocket of Mr Watt's shirt. He pulled out a very old tattered OHMS brown envelope, which was almost falling to bits. His home address was on the front, and on the top right hand corner a faded first class stamp.

Les turned it over but there was nothing on the back or inside.

Mr Watt held out his hand appealingly, so Les placed it in his palm for him.

Mr Watt just looked at it, smiling to himself.

Les went up to Ray and said quietly,

"What do you make of that, Ray?

Do you think his mind has been affected by the isolation or something?"

Ray stopped what he was doing and watched for a while, then went across and looked at the envelope, still lying on Mr Watt's hand.

He jerked his head sideways to bring Les across, and pointed to the stamp.

"When did you ever see a first class stamp, on an OHMS official brown envelope Les?"

Les looked at him and shook his head.

"You don't, do you.

They're either franked with a franking machine, or it's on official business."

Mr Watt looked up at them and said weakly,

"They made me pray with them five times a day. Had to bow to Mecca.

Put envelope with Queen's head under prayer mat.

Bowed to the Queen, five times a day for four years.

It kept me going."

The exertion of speaking was heavy for him but he continued.

"I fooled them.

Didn't I?"

Les lifted up the envelope and saw the faded, unfranked stamp of the Monarch, stuck neatly in the top right hand corner.

He looked down at Mr Watt.

"Mate. You certainly did, and if I have anything to do with it you're going to walk up to Buck house yourself and do it in person; and if she doesn't tap you on the shoulders with her sword there'll be merry hell played."

Ray shook Mr Watt's hand.

"That goes for myself and Peter.

Well done Mr Watt.

Very well done."

Les gave him the envelope back, and within five minutes Mr Watt was having the most restful sleep that he had for years.

He deserved every second of it.

Chapter 29. Russian Drinks

As soon as Andy realised the urgency of the situation he contacted Michel and told them to make for Kuwait City.

The mainframe computer had taken both aircraft's positions, headings and speeds, and had come up with a rendezvous near the city. He passed instructions to Peter to head there and if possible, with Michel's assistance, try to make Socotra.

It was about fourteen hundred miles away from them, across the deserts of Saudi Arabia. If it could not be done then a reappraisal would need to be made. The Vulcan would still be close enough to the waters of the Persian Gulf for abandonment and destruction.

A further decision could be made as soon as Peter and Ray could feed the aircraft data to them for a full examination. It was obvious that they had problems of greater seriousness to deal with; therefore his final decision could wait for another hour or so.

He advised MOD special operations of the situation, and that Mr Watt was on board.

"Good," said Andy's superior on the other end of the telephone.

"That's going to set the feathers flying in the Foreign Office. I expect there will be a few red faces when they find out.

They should never have cancelled in the first place."

"Do you still want them at Socotra?" Andy asked.

"That's the priority if the aircraft can make it, and if Mr Watt is up to it.

Ask them how he is. You can put him into Riyadh hospital if it is necessary."

There was a moment of silence on the line, before he spoke again.

"Andy, a delicate point. How quickly can you get him out of the Vulcan, and into the Bear, if needs dictate?"

Andy checked the clock on the computer screen, and read the countdown readings.

"I've got that ready for you.

The microjet can get there in fifteen minutes. It's on its way now.

The other one is en route to Kuwait City hospital, for Doctor Pachandra. It can pick him up and get into the cabin within an hour, assuming it's safe to do so."

"Can they stay airborne long enough for a transfer, do you think?"

"I can't say as yet. They're too busy gathering bits and pieces together.

I'll send a full report of this as soon as possible.

At the moment all I can confirm is that they are airborne, and nothing else."

"Ok, call every fifteen minutes and keep me updated."

* * *

It was another ten minutes before Peter managed to get some data through.

It looked bad, especially with the fuel leaking away.

Eventually Ray was able to send more to them, as he scanned around the various systems.

The two major points, as far as Andy could see were the excessive fuel leaks, and that the consumption rate with the undercarriage down wouldn't even get them to Kuwait City, let alone Socotra.

It was looking more like a ditching job, no matter which way he looked at it.

He pressed the keys on the computer, to connect him with the Vulcan's radio link.

"Peter, what is the fuel situation?"

"It's pouring out of the wings Andy. The tanks are all shot up on each side, and the port wing main tank is completely ruptured.

I'm using the fuel up as quickly as I can before it all goes overboard, then I'll only have the fuselage tanks left. They're all right. They never got hit, but there's only half an hour of fuel remaining at the rate were using it."

"That's better than I had hoped for.

Is Mr Watt fit enough for a transfer to the Bear, if you have to do it?"

"Yes. He's tough enough. After what he's been through lately, that will be a pleasure ride."

"Ok. Ivan will be with you in five minutes. He can stand off until we decide what to do.

Kuwait City is eighty miles ahead of you now. Michel will meet you there.

Try to isolate the wing tanks from rest of the fuel system, so that he can refuel your fuselage tanks."

Ray and I looked at the fuel charts in the screen together, and he found that he could physically turn off the fuel pipes leading from the wing tanks to each engine, using the main fuel cocks in the engine bays.

The fuel from the fuselage tanks would then only feed the engines, and not drain away through the damaged piping.

The number four engine fuel line was already turned off, so all he needed to do was to turn off the fuel lines to the other three engines.

Kuwait city was twenty minutes away, and I was reluctant to do anything until I had used up as much wing fuel as possible.

Ray scanned the tanks as we emptied them one at a time, and let me know when the time came to isolate them.

"Go to each engine Ray. I'll switch on the fuselage tanks, then you turn off the isolation cocks."

When we completed the switch over, we had used as much wing fuel as possible, and had about twenty minutes flying time remaining.

Ray was now back at the main computer, and had switched the video screen onto the Big Bird satellite display. I could see Michel south east of us, on an intercept path; we would reach each other in ten minutes.

Ivan was now on the port wing tip, reporting all the damage back to the Bear; Gan would analyse what he reported, and cross reference it with our flight data output to them.

The fuel leaking from the trailing edges had now stopped, and the wing vents were clearing the fumes from the internal cavities of the wing.

We filled the tanks with nitrogen, and just kept blowing the gas through the holes. There was enough to last at least six hours, which was more than we required.

I also found that I could close down the number one engine, and fly on the two inboards. I needed a bit more power from both of them, but was not using as much fuel this way; not as much as three engines running at less power.

That was a bonus. I was expecting to close down number three, and crab sideways all the way to wherever we decided to go...

It also gave us another five minutes of flying time.

Socotra was looking more hopeful the more we fixed the aircraft.

Most of our navigation gear, which was stored in the wings, was shot up.

But that was no problem with Michel around as the good shepherd, so I spoke to Andy.

"I suggest we refuel the fuselage tanks, then both proceed en route for Socotra.

If we get any further problems we can fly Mr Watt into Kuwait international with the micro, and then dump the Vulcan into the desert."

That was agreed by all.

Gan checked the engines by reviewing our data output and cleared them. The new fuel system which we had managed to achieve was not leaking anywhere, and the fire risk within the wing tanks was now negligible.

With the undercarriage down, and flying at a height of six thousand feet to take advantage of the southerly winds we would need constant refuelling from the Bear, but we should be able to manage Socotra in about four and a half hours.

It was all on the computer at Gan, and that was where any final adjustments could be made. Michel and I were both sending the data to Andy, and were both getting readouts from him. The computers were again operating in harmony as they did for the Indian Ocean link up... which seemed years ago.

It looked as if it was going to work out at last.

I could now see Michel turning ahead of me on the left hand side, at the same height as me. We had linked the computers together for this part of the rendezvous. Our main computer and the flight computer had received very little damage, and could be trusted. Michel's computer had verified this, and Gan had agreed with it.

The Bear was already trailing the refuelling pipe, and the two computers were judging the distance between the two aircraft and flying them together, to join up with the minimum of time delay.

It worked well.

I saw Michel's Bear turn across my path, about three hundred yards ahead of me, and slowly level off its wings as it took up the exact heading. The Vulcan closed up behind it, and I watched in fascination as the two throttles edged their way backwards the closer we got to the refuelling connecter.

The front television camera locked itself on to the centre of the eight equally spaced lights flashing around the edge of the circular funnel, and it was a great humiliation to me, the now redundant pilot of the aircraft, to see the probe place itself neatly and firmly into the funnel and stay there as the two aircraft flew along together.

I pressed the radio transmit button...

"Michel, are you flying your aircraft at the moment?"

His heavily accented reply was simple.

"No."

I sniffed.

"Well. That's put both of us in our places."

Ray had the fuel switches open, and the wide smiling Piotr was hard at work again in their rear turret.

We filled up the tanks again to give us another half hour of flying, and then I took over the controls, switched out the computer and pulled the aircraft back to about four hundred yards behind the Bear.

The main computer and the systems computer advised Gan of the success of the transfer. The microjet then pulled up behind the funnel for its own little drink.

Piotr squirted a couple of gallons into it, which was all it needed.

It was a bit like filling a Mini, after a heavy goods vehicle at a petrol station.

We collected more stamps though!

* * *

"The flying doctor's coming up on the starboard wing." Ray advised me.

He had received a message from Gan; to expect the second micro any minute, with a doctor from Kuwait City General Hospital.

He had been collected from his private apartment in the staff wing, and driven to the airport ready to be picked up by Boris, the fourth member of the Bear's crew.

He usually did most of their navigation, but this part of the rendezvous was all done by computers, so he was free to pick the doctor up.

I looked to my right to see him holding off about two hundred feet away, waiting for clearance to dock.

But before that took place, Gan and I would decide what we going to do.

Andy wanted us to go to Socotra, and I was game to try it, but there was Mr Watt to consider.

I asked Les to come up for a chat.

"Give Mr Watt the facts, Les. We can get him to Kuwait now if he wants to in Ivan's microjet, or he can come with us to Socotra.

Tell him that Riyadh hospital is about an hour ahead, so if he does decide to come with us he can go there if necessary. After that it's about two hours to Salala, then a flight across the ocean to Socotra.

You seem to have made a hit with the man. Ask him what he wants to do, will you?"

"I don't think it matters, Peter.

He's fast asleep.

I suggest we leave him as he is.

Let's take him with us."

I looked at Les and noted the 'with us' bit.

"Ok Les. Thanks for your help. I'll fetch the doctor across now.

Can you do the cradle, while Ray operates the computer?"

He gave a thumbs up and disappeared.

He did the lot for us. He was getting quite proficient with that particular system now.

He saw the micro aboard, helped the doctor out and showed him up to the cabin, before dropping the cradle back again into the slipstream.

Boris returned straight away to the Bear, and I saw him link up with the cradle in front, and disappear five minutes later into the bowels of the huge fuselage.

It was like a flying hangar, as it thundered along in front of us. It could probably have eaten half a dozen of those little aircraft for breakfast, and belched them out of the engine exhausts without anybody noticing them...

... And I was grateful for the huge capacity of fuel it was holding, as it would have to take both aircraft about fourteen hundred miles before it could be refuelled again.

* * *

I was looking ahead at the Bear when I heard someone climb up the ladder, and walk steadily across the narrow platform to stand beside me.

It was Doctor Pachandra.

He had obviously been dragged away from what he was doing at very short notice, and most probably would have had no choice in the decision at all. I didn't envy him one bit having to be forced into a small aircraft, then flown up into the belly of another.

Not many people would have liked that thrown at them, let alone be told that they were joining a bunch of misfits in an aeroplane that could fall out of the sky at any moment.

He looked at me, his head forwards, deep in thought as he approached me.

"Captain Barten, I am not very happy about this.

First I was told that the patient was arriving at Kuwait City International Airport, and then I was told to come up here into this aeroplane... to find the patient sound asleep.

Perhaps you can tell me please, just exactly what is it that you expect me to do?"

He was very polite in the circumstances, and I could understand his reasons.

He had not been told the full facts.

"Dr Pachandra. We have a man here who has been held hostage for over four years in solitary confinement, and he is very weak.

He forced himself into surviving by his strength of character, and I would like to take him to the island of Socotra, which is about four hours ahead of us.

I can fly him to a hospital at any time in one of our small microjets, but prefer to keep him asleep during the flight.

Would you be prepared to stay with him, and look after him for us?"

He looked down into the cabin at the sleeping figure.

"Oh dear. I didn't know that.

I'd better go and have a look at him.

Oh dear."

I sensed by his remarks that he was going to stay.

I watched him descend the ladder. The deer stalker hat he was wearing got knocked off by the side of my seat, but he didn't even notice. Our little Indian doctor was too absorbed with his new patient.

I knew that Mr Watt was in good hands. The hands, I found out afterwards, of a trained surgeon, who took his work very seriously, and accepted his responsibilities with equal demeanour.

Les was there watching the doctor, and told him what he had done so far. I could see Doctor Pachandra nodding away in agreement. Then he started a full examination.

I left him to it.

I had my own 'patient' to look after, and it needed another drink!

It was rather like Mr Watt in a way.

Both patients were very weak and jaded, and both were being fed by tubes and drips.

I took hold of mine and fed it into the 'glucose' bag in front of me, and filled the tanks up again. Ivan followed suit; and that's how we crossed the Saudi Arabian desert...

Doctor 'P' looking after Mr Watt, our very important patient,

Captain 'B' looking after the private ambulance,

Michel leading the way with his lights flashing,

And Ivan riding on the port wing as official escort.

Even the British police force couldn't have done better than that.

* * *

Just before midday I heard Gan's message.

"Gan control to all units. Detonation in five minutes."

Michel and I acknowledged the message, and Ray selected the channel so that we could hear the countdown.

We would be too far away to be affected by the blast waves; the weapons had been designed to concentrate the waves in a vertical direction, and they were sunk deep into the ground.

From our point of view it was an anti climax, which suited me fine. The boffins could get on with whatever they wanted to do. We had our own problems.

At midday we just heard the final "three, two, one, detonation", and that was it as far as we were concerned...

* * *

We saw the video pictures taken from the United States shuttle after we landed at Socotra.

It literally changed the map of the world, particularly at the head of the Persian Gulf.

We didn't even feel any blast wave.

It was the direct opposite of the Bandar Abbas explosion.

We hardly felt a thing.

* * *

... And the aircraft intercom was very quiet as well.

It was as we were passing Riyadh that Doctor P spoke to me again.

"Would it be possible for me to contact the hospital for some information please?"

"No problem Doctor P.

Pick up the handset at the back, and ask Ray to patch you onto the Skynet telephone circuits.

Just tell the operator who you want."

He went back down again with a big beaming smile. He was a lot happier than when he arrived. We heard him chat away in his native language to another of his fraternity.

Then there was a gloomy session.

He looked very heavy and worried.

I heard Ray say to him,

"What's up Doc?"

"They have the information I want, but it is on their computer data banks. I cannot get into it and get a reading I need," he replied unhappily.

Ray went on the line and spoke to the computer operator for a few moments. He passed them some Skynet channels and some specific details concerning our main computer, then placed Doctor P in front of the monitor.

"Try that Doc. See if you can get in. If not, they can send it to us, and we will record on the memory disc.

We use this system for transferring military casualty information, and it can link with most system 'x' networks.

Tell them you have a priority 'z' and watch them fill their nappies.

He did...

And they did!

We couldn't stop him or the hospital operator. They were both at it on their keyboards all the way to Socotra. He knew more about Mr Watt than the man knew about himself, and when that enquiry was over he started taking over the aircraft computer.

Ray went wild. The man was a computer buff.

He reprogrammed some of the operations for the better, and gave Ray a full indoctrination in the new system.

By the time we were abeam Salala, on the south coast of Dhufar, we already had an improved flight systems data collector.

"I use this in the Kuwait hospital for monitoring tropical diseases, which is then transmitted daily to America, for their tanker protection conveys.

You will find it better than your previous system."

I called up Gan.

They saved it on the mainframe for the Bear.

I think we all gained from Doctor P's visit; he was treating two patients by the time we landed!

* * *

"Zero One. This is Socotra. I see you coasting out from Dhufar, abeam Salala.

Message from Gan.

Double check all aircraft systems before the sea crossing."

Ray did a full system check on everything. Dr P checked Mr Watt and the new flight data system, and I called up Michel.

"How's the fuel Michel. Ok for both of us?"

"Yes. No problem. I can get to Gan if I wish afterwards.

We fill you up now, half way across, then just before you land."

I was getting as good as Ray now at this flight refuelling lark.

The tanks filled up, then Ivan fuelled his micro ready to return to the Bear. He had stuck on our port wing all through the three hours since we left Kuwait, just in case Mr Watt needed a rapid departure from the Vulcan.

The nearest hospital now was at Salala, and if it was urgent, we could have landed there and dropped him off, before carrying on to Socotra.

The sea crossing took about an hour.

Ray picked up the island on the forward camera when we were within one hundred miles, and set up the flight computer with the airfield as the datum. The readouts on the screen in front of me showed the exact position of the aircraft to the airfield.

I now knew how to get there, even if the navigation system started to go backwards or blow up in our faces.

Michel filled us up for the final time at the twenty mile run in point from the main runway, and led us in all the way down to the touch down point.

* * *

The airfield used to be a Royal Air Force maritime reconnaissance airfield during the Second World War, but had been neglected after that; until it was taken over by the civil sector of the United Nations.

It was now an important centre for their operations in the Indian Ocean and Persian Gulf area.

It was positioned on the northern coastline of the island, and we were running straight down towards the runway from over the sea.

I just followed Michel as he approached. He flew low over the airfield, and circled around to the left as we did our own approach.

The undercarriage was no problem as we landed, but the tyres eventually gave up on us.

I wasn't surprised.

They had taken a hammering during the take off at Khorramshahr, and all the tyres had been cut to ribbons.

They all burst without exception.

I was prepared for that, and as I couldn't use the tail breaking parachute to slow the aircraft down - it was lying in the road by a level crossing at the time, I had to use the full length of the runway to slow the aircraft down.

The touchdown was smooth, but rolling down to the end was very rough.

It was steel wheels travelling on a rippled concrete surface, and it rattled our eyeballs like peas in a pot.

I was glad when we stopped.

I put on the parking brake and looked around.

There was nothing to see.

No hangars.

No control tower.

No buildings at all.

There were no people either. It was not only completely deserted, but devoid of any form of life at all...

Not even sea gulls.

Ray looked around the airfield, and agreed with me.

"You can't even call it a ghost town Peter. At least that would have some buildings around somewhere."

* * *

Then a solitary Landrover, with one man in it emerged from the ground about half a mile ahead, and came down the runway to meet us.

He stopped in front of the Vulcan, took out a handset and spoke into it.

"Zero One. This is Socotra. Welcome to Qadhub airfield.

Please chop your engines and remain in the aircraft.

 Thank you."

I just sat back and relaxed for the first time in hours. What a trip that had been.

I promised myself that one day I would write about it, but at the moment all I wanted to do was sit back and do nothing.

Ray spoke to me after a couple of minutes.

"You're supposed to pull the throttles back when you chop engines..."

Oh god.

One day I'd forget my head.

As the turbines whined down, and the noise gradually reduced, Dr P came up to speak to me. He whispered quietly in my ear so the others wouldn't hear.

"I am sorry that I was so angry when I came in, but I want you to know that I enjoyed the whole trip very much, and so did Mr Watt."

I took his hand and shook it warmly.

"Thanks Doctor P. I couldn't have done this without you. Thanks for all your help."

He looked behind him secretively to see where the others were, and gave me a little brown bottle marked 'poison'.

"Here is some special medicine for you.

Don't worry about the label. Drink it up."

I crossed my fingers and had a little sip.

It was the best champagne brandy that I had ever tasted.

"I keep it for my best patients," he remarked.

"The 'poison bottle' keeps my reception staff away. It wouldn't last a minute if they ever found out."

He put his finger to his lips,

"Mum's the word. Keep the bottle."

I winked at him and sipped slowly.

"Medical - in confidence, Doc.

Strictly confidential."

I just sat back, and waited for the aircraft tug to come and tow us away.

Michel growled low overhead and rocked his wings.

"Greetings little brother."

I raised my brandy to him.

"Cheers big brother. Thanks for the drinks. We'll see you later."

"Don't worry, my friend", Michel replied.

"Next time we pour them; you drink the best Russian vodka, and get the best Russian glasnost.

Give our regards to Mary Jo when you see her."

"Who is she?" I asked.

"She's our adopted little sister.

She works at the hospital for the famine relief.

We tell you all about her on Tuesday. She is a good girl. You look after her until we see her."

"It will be our pleasure Michel, thanks again. See you Tuesday."

I watched his aircraft as he banked steeply to starboard across the airfield, and flew low level along the edge of the hills towards the hospital, which was hidden on the eastern side of the island.

It had been built into the hillside to keep out of the intense heat of the overhead sun, and the windows had a panoramic view of the island, from a height of about one thousand feet.

Michel flew right past, level with them, and rocked his wings at the people inside.

He banked his aircraft hard to starboard and climbed steeply away, directly in front of the windows for all to see.

Then he returned to Gan.

His mission accomplished!

Chapter 30. The Best Medicine

The man outside was Bob Marshall, the chief aircraft engineer in charge of all technical servicing on the island.

He waited patiently until the engines fully wound down.

He heard the final rattling of the turbine blades as they loosened up in their mountings, freed from the centrifugal force of rotation, and when the last blade 'clicked' to a standstill, he spoke into his handset.

"Socotra Control from Mobile One. The engines have now stopped."

"Thank you Mobile One.

Zero One, do you need a bomb disposal team to check for unexploded shells or missiles inside the aircraft?"

"Stand by."

I asked Les for his opinion.

"Shall I just speak with them, and have a chat with their team leader?" he replied.

It was his party for the moment, so he held the stage.

He indicated the type of weapons used against us, and it was concluded that there was very little probability of any live explosive bullets being fired from the machine guns; and that the armoured cars did not have an opportunity to deliver their high velocity armour piercing shells...

If they had, we wouldn't be here.

When they finished their little discussion, Socotra Control broadcast to the man outside.

"Mobile One, clear to carry out external examination.

Pass in the canister for cabin disinfestation."

Doctor Pachandra explained that all aircraft coming to Socotra received this treatment. It resulted in the island remaining clear of all nasties, and that the hospital was the cleanest in the Middle East.

We all put our masks on, whilst our personal doctor sprayed the inside of the cabin as if he was painting the outside of his car.

"We have to wait two minutes until the nasty bugs are all dead," he said.

At the rate he was spreading it around, I doubt if they would have lasted two seconds.

Bob was back on his handset:

"Socotra Control, we are going to need the mobile jacks.

All the tyres have blown, and the whole aircraft is covered in fuel and oil.

The other damage is safe until we get it into the hangar.

We'll give it a foam wash now, and get all the flammable muck off it."

"Thank you. The jacks are en route now.

Zero One, will you please take fire drill action on your other three engines, and fill them with fire extinguisher foam.

Then put the wing tank nitrogen system onto full pressure. Stand by for foam covering."

I did as requested, switched off the fuel to the other engines, and pressed the fire buttons. There was a sharp cracking sound as the fire extinguisher bottles fired, and a loud 'shushing' sound as the foam filled the containment tubes at the front, centre and rear of the engines.

Because we weren't moving forwards, it poured out of the front intakes as well as the rear exhaust tubes, and very soon there was a huge pile of foam spreading all over the runway around us.

Along each side of the runway I could see small wide barrel shaped objects, which looked like mortar tubes. They were spaced out every fifty feet, and I noticed that the ones in the immediate vicinity of the aircraft were all pointing towards us.

If I didn't know otherwise, I would have assumed that they were some form of gun, because that's what they looked like.

The ones closest to us started to dribble water and foam onto the runway in front of them, and then they all let rip.

The aircraft was covered in the stuff, from all sides, and we disappeared under a mountain of white foam.

We must have looked like a huge blob of shaving cream on the runway. It was just like sitting in a pot of white paint as it covered our cockpit windows.

"Zero One, you'll be like that for about ten minutes, until the fuel and oil is all dissolved. I suggest you try and amuse yourselves for a while.

How is your patient?

Will he need an ambulance, or can he wait until we get you into the hangar?

It takes about fifteen minutes to get there once you start from the runway."

I looked behind me and saw them all sitting on the floor of the cabin, leaning against various bits of equipment; with paper cups full of neat brandy, watching a television monitor that had been strapped to the side of the navigation table using black adhesive tape.

Mr Watt was propped up against a couple of blankets which acted as a pillow, and was drinking a cup of warm liquid which Doctor Pachandra had prepared for him in the galley.

All five of them were wearing headphones, and were laughing at a Tom and Jerry cartoon being played on the television.

"What the hell's going on?" I asked.

It's Doctor P's idea," said Ray.

"He's fixed up the aircraft's main computer, so that he can play his laser discs on the monitor.

We've been sitting here watching all his cartoons for the last two and a half hours, while you've been flogging yourself to death getting us here.

It's a great idea. I've recorded all his discs, and they're in the memory banks now."

Doctor Pachandra came onto the intercom.

"Mr Preston, could you look into my little black bag, please, for my Fred Flintstone series?

You'll find them filed under 'aspirins', next to Mickey Mouse."

"Ok Doc...

... Sorry Peter, we're far too busy down here to be bothered with 'them' up there."

I groaned.

"Will you ask the Doc if he wants an ambulance for Mr Watt?"

Doctor P spoke to me himself.

"Captain Barten. Please tell them that under no circumstances must the patient be moved."

There was a great howl of laughter, as Tom smashed into the side of a ship and scraped his way down the paintwork into the water, trailing scratch marks with his claws.

"Anyway," continued the doctor, "he cannot leave at the moment.

The cartoon is not yet finished."

I despaired.

He was as bad as they were.

They had infected him with their lunacy!

I shook my head at the thought of five grown up men, watching a kiddie's cartoon inside a nuclear bomber aircraft; covered in 'shaving cream', in the middle of a disused airfield somewhere on Socotra island in the West Indian Ocean.

Try telling that one to your bosses on the radio, when everybody from Gan to New York could listen in, and most probably were.

"Socotra Control, Zero One. The ambulance will not be required.

Doctor Pachandra has administered a placebo, and the patient is comfortable."

There was another howl of laughter, as Tom got flattened by the ship's funnel!

* * *

"Thank you. Stand by for water cleaning."

I could see the windows clearing from the foam, as the water sprayed over us and wiped us clean. Bob Marshall then inspected us, and declared us free from fire risk.

There were three 'trucks' standing on the runway in front of the aircraft. They had been sent to take us to wherever we were going. Bob gave them instructions over his handset.

"Take up positions."

They were driven in reverse towards us.

Each had four enormous tractor wheels, with heavy treads on the tyres, which were independently suspended at the four corners of a steel rectangular box, open at the back end, with the base scraping over the concrete surface of the runway.

Two men were in an enclosed cabin at the front.

They drove the trucks slowly under the fuselage and wings, until the back end of the boxes were lined up with the undercarriage. A thick steel hawser was then connected to the centre of each axle between the wheels, and the two side trucks were electrically connected by a cable to the centre truck.

I heard the instructions on the radio.

"Take up the slack."

The engines roared, and I felt the aircraft judder as the trucks were pulled towards the undercarriage by the hawser, until the rear end of the floor of each box was lined up underneath the wheels.

"Full power."

I heard the engines rev up, and felt the aircraft moving slowly forwards as the hawser pulled the trucks and the wheels together; until the aircraft undercarriage was sitting inside the three boxes.

"Power off. Chocks in position. Secure the aircraft."

When they had finished, we were chocked into the three boxes, and steel bars were pushed through the axle mountings to fix us securely onto the three trucks.

"Power on."

The engines roared again.

"Lifting now."

I could feel myself rising gently, as the hydraulic jacks raised the boxes in the framework of the trucks, and the aircraft was lifted up off the runway to a height of about nine inches.

"Locking bars in."

I had now acquired a new set of wheels!

"Zero One, are you ready far taxiing?"

"Yes, go ahead please. I'll just sit back and enjoy the view."

"I don't blame you. Get a pair of binoculars and look at the hills ahead.

Look for a quarry in your one o clock position."

"Mobile One. You're clear to move."

Bob got into his Landrover, switched on a 'follow me' sign on his roof and spoke to the three trucks.

"Slow ahead. Pick up my speed."

All four of them moved forward at the same time, and I went rolling along the runway, just sitting there watching it all without a care in the world.

* * *

There was another burst of laughter behind me.

I heard Doctor P remark to the others,

"I have seen that bit hundreds of times, and it still makes me laugh."

I looked back at them. Even Mr Watt was giggling away.

Doctor Pachandra saw me, took off his headset and climbed the steps up to my seat.

"Captain Barten. These cartoons I carry for my patients, when they came to see me.

They are very good for the little children, when they are frightened and worried. It relieves the stress.

Sometimes we adults need to be reminded that we were children once.

It is very good for us.

I knew you wouldn't mind."

I looked down at Mr Watt, Les, Jock and Ray; then at Dr P...

"Excuse me, Doc. You're in my way."

I reached past him and flicked a switch, so that I could listen to the monitor too.

He grinned and returned to all his patients.

He'd caught us all now, lock, stock and barrel, including the aircraft!

* * *

The trucks had some form of computer on board the middle one, which controlled their relative speeds, as they turned round the bends of the track leading to the quarry entrance.

It took about twenty minutes to reach it, and in that time we went through three more Tom and Jerries and a Fred Flintstone.

I had done as the controller had suggested, and had examined the hills ahead of us.

They were part of the Hajhir range of mountains, on the eastern half of the island, the highest point rising to about four and a half thousand feet.

I could see six quarries ahead of me about half a mile apart, some of them active, and blasting was taking place in the one farthest away as we approached. The two nearest were disused, and it was to one of these that we were being taken to.

The Landrover and the trucks stopped at the entrance, and waited until a bulldozer scraped the surface of the quarry as flat as it could. The rocks and stones were crushed under its heavy tracks, as it crunched back and forth.

Ray came up to the front and watched. There was a sign at the side of the road that said,

: **DANGER. QUARRY BLASTING. KEEP OUT:**

: **PRIVATE PROPERTY:**

: **ASB ASSOCIATES. PLC:**

The hole that had been gauged out of the ground was enormous.

We looked at the towering cliffside ahead of us, and the slabs of rock all over the floor. The bulldozer was at the far end clearing rocks and stones, and piling them into a heap at the side of the cliff.

Ray pointed down to the ground and asked,

"What are all those coloured things there?"

They looked like flattened plastic dinner plates, all splayed out.

There were dozens of them all over the place, all different colours; red, blue, yellow and white.

"Dunno, unless folks have dropped their hard hats, and the bulldozer's flattened them, otherwise they've got multi-coloured hedgehogs on the island."

As we were talking, a brand new Saab turbo 9999/90 screeched around the corner ahead of us and skidded fifty feet to a halt, sending up fountains of big jagged stones in all directions, some of which bounced off the brand new paintwork.

A young man got out of the driver's seat and a young lady from the passenger's. He leant into the car and picked out two stainless steel hard hats, which they both put on their heads, and looked across at the Vulcan for a few moments.

Ray said casually,

"He must be the big chief. He's wearing a shiny steel hat."

"Don't you believe it, Ray" I replied.

"It's probably just to stop it getting crushed by the bulldozer or something. What's he doing now?"

We watched him as he went into a small shed, with 'DANGER EXPLOSIVES' warning notices painted all around the four walls.

Inside he opened a wall cupboard marked 'DYNAMITE', and switched on an electrical panel screwed behind the door.

There was a red button, which he pressed.

A siren screeched for five seconds, and then he pressed two green buttons beside it.

As this was going on I was looking at his young lady, and gave her a little wave. She grinned and waved back at me.

I noticed a flash of sunlight from the big diamond ring on her left hand, and then a movement in the cliff wall took my attention away.

The quarry wall ahead of us was slowly moving apart, producing an ever widening gap.

It continued until the two camouflaged doors reached some marks on the hangar floor inside. At this point an engineer waved his hand, and the doors stopped.

The engines of the three trucks revved up and carried the Vulcan slowly across the surface of the quarry, through the gap in the doors, and up to the far end of the hangar where they stopped.

The safety securing bars were removed from underneath the boxes, and then they were gently lowered until all three rested on the hangar floor. The trucks detached themselves from the boxes then drove back out through the hangar doors into the quarry.

I could now hear the dull rumbling of the doors, as they slid across the rails towards the middle of the entrance behind us, and heard a dull boom as they closed up tight.

The echo resonated around the cavern for a full minute, and during that time I looked across the hangar floor in all directions to see if anyone was around.

It was completely deserted.

The cavern was enormous. The ceiling must have been at least one hundred feet above us.

All we needed were a few bats flying around and we could have been in Transylvania.

"Christ, I hope this isn't Dracula coming towards us," Ray said.

He had come up front for a look.

A huge matron figure, with winging cape was marching across the floor, with two other nurses in escort pushing a stretcher in front of them.

"I don't mind the two young ones, but I don't fancy yours much." he said.

I was about to tactfully remark about his choice of selection, when a message came across the radio to us.

"Zero One. From Socotra Control.

Well done everyone.

Welcome home."

The girls took Mr Watt away to the hospital, with Doctor Pachandra and the Senior Surgeon, for an immediate examination.

Before he left the hangar we both held his hands as he looked at the Vulcan.

"Did I cause all that damage to that aeroplane?" he asked.

Ray looked down at him.

"Not really, and we've both seen a lot worse than that.

It's a bit like you, Mr Watt. It can take punishment and still keep going."

Bob Marshall butted in at that point.

"Mr Watt, I'll fix it up in time for these two to fly you back to England when you're better.

Is that a deal?"

I felt has thin hand grip mine with emotion.

"It's a deal," he whispered, "it's a deal."

And then they took him off to the hospital.

I looked at the aircraft. It was a complete mess. I had seen pictures of war damaged aircraft in the history books, but this was beyond a joke.

"You must be out of your tiny head, Bob. You don't stand a chance.

The bloody thing's dropping to bits as we look at it. Have you seen the back end?

There's nothing left of the fuselage after the rudder and fin.

You're going to need more than sellotape to fix this heap of junk."

He looked at me and shook his head.

"Who do you think built it in the first place.

Have you seen the plate in the undercarriage bay, Mr Barten. Take a look."

He led us across the floor. and there it was for both Ray and I to see.

: CONSTRUCTED BY ROBERT MARSHALL ENTERPRISES. JULY 1995:

"I don't understand this at all.

I thought that this was the RAF display Vulcan from Waddington." I said to him.

"No. We've had this under wraps for some time at Cockfosters. We got it activated last month when MOD asked us to.

The display Vulcan was flown here under the pretext of a refit at RAF St Athan. It's over in the inner cavern with the other Mark 2 Vulcans, except of course the one at the Waddington gate. That will stay there. The others will stay here."

He looked up at his aircraft.

"Two months will do it, then you can fly Mr Watt home.

By the way, these are for you, compliments of the management."

He passed over two cans of beer.

There were two 'pssssssts', two 'gulps', two 'burps', and two satisfied people two seconds later.

"By God, I was ready for that." Ray said, as he sucked the can dry.

I was too busy looking across the hangar to reply.

A young lady in her early twenties was walking slowly across towards us.

"Ray, I think we have company."

She was about five feet in height, nicely built, dark hair, and walked sedately up to us.

"Mr Barten?"

"Yes", I answered.

She held out her hand.

"How do you do Mr Barten. I'm very pleased to meet you.

My name is Mary Josephine Kennedy."

We had met Mary Jo.

Chapter 31. The Umbrella Principle

It was nine am in London, and four am at the United Nations building in New York when the detonation occurred.

Mr Luanda had taken his place in the auditorium one hour before this as President, ready to receive the Secretary and witnesses to his signature of authorisation. He had to sign the document which had been presented to him twenty four hours previously.

Before doing so, he listened to a full briefing from all Ministers and representatives concerned with the evacuation from Shatt El Arab; the new country, not the waterway!

He had read all the reports from the United Nations patrols in the area and apart from a few minor skirmishes, and an aircraft accident in Khorramshahr, the truce had been satisfactory.

The television and radio broadcasts had done more than evacuate the immediate local area. The population within a radius of about one hundred miles had decided to retreat to safer distances.

Kuwait City was deserted. The trains had evacuated most of the citizens to the Mediterranean area, which was upwind of any suspected fall out. The roads had been jam packed with motorists and buses going south to Riyadh, and the international airport had been busier than anyone could remember. All the major operators had sent their aircraft into the airport, which coordinated flights by the minute.

The major Gulf States took no chances either.

Bahrain, Qatar and the Trucial States moved their populations to Muscat and Oman; and Saudi Arabia moved everyone living within fifty miles of the shoreline inland to Riyadh and Al Hufuf.

The Shamal wind was blowing gently from the north west that day, which put them all in the fall out area.

The Iraqis had taken advantage of the international railway system, and had moved all people south of the river Tigris barrage at Al Kut, up country to Baghdad and beyond. They needed little persuasion once the broadcasts started.

The railway system coped with both the evacuation of the Basra bodies and the rest of the fleeing populations.

There was panic in certain areas, as is usual with fear, but in general everybody got away to the north.

The Iranians had already retreated from previously occupied war zones in southern Iraq, and were pleased to do so. They had the least distance to go. They moved east to the Kuzestan region to their mountains, and the main towns of Dezful, Shushtar and Khorramabad.

It had been the greatest mass exodus of people known to the historians.

Everyone just moved outwards as fast as they could possibly do so. By the time Mr Luanda had to make his decision, there was nobody at all in the area.

* * *

The delegation was looking at pictures on a large screen, on the wall at the front of the auditorium.

It was showing images from the Big Bird satellite, in geostationary orbit over Kenya.

The cameras were all pointing to the intended explosion area, and would be able to track the fall out cloud, which would settle along the line of the Persian Gulf and dissipate through the water. The radioactivity should be minimal, and have very little effect after two years had passed.

The war would be long finished by then.

At least, that was the theory.

It was just as well that they used the Big Bird as it turned out, but for an entirely different reason.

The scientists would be able track the fall out cloud all right, but there was something else hidden in their calculations.

Part of this was to do with human nature...

The 'umbrella principle' describes the tendency of individuals to ensure that they are covered, if anything goes wrong.

It manifested itself in this scenario by various scientists, all involved in the calculations for the required explosive power of the weapons, covering themselves by adding a few extra percentage points into their figures.

When this is done a few times in the process, it only needs a few extra 'per cents' to end up with a final weapon yield far in excess of that which is required.

Multiply this by five thermonuclear weapons, set underground, spaced at ten mile intervals, and the final results will end up producing quantities of power that will be measured as *enormous*, as opposed to *large*.

The other mistake they made was the sequence in which the weapons were detonated.

They should have been detonated from the Head of the Gulf first, with the bomb nearest to Basra detonated last of all, but it was decided to explode them in the reverse order...

Both of these were compounded by a final unforeseen factor, when the third weapon exploded.

With devastating consequences...

* * *

It was important that the whole area was evacuated, as the combined effect of the five explosions could have resulted in the greatest toll in human life ever recorded, since records had first been kept.

What turned out to be a simple moment of compassion by the Iranian representative, to bury the dead of Basra, could have saved the world from having to bury millions more, from Iraq, Iran, Kuwait and Saudi Arabia.

Could have...

* * *

'Mr President, I think we are all satisfied."

It was the Secretary of the delegates who addressed him.

'We have the papers ready for your signature."

Mr Luanda looked around the group, before he gave the final authorisation.

"Is it still your wish that I do this, Ladies and Gentlemen?

We can rescind our initial decision, if you think otherwise."

The Secretary addressed him, on behalf of the others.

"We have considered that factor, Mr President, but we think that if we did not do this now, we would enflame passions in the region, and cause an extension to hostilities into the foreseeable future.

We consider this to be the lesser of many evils; we are all in agreement to proceed, and ask you to take the ultimate decision."

Mr Luanda looked down at the table at the single document in front of him. He took his fountain pen, unclipped the top with his good hand and signed across the page underneath the writing, giving the final authorisation for detonation.

He then got up from his seat, walked across the floor, and took up his position as the representative of the newly founded country of Shatt EL Arab; he sat on the small hard backed chair, in front of all the others, and gazed up at the screen.

It was fifteen minutes to midday.

The rest of the group signed as witnesses, and when this was completed, the Secretary came forward to speak to him.

"Mr President.

The formalities are now complete.

I will contact our controller now, with your permission?"

Mr Luanda looked into his eyes and said simply,

"Yes, please go ahead."

Nothing else was said.

The Secretary picked up the green telephone on the table in front of them, and spoke quietly to the United Nations controller in the communications room. The countdown had been stopped at zero minus ten minutes, and would be resumed at the correct time to the nanosecond, by the same clock which had warned the two belligerents in the first place.

The message went to Gan control, and now the media waited.

It must have been the largest television audience ever. It was incalculable.

It could only be assumed that those who had access to a television screen were watching it, no matter what time of the day it was around the world.

They all saw the same picture from Big Bird:

A clear scene, devoid of all cloud; showing the head of the Persian Gulf as far north as the Hawr Al Hammar inland lake, north of Basra.

The rivers Tigris and Euphrates could be seen joining together at Al Qurna, then flowing as one, the Shatt EL Arab waterway, onwards to Al Faw.

The original Holy Lands!

At ten minutes to four in New York, ten minutes to nine in London, and ten minutes to twelve in Basra, the figures on the screen suddenly moved on from 10.00.00, and rapidly reduced as the countdown restarted.

* * *

Mr Luanda had a stop button on the table in front of him, if he wished to press it.

He wished that he really had a choice.

He wished that they had never started on the venture in the first place.

It had seemed so cut and dry a few months ago, when the final theories were resolved.

It was so simple.

Hit one country hard, and then the other, until they both gave in.

He looked up at the screen.

It was so tranquil.

If it wasn't for the odd judder on the film, as the satellite adjusted its position in orbit and altered the focus, it could have been a snapshot taken from one of the monthly NASA Shuttle flights.

The counters wound down to zero minus five.

The button was tempting, but he did not do it.

He sat and he watched the screen, as the numbers sped downwards towards the set of zeros.

He reflected afterwards whether he was a coward or not, by not pressing the stop button.

It would have been easy.

All he had to do was lean forward, rest his good hand on the table, and drop his index finger.

It would all be over, then he could give his resignation...

But that would only have lifted his personal burden.

Someone else would have to take over, and do it all later.

And that's why he couldn't do it, why he had to make the ultimate choice...

He watched the screen quietly, and saw the numbers reduce all the way down, until they showed 00.00.00

... And then they flicked off.

* * *

At first nothing happened.

He looked carefully, in case he had missed anything, but it looked exactly the same as before.

He was expecting a mighty eruption from the whole area, but it was a bit of an anti climax at the moment.

He looked very carefully.

There was a little blob appearing in the surface of the desert, about five miles south of Basra. It looked like a small yellow mushroom, growing on the surface of the ground.

It got bigger and bigger until it reached the outskirts of the town, and continued growing until it reached the other side. Burning buildings perched on the curved surface of the mushroom, and then the skin burst!

There was no noise.

It was all visual.

The cameras showed an enormous volume of sand, smoke, flames and desert material being flung up into the atmosphere.

The shockwave could clearly be seen flying radially outwards from the epicentre, lifting up sand and dust, creating another mushroom of dust storms.

The stem of the mushroom got wider and wider, until it was six miles across, and pulling millions of tons of earth from the ground.

The camera panned back for a moment, to show the clouds shooting skywards.

They were climbing vertically, but very soon the wind would blow it south east, over the rest of the waterway.

And then the second weapon exploded.

The same picture came from space.

An ever widening mushroom, growing slowly over the surface of the desert; about seven miles south of the first stem.

The rim of the mushroom reached the side of the first stem, and then its skin burst, with the same gigantic eruption of material from the ground.

The effect was now twofold.

There were two clouds of earth, sand, rocks and balls of flame, flinging their way skywards…

All of it once belonging to Iraq.

* * *

The delegates gazed at the screen.

The awe of seeing something that nobody in history had ever seen before.

It produced complete silence.

The Secretary was going to say something, when the third weapon went off.

* * *

This had been dropped on the western side of the waterway, opposite Abadan.

The same pictures were seen as in the other explosions, up until the skin of the mushroom burst.

The stem of the mushroom cloud got wider and wider, blacker and blacker; then wider and wider again, until it reached an enormous width of fifteen miles in diameter.

It was colossal, as black as tar, with huge rolling balls of fire within it.

It was terrifying to watch.

A solid column of black smoke, pouring into the atmosphere...

And suddenly there was another gigantic explosion, as the fourth weapon detonated prematurely.

* * *

The United Nations controller in New York hit the stop button immediately, and halted the countdown.

He also hit an alarm switch, which sent warning signals to Gan control and the auditorium where the delegates were watching.

They looked at each other.

The telephone rang in front of them on the table.

Mr Luanda picked it up and listened to what the controller told him.

"Mr President. I had to stop the countdown.

Number four went off by itself, as the shockwave from the third bomb reached it.

Something has caused an additional explosion in the immediate area, which resulted in excessive shock waves, beyond our computer predictions.

We don't know for sure what it is yet, but we think it's related to the Abadan underground rock structure.

The seismometers there are indicating powerful ground movements in the fault lines."

Mr Luanda had selected an open channel on the telephone, which allowed all the delegates to hear the message.

They looked at the screen as the controller told them the bad news.

There were huge volumes of dense black smoke, pouring out of the ground from where the number three weapon had detonated, but this only lasted for a further ten seconds.

They had watched as the surface of the desert blow upwards from number four, watched its mushroom cloud developing, and seen it mixed up with the smoke, the earth and the rocks.

... And then an enormous fire ball, ten miles in diameter, emerged from underneath the desert floor, exploding outwards.

It was Hell on Earth.

* * *

An enormous flash fire then occurred, as the fireball vaporised the oil bearing rocks, and set off a chain reaction of underground explosions, bursting outwards beneath the desert surface.

The orbital cameras recorded everything.

The desert surfaced rippled at first, as the faults in the rock structure heaved under the enormous pressures underneath.

Minor eruptions and explosions appeared all over the area, within a radius of fifty miles.

More and more of these occurred, as the rocks gave way, and eventually produced an enormous volume of black smoke and flames over the entire region.

The explosions became more and more frequent and excessive, and spread north eastwards into Iranian territory, and south westwards towards Saudi Arabia.

Towards the Saudi Arabian oil fields!

The camera in Big Bird panned back even more to show the area of fire.

It stretched from Basra down to Khosrobad, ten miles south of Abadan; then north to the disused airfield just to the north of Khorramshahr, and down south west towards Om Qasr.

As they watched on the screen they could see ground explosions flinging the desert floor skywards, as more underground rocks vaporised, and blew the strata layers apart.

* * *

"Oh, my God.

What have we done?"

It was the Secretary who broke the silence.

"The whole oil field has caught fire."

Mr Luanda realised what had happened, and wished that he could go back ten minutes in time.

But how many of us have often wished that.

The bombs had done the worse thing imaginable.

There had been far too much power in each of them individually; but when combined together, with all the extra 'percents' added in, they had set fire the outer layer of the Earth's mantle...

... Right in the centre of the Middle East oil fields, the largest in the world.

The delegates looked in horror at the pictures.

The explosions had now reached Om Qasr to the north of the rich Kuwaiti oil fields.

The north and western coastline of Bubiyan Island suddenly disappeared, in an eruption of black smoke and flames.

The whole area to the west of the Shatt El Arab waterway was now a mass of black smoke and flame, and it was increasing rapidly southwards as they watched.

There was nothing they could do.

Nature had taken control.

They had set off a chain of events, which was now uncontrollable by anyone.

How far it would go was beyond their capabilities for calculation.

In addition to this, to make matters worse than they already were, the weather forecasters had miscalculated the upper local winds.

They had received very little wind information from the Iranian war area, and only used forecasts from the weather satellites; and they had got it all wrong.

* * *

The local Shamal wind, usually blowing south east over Iraq, had joined with the tropical maritime winds blowing from the Indian Ocean towards the main Asian continental land mass; and it was now blowing the fallout from the initial nuclear explosions, and the resultant oil field explosions in a north easterly direction instead...

The radioactive clouds of fall out began to settle on the south west coast of Iran, but there was worse news to come, as the weather men soon found out.

The Seistan wind is another local wind, and at the time of the explosions it was also blowing in from southern Russia, towards Iran and the Persian Gulf.

The result of this could now be seen on the screen in front of all the delegates:

A solid black column of smoke, with all of the nuclear fallout intermixed with flames and fireballs, stretched over a width of over sixty miles, from Basra to northern Kuwait; it was increasing in size as they watched, and it was all being blown towards Iran.

* * *

The controller spoke gravely to Mr Luanda.

"The computer now predicts that ninety five percent of all fall out will land in an area between Shiraz and Mashad, at the north eastern boundary of Iran.

The rest will be dispersed over the Himalayas by the upper winds.

Also, the seismometers are now indicating earthquakes occurring in the Kuwaiti oil fields.

If they catch fire, then nothing can protect the Saudi Arabian oilfields."

It didn't take very long.

The explosions had penetrated the horizontal fissures across the surface of the desert, and had made their way south faster than anyone could have imagined.

They could see the line of underground explosions, rapidly tracking their way southwards towards Kuwait City, and then there was an almighty eruption as billions of tons of desert blew up into the sky.

The oil deep in the ground had vaporised, and had taken the line of least resistance, being thrown upwards.

The coastline at the north western end of the Persian Gulf suddenly rearranged itself,

And Kuwait City no longer existed.

***

It was difficult to call it an explosion, because it was so huge.

The cameras could not record all of it, as it combined with all the others, which were occurring at the same time in the region between Basra, Abadan and now Kuwait.

... One of the richest oil fields in the world.

It was now consumed entirely by fire, heading towards the Saudi Arabia oil fields.

The telephone rang again.

"Mr President. I regret to inform you that it is now out of all control.

We fear the worst.

We expect the whole of the north eastern section of the Saudi oil fields to catch fire within the hour."

Mr Luanda slowly replaced the receiver on the cradle, and looked at the screens.

All he could see was a mass of black smoke and flames, pouring out of the ground between Abadan and Southern Kuwait, and blowing across Iran.

"Ladies and gentlemen.

We appear to have unleashed uncontrollable forces, perhaps we ought to reflect for a moment on any possibilities that could stop this catastrophe from getting any worse."

They looked and they reflected, but as they did so, the ground containing the largest and richest oil fields in the world continued to explode, and there was nothing any of them could do about it.

The power of the largest nuclear bombs designed by mankind was as nothing, compared to the power of nature which they had unleashed.

They could only watch and pray.

Chapter 32. The Devil's Advocate

The Consequence of Ignorance

The whole world saw the fire and flames.

From the Antarctic wastes, where they sat in perpetual night, to the northern tundra of Siberia and Canada, they watched the flames spreading.

It was the most frightening thing anyone had seen.

People feared the worst.

"The end of the world is nigh." was their eternal cry in the streets.

In the British Isles and Ireland people heard all about it on their car radios, or morning television programmes.

For a full hour after the bombs exploded, the fire raged down towards the vast Saudi Arabian oilfields.

The neutral zone to the south of Kuwait was the next to feed the inferno.

The desert skin burst with thousands of explosions, as the subterranean oil deposits rapidly expanded under the enormous heat from the fires.

The oily smoke filled the upper stratosphere, and was blown across the northern hemisphere by the westerly jet streams. A huge trail of black smoke extended for about one hundred and fifty miles to the north east.

The weathermen forecasted that it would travel around the world, and return to the Middle East area in the westerly air current within a week.

They got it right this time!

As far as anyone could predict, the fires would increase in enormity and rage for years, due to the vast oil deposits underground.

It was fortunate that the stock markets were all shut for the weekend; otherwise there would have been a bigger crash than the 1987 collapse, when the computers took over the equity trading and nearly plunged the American economy into another recession.

Only a complete revaluation of the dollar saved a world recession from following, but it would take more than financial management to save certain countries from the present 'oil crisis'.

At the United Nations building, the representatives had returned to the building during the last hour, and had taken their seats around the auditorium to view the screen. Their discussions continued into the early hours of the morning, trying to find a solution to the catastrophe, with little agreement.

What did resolve, however, was an agreement in principle from all parties, including Iran and Iraq, that this was a far greater tragedy than all the past fifteen years of warfare, and that as of that moment, all hostilities were at an end.

Neither of the belligerents were in any position to continue, even if they wished to, but all countries had now resolved to ensure that nothing would interfere with the massive task ahead of them...

Including a ridiculous, unnecessary war!

The airborne tracking aircraft from the Royal Air Force, French Air Force, United States Air Force and the Soviet Air Force had joined forces to plot the track of the smoke and fall out.

As predicted, the Seistan wind from southern Russia was keeping the main nuclear fallout cloud within the territorial boundaries of Iran.

It was a tragedy for that country.

The Soviet experience of the Chernobyl disaster now estimated that fifty five percent of the population would perish within two years, from radioactivity tissue and blood diseases; and a further twenty per cent would produce severe second generation deformities.

The elderly stood no chance of survival within the next five years.

Only the young and healthy, living at the extreme north westerly areas in the mountains, would live radiation free lives; as long as they stayed where they were...

It would take more than seventy five years to clean out the isotopes from the surface of the affected area.

The problem was far too great for a war torn country to tackle on its own.

Iran as a nation was finished, it would be lucky to survive more than three generations.

... And it was simply caused by the fall out dropping in the wrong direction, because everybody forgot about mother nature, and ignored the local winds blowing across both countries.

The big weather computers around the world, and the millions of pounds spent on satellite forecasting had failed to register what was happening in that tiny sector of the globe.

If the forecasters had only bothered to speak to one single Iranian citizen living in the town of Mashad, or one Iraqi living in Baghdad, they could have found out so easily...

But they didn't!

That one Iranian citizen died within a month of the explosion.

The Iraqi died on the day of the explosion, along with thousands of his fellow brethren.

* * *

It was Miss Beryl Martin who inadvertently caused their deaths. She didn't know them at all and she never knew that she had caused it.

She was outside the British Embassy in Washington, dressed in black with a placard across her shoulders; walking up and down, ringing a hand bell and shouting at the top off her voice:

"The end of the world is in sight.

Fire and brimstone will rain down upon you.

The Lord Jesus will persecute you all.

This is his punishment.

He will destroy the wicked and sinful.

The end of the world is in sight."

She kept it up until a patrol car moved her on.

It was four thirty in the morning when she started, and five o clock when she finished; but she woke up a lot of angry people before the police arrived.

One of them was the Reverend Harold Parker, who was due to preach at St Mary's All Saints Church, on Second Avenue, at ten o clock that morning.

He turned the light on to see what the commotion was about, and looked out the third floor window of his hotel room, at the scene below.

He heard everything she said, and could see the placard quite clearly.

He didn't know why she was making her protest, but he had turned on the television set just as the Kuwaiti oil field exploded, filling the screen with red flames, and gigantic balls of fire rolling up into the back sky.

It had an immediate impact on Harold Parker.

He looked at the scene with astonishment. He was fully awake now.

He sat down on the end of the bed, and listened to the commentary relating the hopelessness of the situation, and just gazed at the screen and looked.

That very evening he had prepared his sermon on the same subject, as a warning to all not to tamper with his Lord's power over evil,

... And now it was all coming to reality.

He couldn't believe it.

The camera panned back in the satellite, to show the full breadth of the Middle East area, from the Strait of Hormuz at the bottom right hand corner of his screen, to Syria at the top left.

"My God,' was all he could say.

He was stunned.

He reached behind him, picked up his book, and turned to page eighteen to read the words once more.

... AND HE LOOKED TOWARD SODOM AND GOMORRAH, AND TOWARD ALL THE LAND OF THE PLAIN, AND BEYOND, AND, LO, THE SMOKE OF THE COUNTRY WENT UP AS THE SMOKE OF A FURNACE...

"Oh My God."

And he held his head in his hands.

To the Reverend Harold Parker, those words, and the scene in front of him, held a meaning.

He looked at the book in his hands. It was the Gideon Bible.

The book at the bedside of every bed in every hotel in America...

He didn't need it, as he had his own in his suitcase, but this one was nearer to hand.

He held it up to his eyes, and looked at his reflection in the dressing table mirror.

That's how his congregation saw him in the pulpit.

"The answer to this is in here as well, Harold.

It's all in the good book.

Seek and ye shall find."

He looked at himself once more, then started reading.

It didn't take him very long to find the relevant chapters.

He read them again to refresh his memory,

He now knew how to do it.

He had found out how to stop the fires.

In his eyes there was only one way.

He had to tell someone, even though he knew the consequences would be great.

His father had always told him to be strong and determined, and he was right in every respect.

"Harold, my boy, there is always an answer in the good book.

Find it, then be brave, and do it."

He said a quiet prayer to himself, for he knew what the outcome would be, then picked up the telephone at the side of the bed.

The hotel receptionist answered.

"Yes, Reverend Parker."

"Miss, I wonder if you can help me please.

Could you get me the United Nations building in New York?

I have a most urgent message to deliver to the General Assembly."

* * *

Mr Luanda was in the Presidential chair when one of the private Secretaries arrived.

He whispered a few words in his ear, then gave him a radio telephone.

"We think it's a crank Mr Luanda, but he is very persistent.

He says he will speak to nobody else."

"Thank you. I will listen to what he has to say."

He spoke into the telephone, and listened carefully to the Reverend Parker.

When he had finished Mr Luanda thanked him; then asked for a copy of the Bible.

The Secretary gazed at him.

"Of course Mr Luanda, they have one in the Justice Department. We will bring it to you immediately."

It took only a minute.

Mr Luanda turned to the Secretary of the witnessing delegates, and asked him to take it.

"Mr Wilson.

Would you read Genesis Chapters Six and Seven to us please?

It may assist us in our search for an answer to this problem."

They all listened as Mr Wilson read the verses from the book.

When he finished there was complete silence.

The auditorium was as quiet as a tomb.

* * *

The three members of the British delegation spoke quietly to Sir Percival Brown. He nodded his agreement, and stood up to address the assembly.

"Mr President, ladies and gentlemen, we need to take action immediately before the situation worsens.

I propose that we use the fifth weapon immediately, before it is too late."

The United States and Soviet delegates had an equally quiet consultation between themselves, nodded in agreement, then the American representative stood up.

"Mr President, we jointly second the proposal.

I suggest a vote with all delegates participating, except Iran and Iraq."

Mr Luanda addressed all the delegates.

"The proposal is: That we use the fifth weapon, to quench these fires with the waters of the Persian Gulf.

Those for?"

The captions lit up on the screen behind him.

It was unanimous.

"Let the records show a unanimous decision for proposal 765, by the British delegation."

It was at this point that Mr Khalid Shakir, the Iraqi representative, stood up.

"Mr President.

Please give us one hour. That is all we need."

He looked around the auditorium for a seconder.

Mr Hassan Rejad caught the eye of Lee Luanda, and nodded.

"Those for?"

It was again unanimous.

* * *

Lee Luanda picked up the green telephone and spoke to the United Nations Controller.

"Please advise our Gan control to commence countdown for the fifth weapon, to detonate in one hour.

Give all assistance as necessary to the Iraqi population, to evacuate their country."

As he replaced the telephone, he thought of the Reverend Harold Parker. He may have provided the answer to the fires in the oilfields, but at a terrible price.

It could cost thousands of lives.

The devil's advocate could not have come up with a worse solution.

He picked up the bible which Mr Wilson had left on the table in front of him, and read one of the verses again to himself.

... AND, BEHOLD, I, EVEN I, DO BRING A FLOOD OF WATERS UPON THE EARTH, TO DESTROY ALL FLESH, WHEREIN IS THE BREATH OF LIFE, FROM UNDER HEAVEN; AND EVERYTHING THAT IS IN THE EARTH SHALL DIE...

They all had voted to kill the underground fires and explosions with the waters from the Persian Gulf; but at the same time risk the consequences of a second great deluge in the ancient Garden of Eden,

... Only this time the occupants had less than an hour to 'build an ark'.

A lot of the animals were not going to make it to safety this time.

A lot of the population wouldn't either!

The telephone buzzed in front of him.

"Mr Luanda, the countdown has re commenced.

Detonation will occur at six fifteen New York time, two fifteen Basra time."

He shook his head sadly and looked down at the book.

"Fire, brimstone, storms, floods, and disease... I sincerely hope this is the end."

He picked it up in his good hand.

"Genesis, you had better be right, otherwise it will be Exodus for us all."

* * *

The United Nation's scientists had calculated that the size of the crater produced by the Basra detonations would be about two hundred feet deep, ten miles wide and about fifty miles in length.

Unknown to them, due to the secondary explosions, the actual depression was pear shaped, with the narrow end at Basra about twelve miles in width, and the wide end at Kuwait city about one hundred miles across.

The depth varied from the calculated two hundred feet in the north, to over four hundred feet deep in the south.

It was an enormous depression in the surface of the earth, getting larger every minute; and into this they intended to pour the waters of the Persian Gulf, hoping to put out the fires raging underground.

The fifth bomb had been planted five miles north of Al Faw, and had cut deep into the soft silt which had been building up over the centuries. At present it was nestling itself in clay about two hundred and fifty feet under the bed of the waterway.

The debris from the previous four explosions had cratered out an enormous cavity to the north of it, and the waters of the Gulf were being held back by a large barrage of debris, which extended in a semicircle of radius twelve miles around Abadan.

The ground explosions had also thrown more debris further down the Gulf, as the line of explosions moved southwards.

The existing coastline had now disappeared altogether, and the huge barrage of mud and rocks was now the only thing holding the Gulf at bay.

The ground shock waves had produced a series of tidal waves, which travelled down the length of the Gulf, to rebound again six hundred miles further south.

They had little initial effect, but caused a disaster on their return.

The Iraqi Government had an enormous problem.

Somehow they had to warn the population living in the towns along the two rivers to move out as soon as possible, without causing a panic.

One hour was little enough time to do it, and the people had already been moved out of their homes and resettled further up country, to escape the effects of the blast from the nuclear explosions.

Unfortunately, their Government underplayed the second warning.

They did not emphasise the urgency of the situation, mainly because even they did not know what was going to happen.

When the population eventually moved, it was with a lethargic reluctance to move for the second time that day.

A lot of them didn't bother moving out. They were fed up with everything, and stayed where they were.

It would have been different if transport had been arranged, as had been for the first move, but now it was everyone for themselves.

The quick ones got the few remaining buses and lorries, but the rest were on their own two feet...

... And you cannot travel far in one hour, when you're tired, fed up, and walking.

The result was that after the warning time had elapsed, the vast majority of the Iraqi population were out in the open, travelling slowly up country, not knowing what was going to happen, and simply hoping that they could return home as soon as possible.

It was a bit like the blind leading the blind; nobody knew where they were going to, or why they were doing it in the first place.

* * *

The detonation message was relayed to Gan control from New York, and Andy set up the countdown once again.

He had been waiting for instructions since the United Nations controller had terminated the initial countdown.

It had been obvious to all at Gan that something serious had gone wrong, when the number four had prematurely detonated, fifty seven seconds before it should have done.

They didn't tell New York, but Andy had hit the stop button for the number five bomb two seconds before New York did!

"It's all set up, New York.

Check the time phasing circuits.

You should be reading zero minus fifty five and thirty seconds in three... two... one... Now."

"Thank you Gan, That agrees.

I will advise the delegates."

The whole of the Gan complement were in the control room, looking at the monitors spread around the room.

There were none of the usual ribald comments, which you normally get amongst people watching the disastrous activities of others; when they were slowly but surely dropping themselves deeper and deeper into manure.

This was too serious.

* * *

"Where are Michel and Peter now?

Can you pick up their radar transponders?"

John pointed to the wide range screen.

"That's them, to the south east of Riyadh.

So far so good.

Their fuel's holding in the aircraft fuselage tanks.

If it does leak for any reason, Peter can fly it on the refuelling hose all the way down to Socotra, and Michel can land in front of him on the runways.

They can still make it."

The green telephone rang in front of him. It was the Ministry of Defence in London.

"Andy. We've had a call from Sir Percival Brown in New York.

It concerns Operation Deluge.

On a request from the Saudi Arabian representative at the United Nations, and the Saudi Ambassador in London; be prepared for a short notice detonation, well in advance of the timed one hour, if those oil fields south of the Kuwaiti neutral zone begin to quake.

The seismometers are already reading heavy shockwaves."

Andy replied carefully.

"Will you be authorising an earlier detonation, or will New York?"

"There is no question about that, Andy, New York will authorise.

They have the new detonation codes.

We are only in an advisory position.

You will be asked to set up the new code at five minutes warning, for a restart at zero minus five.

They've just told us now via our discrete telephone in the auditorium, direct from Sir Percival.

Keep this line open, I've a feeling it won't be very long in coming."

Andy gave the phone to John.

"Listen out on that, and shout if it sounds like panic again."

He pressed the keyboard to speak to the computer operators.

"Set up a secondary timing circuit for five minute duration, and be ready for release coding."

"Ok Andy. Call you back in two minutes."

They watched the screen as the explosions moved south, towards the southern boundary of the neutral zone between Kuwait and Saudi Arabia.

As soon as it reached the territorial boundary, the new coding would be sent by New York.

"Andy, it's London for you.

They've got new release codes.

Get on to New York via Sky Net.

They're waiting now."

"Bloody hell. That was quick"

He sat at the console and typed out on the keys. The New York controller was holding the new release code for him.

Across the screen was a series of figures and letters, split up with semi colons and full colons.

He had to retype them carefully onto the other keyboard, and then match them up. If he made a mistake he had to continue until it was correct.

It was the two man principle of nuclear detonation.

The double key release technique used by both the RAF and USAF, only electronically updated.

He had done this for the four previous detonations, and was careful with his keying. It took about ten to twelve seconds, then the curser locked onto the numbers, indicating the correct code.

He pressed the keys to the five minute release circuit, and fed the code into the main computer.

It locked on as well.

All was ready.

He spoke to MOD.

"All circuits ready. Awaiting New York."

"Thank you Andy. I'll tell Sir Percival."

The message was passed on eventually to the Saudi representative, to the Ambassador, and of course, to the Royal Saudi household in Riyadh, from where the original request had been made.

* * *

It wasn't long coming.

The seismometers were now giving their final warning signals, and the graphs were swinging wildly on the printouts.

The Saudi representative in New York made his way to Mr Luanda.

"Mr Luanda.

With our greatest respects. I feel that I must insist on corrective measures being taken as soon as possible.

I'm sure the other delegates will agree."

Mr Luanda nodded in agreement, and looked at the electronic board recording delegates' votes on the point at issue; an immediate explosion of the fifth weapon, to release the flood waters as soon as possible.

It was showing a unanimous decision for the five minute warning.

Mr Luanda looked with sorrow at Mr Khalid Shakir.

"I am very sorry Mr Shakir. We must do it now. It is vital.

For the General Assembly records, do we have your acceptance of the situation as being extremely serious?

Far beyond your national responsibilities in this chamber?"

This was Mr Shakir's diplomatic recognition that he had done all that was possible for his country.

Mr Luanda was giving him a chance to show that he had done all that was possible in the circumstances.

"Thank you Mr President. I cannot agree with this action, but I fully understand the circumstances enforcing this decision.

Please excuse me. I must retire to my Embassy."

He then turned and slowly walked towards the auditorium main door.

As he was crossing the floor Mr Rejad caught up with him.

"If you have no objections, Mr Shakir, perhaps we could share the same taxi.

They are so difficult to find at this time in the morning."

Notwithstanding the fact that the New York cabbies were lined up six deep outside the United Nations building, Mr Shakir nodded his agreement, and they both departed through the same door.

It was the first time that either of them had accompanied the other out of the building since the war started.

It was a shame that they had not done so before, as it could have saved many lives.

Mr Luanda picked up the telephone and spoke to the controller.

A message went to Gan; Andy evaluated it, and double checked the coding.

It was correct, so he started the five minute countdown.

The new timing circuit gradually reduced from 05.00.00 to 00.00.00

At that point he looked at the screen, and after three seconds saw the mushroom grow on the desert surface, pushing itself outwards to the Al Faw peninsula, then further out beyond that into the waters of the Gulf.

The explosion was more pronounced than the previous ones.

Half was underground, and half was underwater.

The water offered the least line of resistance to the expanding gases, and there was a sideways vector to the spoil, as it was flung skywards.

It was like a cannon. shooting earth and rubbish up at an angle of about seventy degrees.

The stem of the mushroom initially deflected out towards the Gulf, as if the water was attracting it, and then it climbed vertically upwards.

It looked as if the mushroom was growing towards the south east.

The shock wave threw the waters of the Gulf down its southerly line, and formed a massive tidal wave.

It travelled right down the six hundred mile coastline, and after causing considerable damage en route, rebounded from the Trucial States coastal plain, then returned back up towards the explosion point again.

It took just over a day to do so, but the initial deluge had already done its own disastrous work by then.

The returning tidal wave caught the Iraqi rescue services at their lowest ebb, and increased the already high number of casualties.

The fifth detonation breached a point in the barrage facing the Shatt El Arab waterway, and the tremendous weight of the water immediately behind the breach gradually took effect.

It started to leak through slowly at first, and then pushed the rocks and mud aside as channels flowed through.

Very soon there were torrents of water pushing their way into the bomb's crater, as great walls of mud slithered away under the impact of a whole sea, finding new areas to fill.

It was more than a dam bursting.

It was a massive head of water, one hundred miles wide and five hundred feet in height, being pushed forwards by the sheer volume of water contained in the Persian Gulf, which measured six hundred miles in length and one hundred and fifty miles in width.

The water filled the cavity in the Kuwaiti region first.

It didn't put the fires and explosions out immediately; that took days, as nature fought nature.

Until it did, the surface of the sea boiled like a saucepan full of water on a fire, throwing up huge geysers of steam mixed with black, tarry smoke into the atmosphere.

The immediate impact of the detonation, however, was produced by the water travelling up the line of the old Shatt El Arab waterway.

The waters rapidly filled the pear shaped depression, and the tidal wave which developed surged northwards, towards the narrower and shallower section of the crater.

The Persian Gulf, unfortunately, didn't know about these important alterations; it just kept pouring millions of tons of water into its new sea bed.

The tidal wave became higher, as the slope of the crater pushed the waters upwards, and its speed increased, as the width of the crater became narrower; and when the waters reached Basra, the wave had reached a height of three hundred feet above the surface of the desert, and was travelling at a speed of over seventy miles per hour.

... Ahead of it was the Garden of Eden, between the rivers Tigris and Euphrates!

The second great deluge in the history of mankind was about to commence.

* * *

Genesis 6.7

"I WILL DESTROY MAN WHOM I HAVE CREATED FROM THE FACE OF THE EARTH"

The ancient city of Ur was the first town to go.

The deluge swept over it, and blasted the old monuments to bits.

It was from this city that Abraham had set off, on the Great Hebrew trek to the land of Canaan.

The ancient Sumerian city was no more.

Neither were Erech, Kish, Lagash and Eridu.

The deluge surged northwards, up the valley of the Euphrates, sweeping everything forwards in its path.

The towns of modern Iraq had been evacuated, but the buildings were waiting to be destroyed. Those that survived the war were now blown apart by the force of the water, as it raced across and through them.

The towns of An Nasiriyah, Diwaniyah, An Najaf, Al Hillah and Karbala were deluged, and all buildings destroyed.

* * *

That was the Euphrates, getting her own back for all the fighting that had taken place around her during the past four thousand years...

The Tigris did the same to Al Qurna, Amarah, Al Kut and Baghdad...

* * *

There wasn't much left of these towns by the time the water had finished, but there was more to come.

The two rivers joined forces after the Euphrates destroyed Habbaniyah, and the Tigris destroyed Samarra.

They flooded the upper half of the country, as far as Tigrit on the Tigris, and Anah on the Euphrates.

In doing so they managed to catch the remaining refugees out in the open countryside, who were still wondering where they were all going...

They were only going one place now.

And that was oblivion.

* * *

Genesis 7.20

"FIFTEEN CUBITS UPWARDS DID THE WATERS PREVAIL"

The floods stayed in place for two days, before slowly receding back again towards the new head of the Gulf; which was previously the northern coastline of the Hawr Al Hammar inland sea.

Before they reached it, however, the rebounding tidal wave from the Gulf swept up the country, passing previous upper limits; and caught the rest of the population unaware, as they struggled for survival.

The combined deluges wiped out eighty five percent of the Iraqi population in less than twenty four hours.

It was the biggest single disaster in the history of mankind.

* * *

The biblical deluge had occurred in exactly the same place, when the two rivers flooded due to excessive storms and heavy rainfall;

Drowning the ancient Holy Land of Mesopotamia, between the Tigris and Euphrates rivers; where Adam and Eve fell victim to the temptations of the tree of knowledge.

The present population had once again fallen victim, only this time it was to the hubris of nuclear knowledge, and a lack of understanding of the power of nature.

When the second great deluge receded, a very different country emerged to that which preceded it.

The population had received a greater shock than anything previously experienced during the fifteen years of warfare.

They had been playing their war games with Iran, over which of them should control the Shatt El Arab waterway; and now they all knew.

It is nature who controls nature.

The human being, in its brief life span on this Earth either lives with nature; or perishes with the consequences of its own ignorance.

The deposits placed over Iraq, by the very waters over which they had been fighting Iran, were now infused with radioactive elements from nuclear explosions.

The rich oil fields, which supplied the vast bulk of their export income, had either disappeared or were contaminated by radioactive isotopes.

The population had been decimated at a stroke.

They would be lucky to survive, let alone continue to fight a war.

Iran had suffered oil rich territorial losses as well.

Their population would slowly die over the next five years, as the fallout took its toll.

They could still have mounted an immediate strike against Iraq, if they still wished to have the President's head on a plate for the Ayatollah...

... But nobody suggested it.

The steam had all gone out of the fervour for war and revenge, which was just as well, otherwise there would have been an internal revolution in the country; if what Mr Watt eventually told us had been revealed to them!

The bombs had unleashed the power of nature, and this eventually resulted in a cessation of hostilities, but it had been a close run thing.

The Kuwaiti oil fields had been completely destroyed, and the fires would have taken out the northern Saudi Arabian oil fields next, if the waters hadn't poured into the bowels of the earth.

The nuclear scientists got a shock as well.

They had started something that they hadn't a snowball in hell's chance of stopping.

Those who just added in their extra few 'percents' got their fingers burnt all right. A lot more people thought twice after that.

There hasn't been a nuclear explosion since that day.

Especially underground...

Nobody is taking any more chances!

* * *

And the Two Rivers?

They still flow quietly down to the Gulf.

They have the added knowledge that if anything starts up again, they'll have another great deluge to sort something out once and for all.

They've had two so far and the third could be the last!

They're the only ones laughing all the way to the bank now, only this time it's the river bank.

The bank where Adam met Eve, and both bit into the apple from the tree of knowledge.

... Its full title is the 'Tree of Knowledge of Good and Evil', and it has to be treated with care and respect.

The first biters into the forbidden fruit were thrown out of the garden, and their descendents faced a flood in the same way as the Iraqis just did.

Before the first deluge, only Noah and his family were chosen to escape in the ark, to produce the next generations.

Now some of their descendents have been further selected, to continue their future populations.

Maybe there's a message somewhere that everyone is missing!

* * *

The pall of smoke from the burning Iraqi oilfields mixed with the smoke from the firestorm still raging in the Iranian town of Bandar Abbas;

And the radioactive clouds blew around the northern hemisphere, carried in the upper winds of the Earth's atmosphere, like a huge black banner in the sky.

Even a blind person could see that message.

Chapter 33. Old Friends

Sir Percival Brown was entertaining Mr Luanda at the British Embassy later that morning, after the General Assembly meeting was over, for a working breakfast. They had their private aides and secretaries in conference and were reviewing the whole situation.

The deluge had pushed its way up the country at that specific time, and Mr Luanda was in a dilemma concerning the decision he had taken.

The choice he had made.

His name was now well and truly embedded in the history books as the person who had authorised the dropping of multiple nuclear weapons on two countries.

Not exactly the claim to fame he would have liked.

"There was no other way, Mr Luanda. It was a Jehad, a Holy War. Nothing could have stopped it except common sense in each of the countries, and that was hardly forthcoming after fifteen years of warfare and revenge."

Mr Luanda noted Sir Percival's point of view. But shook his head sadly.

"No. There must have been another way. This has turned out disastrously for all concerned.

Look what we've accomplished.

The decimation of the population of two countries.

The total destruction of a capital city, and probably the whole of Kuwait.

The complete desolation of a vast area of the Middle East by nuclear fallout.

The destruction of some of the richest oil fields in the world.

Probably the elimination of the Iranian nation by radiation induced diseases, for the rest of the foreseeable future.

The turmoil on Monday morning to the world economic system, when the stock markets and the bank open will be uncontrollable. The repercussions will continue forever.

How can we possibly justify what we did?"

Sir Percival was about to respond, when the telephone buzzed in front of him. His private secretary answered it and held it to Sir Percival.

"It's the Palace for you Sir Percival. The Queen's private Secretary."

You could have heard a pin drop in the room.

Mr Luanda rose in his chair to leave the room with his retinue.

"It's all right, Mr Luanda, I can take it next door. Please remain where you are."

He went into the adjoining study, and took the phone call there.

"Sir Percival, are you there? This is most urgent."

"Yes, I can hear you very clearly. Please pass on your message."

"Do you remember Freddy Watt, back in the fifties, when you were in the Diplomatic Corps at Teheran?"

"Yes, of course, we were very good friends, but he went missing four years ago. Held hostage somewhere. The last time I heard about him was about two years ago. He must be dead by now. We refused the terms of release. Why do you ask?"

"Well, he's alive and safe. He wants to speak to you for some reason. Says it's important. We got him out of Iran early this morning, before the bombs went off. He's in a private ward at Socotra hospital. Can you speak to him now? I'll connect him through to you."

There was a hollow sound on the line, as Mr Watt was connected.

A weak voice came onto the line. It was amplified so that both of them could hear.

"Percy?"

"Good God. It is you. I thought it was a joke.

Freddy, my dear chap, how are you?"

"Weak, but all right. I want to speak to you about our mutual friend in Teheran, who we met at the Congress in July 1955. Do you remember what I'm talking about?"

Sir Percival thought hard and gestured wildly to his secretary.

"Get my diary will you. The ten year 1950 one. It's in my suitcase upstairs. Quickly man."

The secretary departed... fast.

"Freddy, I think I know who you mean. I can consult my memoirs if you like. I always keep copies of my work. In this line you never know when you need them.

What's the problem?"

"Percy, I want you to listen very carefully and answer my question. What was in the glass tumbler by his bedside?"

Sir Percival suddenly realised what Mr Watt meant.

"I can tell you that straight away Freddy, without my diary, it was his glass eye.

Why do you ask?"

"I'll tell you in a minute. Who else knows about it Percy?"

"Nobody else does, just the two of us. We swore to secrecy.

We had to. We all had a band of friendship.

It was us who disturbed him that evening when we called at his hotel room, remember.

Is this important?"

"Yes. Very important. I want you to corroborate my evidence.

What colour were his eyes, and which was the good one?"

"That's easy Freddy.

The good one was his left eye, because he was good at archery, and he was left-handed; and they were green, but the glass eye was a slightly darker shade than the good one.

Do you agree with that?"

There was a heavy sigh at the other end of the line.

"Yes Percy, unfortunately I do. I knew I was right. I knew it then, and I know it now."

There was a long pause on the line.

"It wasn't him that I saw."

Sir Percival went very quiet.

"What are you telling me Freddy? Didn't you meet him four years ago on your mission?"

Mr Watt was very precise in what he said next.

"I met somebody, who said he was our friend, and looked exactly like him.

He even spoke like him.

But when you know him as well as we do, you get to know personal things, don't you?

It wasn't him."

Sir Percival looked across into the next room at Mr Luanda, who was sitting at the table watching him.

"Freddy. You must be absolutely certain about this. How do you know for sure?"

"It was his eye Percy. His missing eye.

You can put contact lenses in a good eye, to disguise the colour of a pupil, but you cannot make a glass eye see.

The man I saw had a patch over his good eye, but he could see everything that I did.

He even signed his signature with his left hand, without anybody showing him where to sign.

The man I saw could see out of his missing eye.

It couldn't have been done if it was our friend."

Sir Percival hesitated for a moment before speaking again.

"Freddy, my dear chap, that was four years ago, and you've been through a lot since then. It could have been you who made the mistake. You could have got the wrong eye."

"Yes, that's what I thought.

... So I told him that Yvette sent her regards."

Sir Percival dropped the telephone as he sat down, at the shock of hearing that name again.

"Percy. I'm sorry to do this, but I had to."

The secretary took the telephone and spoke to Mr Watt.

"Mr Watt. I'm sorry but Sir Percival cannot reply at the moment."

He caught Sir Percival's eye, nodded and continued.

"What did your friend say, Mr Watt?"

"He was overwhelming in his praise for her, and was pleased that Yvette had remembered him from such a long time ago.

He sent her his best and kindest regards for the future. He then gave me jar of perfumed essence for her."

Sir Percival heard all this on the earpiece, looked up at his secretary and took the telephone.

"Freddy, you were right. It wasn't him, was it?"

"No. It couldn't have been, and yet there are posters of him plastered all over Iran, and they still revere and worship him. There can only be one explanation.

Do you agree Percy?"

'Yes, I'm afraid so. He's dead, and he's been dead for over four years.

They're keeping the image of him alive, to keep the fanaticism going for the war. They have someone else pretending to be our friend.

Oh God almighty. What have we done?"

He walked slowly into the other chamber as if in a dream, slumped down heavily into his chair, and stared at Mr Luanda.

"Mr Luanda. I have heard some extremely disconcerting news. I regret to inform you..."

He paused at this point,

"The Ayatollah is dead, and has been for at least last four years."

He thumped the table hard with his fist.

"We could have stopped that damn war four years ago, if we'd had that information.

That's why Mr Watt was held for so long. They didn't know if he'd found out about their charade, so they held him, and tried to break him; and when they failed, they then tried to starve the poor sod to death."

He bent forward over the table, held his head in his hands and wept profusely.

Yvette had been his dearest wife, who died in Paris sixteen years ago.

Their friend was at her funeral in Montparnasse Cemetery.

It was he who had introduced her to him in Teheran in 1955. They had been married the following year. Their friend had blessed each of their four children.

He would have known about her death.

He saw it happen.

She had caught cramp in her swimming pool and he had tried to save her, even though he couldn't swim, and nearly drowned in the attempt.

Yvette never recovered consciousness, and had been dead on arrival at the local hospital.

Sir Percival's private secretary informed Mr Luanda of this information, and the importance of Mr Watt's message.

Mr Luanda slowly stood up.

"Sir Percival. Please accept my deepest condolences. I will return later today to see you."

He took his walking stick and limped painfully from the breakfast room, deep in his private thoughts.

It had all been a tragic waste.

Not just the nuclear explosions and their dreadful consequences, but the whole damn war, and the attitudes that everybody had to it.

If ever Mr Lee Luanda had an evil thought in his head it was then.

If he could have gone back two months, knowing everything that he knew now, he would not have done a single thing about it, and he would have let them all stew in their own juices...

Every single one of them.

Nobody cared about the suffering.

Nobody cared about the killing,

Nobody cared at all, as long as it didn't affect them, or that they were benefitting from it.

Nobody cared a damn!

* * *

A voice spoke beside him.

"Your car, Mr Luanda."

He looked at his secretary and shook his head.

"Thank you, but I have decided to get some fresh air. I need a walk to clear my thoughts."

He walked painfully across the Grand Central Park in the middle of New York, and reflected on what would happen on Monday morning, when the various City establishments opened for business.

There would be a shake down for a few days.

In two weeks time everything that took place would be forgotten, because some other important factor would replace it as the main economic disturbing influence; but by then the major stock markets around the world would have recovered, and probably one per cent would have been knocked off the world interest rates by the big bank institutions, to stabilise the money markets.

As usual, Mr Lee Luanda was right.

It was forgotten,

They did recover,

And they did drop.

Chapter 34. A Royal Audience

8th AUGUST 1995.   9 00 pm

Her Majesty the Queen was attending to affairs of state at Buckingham Palace.

She was receiving new Ambassadors recently appointed, and members of the Privy Council.

The Defence Secretary had previously received his summons, and was awaiting royal audience. To ensure himself of his facts concerning the issues relevant to the situation he was deeply imbedded in his red folder.

No mistake would be allowed. He must be able to answer all Her Majesty's questions with accuracy and confidence.

It was ten minutes before an equerry appeared and escorted him to the state room, where he was ushered in with the minimum of ceremony.

Her Majesty was most businesslike and very efficient with her affairs. The audience did not take long. Her Majesty had been well informed by the Privy Council and now had the necessary information to hand. Nothing of the previous few days' occurrences had passed without her knowledge.

The Defence Secretary was invited to comment on the part he had played, which he did so with accurate detail. His answers to the Queen's searching questions were concise and clear.

She appeared satisfied, and the Defence Secretary inwardly heaved a heavy sigh of relief. The tower was not for him, he gratefully thought.

The audience over, the equerry was ushering him out in correct protocol.

... You never turned your back on her Majesty.

"One final point."

He stopped and looked up.

She picked up the letter of resignation from the Prime Minister, which she had previously received, put on her glasses and read it.

It was several seconds before she spoke.

... A life time for the Defence Secretary.

He could almost see the executioner's axe!

"I have decided to accept this."

There was a pause.

"There appears, however, to be a minor grammatical error. The incorrect use of an apostrophe in paragraph two."

The axe was now descending with increasing rapidity!

The Defence Secretary could already feel his neck becoming red.

She gazed at him over the top rim of her glasses.

"I sincerely trust that you will not repeat this little mistake, when you send me your own letter of resignation as Defence Secretary."

The axe was now just above his outstretched neck.

The newly 'ex' Defence Secretary was gritting his teeth hard, and looking down into the waste paper basket on the carpet just in front of him.

Her gaze never faltered, but now there was just the hint of a smile...

"Allow me to give you some excellent advice...

... Prime Minister...

Advice which your predecessor appears to have disregarded...

Never underestimate the power of a good woman."

The long stare to him was courteous... but full of meaning.

* * *

The equerry gently took his elbow, and he was ushered out of the state room. The awaiting car was ready to take him to Number Ten, where the other members of his cabinet were patiently waiting.

The equerry opened the state room door.

"Your Majesty.

The Ambassador for Shatt El Arab."

Mr Lee Luanda limped very slowly into the room. It was obvious that he was in great pain.

The Queen saw this and immediately walked across the carpet in order to receive him, and accepted his good hand in hers.

"Mr Luanda, how very pleasant it is to meet you again."

Her handshake, although warm and tender, was unable to console him.

"Your Majesty, I feel as if I have failed in your peaceful endeavours.

I regret to inform your Majesty that I was unable to convince the Iranian government of our intentions."

The Queen led him to one of the two chairs beside the long table in the stateroom, where they sat down together.

"Mr Luanda. In that case the combined efforts of the Royal households of Saudi Arabia, Jordan and the United Kingdom likewise failed.

The Teheran government were fully aware, forty eight hours in advance, of everything; one complete day before you were asked to warn them about the impending strike on Bandar Abbas."

Mr Lee Luanda looked at the Queen in astonishment.

"Your Majesty, I was not aware of the Royal proceedings.

I cannot understand why no action was taken by Iran.

The city could have been evacuated in time.

Nobody needed to have died at all."

The Queen nodded sadly.

"Yes, Mr Luanda, you are correct; and you were also correct when you advised us that the Teheran Government would not heed our warnings. You cannot be responsible for the misdeeds of others."

She paused for a moment before continuing.

"Mr Luanda, we are very, very sorry.

We did not expect their reaction. It was most unpredictable.

Please accept our sincerest condolences."

A tear trickled down his left cheek. He quickly held his hand up to his eyes to shield them from her gaze.

His attempt to regain his composure was as dignified as was possible; in the presence of Her Majesty the Queen of England, in the stateroom of Buckingham Palace.

She watched him silently for a moment, then stood up and walked elegantly out of the room, to leave him to his private grief.

Her head was bowed low as she considered the risks which she and the two other Royal families had taken, in giving as much warning as they dared to Iran.

One whole day would have been sufficient to evacuate Bandar Abbas.

Two days could also have produced an overwhelming defence.

But nobody expected them to ignore both warnings, then carry on as normal as if nothing was going to happen.

She walked into her private quarters, and looked at a personal message which she had received the day before the attack.

It had come from the little boat that had caused all that trouble for the aircraft, as it was preparing for the run into Bandar Abbas.

The little boat, with its crew of ten young men and girls; who were trying to alter the inevitable, as they had done for years previously.

The little boat, that had taken on the giant warriors in the past; as David had done against the Philistines and their mighty Goliath...

Only this time it had failed.

She read the message once more, as she had done every hour since it had arrived.

: FROM GREENPEACE FIVE TO BUCKINGHAM PALACE. LONDON

YOUR MAJESTY

GREENPEACE IS AWARE OF INTENTIONS IN HORMUZ STRAITS. EARNESTLY REQUEST THE ROYAL PREROGATIVE FOR RECONSIDERATION.

YOUR OBEDIENT SERVANTS.

JACK CUSHING

SVEN LARGESSEN

JACQUELINE DUPONT

ARTHUR T JACKSON

PERON DA SILVA

SELINA REBONNA

CHEN SU KUISKU

HASSAN FERU

AKINA LUANDA

MARGARET MACPHERSON

She knew, the King of Saudi Arabia knew, and the King of Jordan knew, that their joint decision to give an extra day's warning to the Iranian Government had allowed Greenpeace more time to get into position.

It had also resulted in one of the most terrible decisions, and the ultimate choice, that any person ever had to make.

And Mr Lee Luanda had taken it.

He had released the aircraft against a fully populated city, which had been led like lambs to the slaughter...

... And in doing so, had caused the death of his only son.

Along with all the other sons and daughters on Greenpeace Five.

Chapter 35. Flypast

Bob Marshall was better than his word.

Not only did he rebuild the Vulcan, but his team produced a mini HOTOL for us.

The United Nations bought the discarded air breathing rocket engine from the British Government, after they decided to cancel it.

It was the only way to keep it independent for general use by all nations, and not monopolised by NASA or the European Space Agency.

At least we now know it is attached to a British aircraft.

Bob and his team did not bother fitting a new fuselage to the rear of the Vulcan. They just cleaned up the wreckage and the bits of metal hanging off, re rigged and strengthened it; amidst various comments regarding useless blankety blank pilots who ruin their handiwork; then fitted the HOTOL rocket engines to the back end underneath the fin and rudder, with the fuel tanks in the main fuselage bay.

That was the main addition to the aircraft.

The air intakes to the four jet engines in the wings were reformed, so that at very high speeds in excess of Mach 3, the shock waves fed the engines with more air.

By the time he had finished, not only could it fly higher and faster than the old aircraft, but it consumed less fuel.

It was not fully orbital, but very close to it.

* * *

The real orbital machine was being built inside the mountain in the main chamber.

It would be called the Vulcan Mk 007, after the designer of the engine.

* * *

Mr Watt made a similar recovery.

Whilst Bob made the aircraft better, the doctors did likewise with Mr Watt's body.

By mid October, a small ceremony took place in the same hangar that we had entered after the flight from Khorramshahr.

Mr Frederick Watt, dressed in his new morning suit, white tie and top hat, walked across the hangar floor accompanied by Doctor Pachandra, the Chief Surgeon of the hospital, and the Queen's Private Secretary.

He mounted a small dais in front of the nosewheel of the aircraft, and turned around to all of us assembled there to watch him.

He was beaming from ear to ear as he gave his little speech of gratitude to everyone, and explained how he had turned down his arranged Concorde return flight to England.

"I've come this far in this aeroplane," he said, "and I'm going home to England in her."

A great cheer went up.

He then turned round, faced the aircraft and said loudly.

"I name this aircraft, The Flying Enterprise."

Then he smashed a huge bottle of champagne onto the nose wheel.

He got covered in it, but he didn't give a damn.

By the time we were all finished, we were as wet on the inside as he was on the outside.

The heads were very delicate for two days after that...

We had to delay all the air tests by a further day because my fellow aviator demonstrated his lack of control when it came to social imbibing. He was last seen swinging across the cavern on one of the overhead cranes, with about a dozen members of Bob's team trying to disprove its safety limits, by adding more and more crates of beer onto the hook.

Needless to say they all fell off!

* * *

All too soon it came time to fly Mr Watt home to England.

The aircraft was satisfactory for the return trip. We were to take him to Heathrow, drop him off at the new Terminal five, then refuel from Michel over the Channel for the trip back to Socotra.

By flying sub orbital we could make it effortlessly in one leg. ASB Associates PLC had extended the runways on the airfield for us.

The main one for the HOTOL take off was ten miles long, and was based on the take off technique which we used with Ahmed at the Tawal Oasis.

The rail track was absolutely flat, and dead straight for the whole distance, with ripple free concrete one hundred feet either side. Two super conducting locomotives were used to accelerate the aircraft along the track, until it could get airborne by itself.

The original plan was to rest the aircraft on a trolley, which acted as the take off undercarriage at the heavy takeoff weight, but our suggested method was much better as it saved engine wear, tyre wear, airframe wear and, more important, pilot wear!

It was bad enough flying the brute, let alone gritting your teeth and hauling back on the control stick at about two hundred miles an hour, with your eyes firmly closed with mounting fear.

I have praised Ahmed and his lovely stewardess many times for their assistance in keeping Ray and I as sane as the next man, which probably doesn't mean a lot.

***

"Zero One from Socotra Control, you're clear for takeoff.

All engines reading OK"

I looked down at Ray and Mr Watt strapped into the rear seats, in front of the main computer screens.

"Ready when you are, Peter" said Ray with his thumb in the air.

I could see Mr Watt smiling through the face visor of his helmet. He was wearing a full environmental suit, similar to the ones that Ray and I were wearing.

Our little 'aeronaut' looked quite happy in the circumstances.

I pressed the transmit button.

"Thank you Socotra, full power now."

As I pushed the Vulcan's seven throttles slowly forward, the two locomotives beneath my feet gently moved along the rail track, pulling the wagons onto which we were fixed by our fore and aft undercarriage.

The wings were resting on high speed wheels, which would be dropped at the end of the runway after takeoff.

It was Tawal Oasis all over again.

The take off was as smooth as silk.

The two locomotives accelerated rapidly, up to two hundred and fifty miles per hour.

We were airborne at two hundred and ten.

Ray dropped the two wing bogies into the dropping area, and we gently climbed away.

If the observers were looking for a shuttle type lift off, after a dramatic reverse countdown from 'ten' to 'one', then they were very disappointed.

It was as exciting as a number four bus travelling along a motorway back to the depot.

"Socotra, Zero One climbing away now."

"Roger, Zero One, call main and secondary engine ignition."

We were using our normal four air breathing jets at the moment, and the new HOTOL engines in air breather mode.

As we flew higher, I would use the three rear engines in the rocket mode, using fuel from the fuselage tanks, and close down our turbojets.

I don't mind helping out with science and new technology, but I'll be damned if I'll be brow beaten into having only the new engines under my left hand, without my own turbos to help me out when the new ones go wrong.

That's why we were a 'hybrid' sub orbital craft, and not a full orbital space craft!

... And also why Ray and I were a lot happier than we would have been if 'they', who must be obeyed without question at all times, had got their own way.

"Socotra, Zero One. Engine ignition now."

The three rockets gradually built up to full power, and we were able to close down the turbojets and pull the air intake covers into place, to form a clean aerodynamic leading edge to our wings.

"Zero One, we see you passing flight level eight, zero, zero.

Call at altitude and in cruise conditions. Have a smooth trip."

And that was Mr Watt on his way home, after four years of solitary confinement.

He was the first passenger on our mini space craft, en route from Socotra to England, arriving at Heathrow within two hours.

We couldn't promise first class, but did promise to get him home in style... and that was still to come, when we got to London!

Just a little something that he didn't know about.

* * *

"Zero One, this is London Control Centre.

You are clear for descent."

I could see the blanket of clouds ahead of us, stretching across the length and breadth of England.

"I see nothing's changed since we left."

That was Ray standing beside me, looking out of the forward window.

He was brown and suntanned after his strenuous sun bathing and swimming on the island. He could have sold his brown skin to the sun tan lotion firms for advertising.

It made me sick to see it.

I was red and blotchy with sun burn!

"It will do you good to see rain for a change. It might wipe that stupid grin off your face," was my jealous response.

"London, Zero One is descending this time. Will call you ten miles running in."

"Thank you, Zero One. You are clear on radar all the way to one thousand feet"

I pulled the throttles back and went down like a brick.

"Send Mr Watt up to the front, Ray, and let him have a look out will you please."

Mr Watt climbed up the ladder, and came up on my left hand side.

"Just reach back behind you, Mr Watt, and pull down the small seat.

You can sit down in comfort and watch us arrive at London Airport.

I might even let you land it if all goes well."

He strapped into the side seat, and watched as we descended towards the English Channel.

Ray was checking ahead on the radar, and steering us clear of the air traffic in the area, in conjunction with the London Air Traffic Centre.

Both the radar sets were interfaced, so the ground operators could see what we could see, and vice versa.

We weaved our way around the airways and reporting beacons, until we reached our run in point at one thousand feet above the ground.

Mr Watt now had a bird's eye view of London, as we flew over it towards the airport.

Not only was he grinning, he was beaming with pleasure.

"This is a fantastic surprise, Peter. Thank you very much.

I expected to land at the airport, and just walk away from you both.

What a splendid sight London is after four years absence."

I switched on the forward television camera and put the picture on the port VDU directly in front of him.

"Keep your eyes on that as well, Mr Watt. You may be in for a bigger surprise."

I could see the Thames winding its way through the City on my left hand side, and looked ahead for Trafalgar Square, Horse guards Parade and the Mall.

"Zero One, London Control, you are clear to continue."

"Thank you London, running in."

Ray was up front now. There were three pairs of eyes peering ahead.

I eased the aircraft down another two hundred feet, and lined it up so that the Mall was underneath us, with Buckingham Palace directly ahead.

Mr Watt looked at both of us with a glazed look on his face.

The Mall was packed with hundreds of people, looking upwards at the aircraft; and waving scarves, hats and papers as we flew over them.

"Just a little homecoming for you, Mr Watt.

Have a look ahead on the screen."

He looked down at the instrument panel at the VDU, now showing the front facade of the Palace.

The balcony had the Royal Standard draped over the balustrade, and members of the Royal Family were standing there watching the aircraft approach.

Mr Watt was now virtually glowing with pleasure.

There were two little boys standing there, jumping up and down with excitement.

One of them had a little black box in his hand, rather like the personal radio sets that Les and Jock had when they jumped into Khorramshahr.

... And that's when Ray and I got the biggest shock of our lives.

I could see one of our Royal Princes talking into the radio, and over our own UHF set came a message.

"UNCLE FREDDY, CAN YOU SEE US, GIVE US A WAVE UNCLE FREDDY. GO ON, GIVE US A WAVE."

And then, as he put it down by his side, he had left his finger on the transmit button, so we heard him say to the other young Prince,

"OUR UNCLE'S FLYING THAT AEROPLANE."

"NO HE ISN'T. HE CAN'T FLY."

"YES HE CAN. THAT'S HIM UP THERE. WATCH HIM WAVE TO US."

"NO HE WON'T."

"YES HE WILL."

Then a different voice:

"BELT UP, YOU TWO."

It was as bad as the argument that Les and Jock had on the undercarriage over Iran.

Ray looked at me, dug me hard in the ribs, held his left hand forwards, palm downwards and rocked it left and right. I looked across and met Mr Watt's eyes.

I sighed heavily.

I could see my new career rapidly going straight down the London sewers, as my right hand moved the control stick left, then right, and the Vulcan flew down the Mall rocking its wings as it approached the Royal Family; who were waving back at 'Uncle Freddy' from the front balcony.

"It's all right for you," I said to Ray,

"You're not flying it. It's me that's going to land in it, when the air traffic violations come in."

I turned to Mr Watt.

"What's this 'Uncle Freddy' then, Mr Watt? You're not related are you?"

He grinned back obviously enjoying my discomfort.

"I think we can say... indirectly on their Mother's side.

I taught them all to ride.

Amongst other things, I look after the Royal stables, and the race horses; but I doubt very much if you will drop in the Royal manure.

I'll see to that."

He dug me in the ribs.

"That's a Royal promise."

I gulped.

"Can we rely on that?"

"Of course you can. You have my assurance that nothing at all will happen to you...

... I hope"

Ray held back his laugh with his hand, and went back to the rear seats; I heard him whisper in my ear as he passed.

"You'd better watch out for the royal gelding irons if I were you mate."

"You rotten sod. It was your idea, not mine.

Ruddy turncoat.

Go on, tell us, how much did you get when you sold your poor old grandmother at the auction the other day?"

*　*　*

"Zero One, this is London Airport. You are clear to land on runway 28 left.

Call finals with three green lights."

It was time to get back on the ground again.

Ray lined us up with the radar, fed in the wind vectors, and I selected the auto land facility on the auto pilot.

Why keep a dog and bark yourself, I thought.

We slid down the glide path towards the touchdown point, and the aircraft greased onto the runway with the minimum of effort. It rolled gently down the full length, and stopped at the far end without even rocking the nose downwards as the brakes applied.

"There you are, Peter. That's how it's done, and I'm not even flying it.

I'll let you have a go on your own when you're a bit more experienced.

Do you think you could taxi it in for us?"

It's a good job that I had switched off my microphone as I took over the controls, as there would have been a bit more than the Queen's English passing over the intercom, no doubt to be reported to the originator by her representative in the cockpit!

The official reception for Mr Watt was to the highest standard.

It was, as we realised afterwards, a royal reception. The royal salute was played, and the lead Rolls Royce flew the royal standard.

We played a very important part; by keeping out of the way, and hiding in the cockpit until it was time to go!

"Zero One, you are clear to taxi now.

Follow the wagon to the runway. Advise rolling for takeoff."

I did as I was told, and followed the yellow ground control vehicle. It led us back to the same runway as we had landed on, and lined us up with the centre line.

I could see the convey of Rolls Royces parked beside the terminal over to my left.

I pressed the transmit button.

"London control, am I cleared for one final fly past?"

The reply came back.

"We will find out for you.

Remain in the visual circuit after takeoff. We will advise as soon as possible."

"Thank you London."

And to Ray,

"Ok Ray?"

"Yes, go ahead."

I just used the turbojets for the take off. We were light, and had sufficient power from the four of them. We leapt into the air after using only a quarter of the runway, and I turned to my left for a visual circuit.

"Zero One from London Control.

You are cleared for one visual circuit, then departure on a southerly heading, for rendezvous over the channel with your tanker.

It is waiting now for your return to Socotra. Have a good trip."

"Thank you London, turning in now."

I could see a figure walk from the lead Rolls Royce, and stand by the edge of the peritrack, looking in our direction.

I turned in towards the airfield, aimed the aircraft right down the centre of the runway, and flew it low and fast towards the far end.

As I approached Mr Watt, I dipped the port wing and held it down until we were past.

He removed his hat, and held it up at shoulder level in his right hand as we saluted him.

* * *

Mr Frederick Watt watched the Vulcan as it turned to the left away from the airfield, towards its rendezvous point with the Bear for its return trip to Socotra.

He watched as it rocked its wings before climbing away, and thought of all that had been done on his behalf.

He thought about the memorial service that they all went to at the Hospital Chapel, for Bill Carter and David O'Mara.

He thought about the strenuous efforts that Bob Marshall's team went to in order to get the aircraft ready to get him home.

He thought about the dedication of Doctor Pachandra, and the hospital team, to get him fit and healthy again; and finally he thought about the wonderful reception that he had received when he eventually arrived home,

He replaced his hat on his head, and remembered fellow colleagues still in captivity in foreign lands, and watched as the aircraft disappeared far away into the clouds.

The wind was blowing directly into his face, but it wasn't that which was responsible for the tears that flowed down both his cheeks.

Mr Frederick Watt was a very religious man.

He believed in the goodness in people.

He now believed in miracles.

He had experienced one.

Chapter 36. Obituary

1st NOVEMBER 1995

The announcement was relayed around the globe in seconds, by the world television agencies.

"It is with deep regret that we announce the death this morning of Mr Lee Akina Luanda, President of the General Assembly of the United Nations, and Prime Minister of the country of Shatt El Arab.

Mr Luanda was well known for his quest for peace throughout the world, particularly in the Middle East.

He died peacefully in his sleep, surrounded by his family in Manila.

He leaves a wife and four daughters, and will be sadly missed by everyone.

Mr Luanda will be buried at sea."

* * *

11th November 1995. 10:54 am

The coffin was positioned at the rear of one of the United Nations minesweepers; at the head of the Gulf in the newly named Luanda Bay, which had been created by the explosion.

It was Mr Luanda's last request that he be buried there; and it was the decision of the United Nations General Assembly to re name the waterway, as a token of his personal contribution to peace.

The coffin was plain teak, with brass handles, and was supported either side by four members of the newly appointed Persian Gulf patrol, with their bright blue berets.

There was a single white sheet draped over the coffin, because as yet there had been no opportunity to produce a flag for the country which he represented.

It was Mrs Luanda who suggested a simple sheet, on which now rested five wreaths with the following inscriptions:

The first one said,

"To my loving husband."

The other four said,

"To my loving father."

* * *

At five minutes to eleven, just before the commitment to the water took place, Mr Hassan Rejad walked up to the coffin, and took out a neatly folded flag of the Islamic republic of Iran;

Equal horizontal bands of green, white and red, with an emblem of the Islamic republic.

He draped it over the top and down the right hand side of the coffin, then stood beside it between two of the soldiers.

At three minutes to eleven, Mr Khalid Shakir walked forward with the flag of the republic of Iraq;

Horizontal stripes of red, white and black, with three green stars on the white stripe.

He draped it over the top and down the left hand side of the coffin, then took his place between the two soldiers on the opposite side to Mr Rejad; after climbing the two steps up to the small dais which had been prepared specially for him.

He looked across to Mr Rejad, at equal eye level, and honour was satisfied.

The service continued until one minute to eleven.

Mr Shakir turned around, and whispered to Mrs Luanda.

'Please, Mrs Luanda..."

She looked up.

"This is very uncomfortable, may I get down?"

She appreciated his discomfort, and nodded to two soldiers beside her.

They went forward, helped Mr Shakir off the dais, and removed it.

Mr Shakir then took up his place again, only this time standing on the deck of the minesweeper.

Mr Rejad turned and gazed down at Khalid Shakir.

The shorter man was staring straight ahead.

He turned his head, and looked up to meet Mr Rejad's eye. He nodded at him, then returned his gaze to the water below his feet.

At thirty seconds to eleven, two silver trumpeters from the band of the Royal Marines marched forward and halted either side of the coffin at attention.

A petty officer marched up and stood immediately behind them. He piped his bosun's whistle for fifteen seconds, then stood at attention with the others.

Between eleven o'clock and two minutes after, the only sound heard was the lapping of the water against the sides of the minesweeper.

A United Nations padre moved up, and laid a cross on top of the coffin. Mrs Luanda had wanted this, even though her husband was a Buddhist.

"We now commit this body to the deep..."

The soldiers lifted the ramp, and the body of Mr Luanda slid over the side of the boat, into what was once the town of Basra.

It was only noticed by the most observant in attendance that Mr Rejad and Mr Shakir forgot to keep hold of their respective flags; and that the coffin became wrapped in both of them, before it came to rest on the sea bed, where the Basra railway station used to be.

The silver trumpeters raised their instruments to their lips and played the last post, as Mrs Luanda and her daughters watched the ripples disperse across the bay.

The final chord rang out clearly, and as it died away Mrs Luanda heard the unexpected sound of jet engines coming from her left hand side.

She looked up, and saw an enormous silver aircraft flying very low and slow towards the minesweeper, with its undercarriage down and its bomb doors open.

It was coming straight at her, the vortices from the wings causing waves on the surface of the bay.

It was almost overhead when a large green object on a parachute dropped out of the bomb bay, then it flew past, dipping its wing towards her in a salute.

She could clearly see two people in the cockpit, one standing at the window saluting her as he flew past, and the other person in the pilot's seat.

The aircraft then levelled its wings, and climbed away quietly to circled round the bay.

* * *

The green object was a ten feet diameter wreath, made from laurel leaves and lilies of the valley.

It was surmounted by an albatross flying with its wings outstretched, made with white carnations.

Around the circumference of the wreath was an inscription, again made with carnations.

: Per Ardua Ad Astra:

It descended slowly on its parachute made of pure silk, and dropped gently into the water, where the other five wreaths were floating,

The wreath had been specially constructed by the disabled ex servicemen working for the Earl Haig Fund, and had been sent to us from the British Legion Poppy Appeal Village at Maidstone Kent.

The Royal Air Force had given Ray and I special dispensation to use our old service motto.

That was us saying goodbye to Mr Luanda.

* * *

Mrs Luanda looked down at the final resting place of her husband for a few moments before the minesweeper moved off.

She could hear the aircraft flying directly overhead as it climbed away.

She closed her eyes for a silent prayer.

As she prayed she felt something fall softly onto her face.

She opened her eyes, startled.

A red poppy leaf fluttered down the front of her dress.

It dropped onto the deck beside her shoes.

She looked down in surprise, and as she did so, another fluttered down and rested beside it; then another, and another, and another.

She looked around her, and saw that the whole of the deck was covered in red poppy leaves.

They were falling from the sky in their millions.

They covered the waters of the bay, the escorting minesweepers, the white uniforms of the Royal Marine trumpeters...

In fact, everything.

She watched in silence as they all gently fluttered down from the sky,

Ten million of them...

That was us saying goodbye to Mr Luanda's companions.

EPILOGUE

We went to the United Nations hospital on the island of Socotra after the raid, and stayed out of sight for a year or so until everything quietened down a bit.

That was an education itself.

Think of any disease, any injury, either physical or mental, across any ethnic diversity of humanity, and it's all happening there.

No advertising, no commercial profiteering, no international companies, with their fingers in the pot.

Just pure medicine for medicine's sake.

There's no politics. It just works.

People come in, get repaired, stay for a while, then go home.

* * *

The runway is in constant use, and tucked away inside one of the hillside hangars is an old Vulcan bomber; one that most people think got shot down after it was stolen.

The Hormuz raid may have been the first one we did, but as we found out, it was really just phase one of a bigger United Nations operation.

We found a number of hostages, we hit another oil field.

We did special ops with our chaps and an old Russian Bear aircraft, that dragged us across the Saudi desert with our probe stuck up its refuelling pipe, and the lovely Olga grinning from the rear turret pretending to shoot us down.

We hid inside reservoir dams, landed on dual carriageways, and terrified a trainload of passengers as we shot underneath them on a bridge as we took off.

But the best 'op' was working with our SAS team to get the Royal hostage out.

It got a bit hairy, when we picked up their Landrover on a desert track, with our chaps inside and one of the terrorists hanging on the back, but that's all history now, recorded somewhere in a black cellar for posterity.

* * *

As well as dropping the poppies to remember the casualties of the 'Hell on Earth' we unleashed by planting the last five bombs, we had another quiet word with 'Those who must be obeyed', and they granted our request;

I hope you will head back to the City of Lincoln, and take a taxi or the bus to Fulbeck village.

Find the front of the gate, and the ten feet high angel with its wings fully outstretched, carved in black marble, its arms reaching forward holding two white doves in its cupped hands, gazing forlornly at the distant twin towers of Lincoln Cathedral on the horizon.

The angel is still standing on a square plinth of plain white marble, with inscriptions on each side in three inch high lettering inlaid with gold, which you can read as you walk around it; alternately in English, then in Arabic.

It now reads:

FULBECK

Twinned With

BANDAR ABBAS

and

BASRA

(Friendship Towns)

Acknowledgements

I would like to acknowledge the help and assistance given to me during the production of the manuscript by the following people.

Mrs Maureen Burton for her constant encouragement, medical information, patience and editing.

Andrew Burton for keyboarding and editing.

Bruce Ward (Tresham) for computer assistance.

Dennis Carlton for weapons and combat information.

George Chambers (Tresham) for weapons and combat information.

Doctor Pirzada for computer operating assistance.

James Burton for electronic advice

Neil Haxton for proof reading.

John Burton for proof reading.

Michael Williams for proof reading.

Printed in Great Britain
by Amazon